# REPORTED MISSING

JOSEPH BIRCHALL

POOLBEG
CRIMSON

This book is a work of fiction. References to real people, events, establishments, organisations, or locales are intended only to provide a sense of authenticity, and are used fictitiously. All other characters, and all incidents and dialogue, are drawn from the author's imagination and are not to be construed as real.

Published 2026 by Poolbeg Crimson, an imprint of Poolbeg Press Ltd.

123 Grange Hill, Baldoyle, Dublin 13, Ireland

Email: poolbeg@poolbeg.com

 A catalogue record for this book is available from the British Library.

An extract from the Seamus Heaney poem '*Mid-Term Break*' is used by kind permission of Faber and Faber.

ISBN 978-1-78199-640-9



www.poolbeg.com

# About the Author

A lifelong writer, Joseph Birchall penned his first play at the age of eleven and later explored screenwriting and fiction, before work and family took precedence. This novel is the second in the Detective Darcy Doyle series, following the success of the bestseller *In Plain Sight*. Joseph is a member of the Crime Writers' Association and lives in Dublin with his wife and three children

## PRAISE FOR REPORTED MISSING

'Totally enjoyable. A missing child, everyone lying, murders, and a race against time: a perfect recipe for a crime novel. I raced through it, hot on the heels of Darcy Doyle and Mick Kelly. Loved it. I highly recommend this series and want to read more of it, and soon!'
PATRICIA GIBNEY

'A fast-paced, gritty police procedural, crammed with high-octane drama and next-level tension. Darcy Doyle and her grizzled work partner DI Mick Kelly are up against the worst of all nightmares – a missing child case. And one thing you can be sure of with Joseph Birchall is that he'll keep you turning the pages!'
GILL PERDUE

'Another gripping case for Darcy and Mick. Believable characters and a deliciously twisty plot. You won't want to put it down. I loved it.'
JEAN GRAINGER (*USA TODAY* bestseller)

'Fresh, darkly humorous … an absolute page-turner from the get-go!'
AMANDA GEARD

'A cracking series that will keep you on your toes.'
@ARCREVIEWS_BY_M (Instagram)

# Acknowledgements

This book would not have reached bookshops without the belief and support of Paula Campbell at Poolbeg Press, for which I am deeply grateful.

Editor Gaye Shortland's insight, care and skill helped shape this book into the polished work you now hold in your hands.

Thank you, Peter O'Connell, for your relentless work in bringing my books to Irish and international media attention. I did a lot of exciting firsts last year because of you.

Early readers (and typo-spotters) included author Jean Grainger, Kay Birchall, Mary Cummins and Pat Moran. Sincere thanks to all.

Special thanks, as always, to Fabian Dunne for his technical advice.

Thanks to David Prendergast for his impressive cover art.

Thanks to all the wonderful and encouraging writers that I've met over the last year, in particular Patricia Gibney, Vanessa O'Loughlin, Gill Perdue and my Poolbeg writers-in-arms Lucy O'Callaghan and Karen Fitzgibbon.

Helen Falconer's input was invaluable in bringing the characters to life. You will always be fondly remembered by us.

A special mention to all the women and men on the front line in An Garda Síochána who go about their jobs without the fanfare they richly deserve.

This book exists because of the unwavering support and encouragement of my wife and best friend, Eileen, which I'm very grateful for.

Thanks to you three too: Kai, Christopher and Jamie (my biggest fan).

And finally, my thanks to you, the reader. Books exist because of you, and because of them the world will always be richer, brighter, and full of possibility.

# Dedication

To Eileen

*Wearing a poppy bruise on his left temple,*
*He lay in the four-foot box as in his cot.*
*No gaudy scars, the bumper knocked him clear.*
*A four-foot box, a foot for every year.*

'Mid-Term Break' by Seamus Heaney

# Saturday

# 14 December

# Prologue

John Scanlan unclipped his four-year-old son, Alfie, from the back seat of his SUV and planted the boy's feet firmly on the ground. In the coming days, he would look back at that moment and remember it as the last time he touched his son.

'Come on, Alfie,' he said. 'We're already late. *You* were the one who said you wanted to go hurling. I was quite happy to stay nice and warm at home.'

John winced at his own words, and he berated himself. His wife was right — he was too hard on the little boy. What made it worse was Alfie's unending ability not to care in the slightest about his father's severity. Instead, the boy looked up at him with his big, bright-blue eyes under a flop of blond hair, and said in the sweetest of voices, 'Sorry, Daddy'.

'It's OK, champ,' John told him. 'Just let's hurry, yeah?'

A raw wind swept through the car park and slithered inside John's open jacket. It seemed to permeate his skin and creep into his bones. He couldn't remember the last time it had felt this cold in the days leading up to Christmas.

They continued into St. Margaret's Park, where the small man-made lake had frozen over. On the icy bank, four large swans huddled together, like ballet dancers on a glistening stage, their heads tucked under their smooth, white wings, as if cowering from some heinous scene in the show.

'Alfie, come on!'

John had planned on spending these two hours watching Liverpool playing at Anfield while he sprawled on the sofa, not standing in a field with a bunch of four-year-olds who couldn't hit a ball straight to save their lives. The last conversation with his wife played on a loop in his head.

'You're the one who signed him up to hurling,' he had told her. 'If you want him to go, why don't you take him?'

'Because I've been with him all week, John,' she replied. 'It's *you* don't spend enough time with him. Unlike your sports.'

'What's that supposed to mean?'

'Nothing.'

'I'm busy at work.'

'We're all busy, John.'

'Some more than others.'

'*Now what's that supposed to mean?*' she had yelled at him before he'd grabbed Alfie and stormed out of the house.

John looked around the sectioned-off park. The surrounding fields still held a thin coating of frost that glistened under a weak winter sun. The area was already full of screaming and running kids. Every week he had to ask which was his son's group.

At the entrance, a box of markers lay next to several white A4 sheets that were divided into tear-off stickers. As usual, he scribbled Alfie's name onto one sticker, pulled off the square strip, and stuck it onto his son's T-shirt.

Eventually, he recognised one of the mothers whose son was also on Alfie's team. She always wore the same see-through yoga pants. Her own son was crying, and she was bent over to attend to him. John stared, but then another woman walked in front of him and blocked his view. He recognised that woman too but couldn't place her.

Alfie saw one of his friends and ran over to him. John found a quiet spot by the wire fence and crouched down, leaning his back against it. He took out his phone, opened the sports app and connected to the game. It had just started, and he stuck in his earphones and listened.

After a while a man walked by, sipping from a takeaway cup, and John remembered there was a small kiosk that sold drinks in the clubhouse. The coffee was instant and weak, but it was hot at least, so he stood up and, with a cursory glance at his son, sauntered off in its direction.

As he returned, he heard a goal being scored against Liverpool through his earphones, and his mood sank lower. He stood watching the kids run around for some minutes before he realised that none of them was Alfie. Embarrassingly, he had been standing beside the wrong group. He looked up and searched for the yoga-pants mother. Walking around, he found her in the far corner of the field where the kids were practising taking penalties. He spotted Alfie in a large group running after the ball, their hurleys raised in unison in the air like Zulu warriors charging into battle. It was chaos just watching them, but the analogy made him smile. He wondered where the coach got his patience from.

He leaned against the fence and sipped on the coffee. On his phone, he heard Liverpool score an equaliser and he raised his coffee cup into the air in delight, some of it splashing out and onto his hand.

The next time he looked up, the yoga-pants mother was putting on her son's jacket. He looked over to Alfie's group. Parents were leading their children hurriedly away and back to their cars.

*Now, where the fuck is Alfie?*

He shoved his phone into his pocket and walked over to where he had last seen his son.

The coach was tidying up the nets and markers. John hurried up to him.

'Where's Alfie?'

'Who?'

John looked around at the children leaving with their parents. The group was thinning out.

'Alfie. The little blond boy,' he said. 'With the Liverpool beanie. '

'I don't know.'

'You don't know? He was right here, wasn't he?'

'Yes. He must have left.'

'*He must have left?* What do you mean, he must have fucking left?'

Most of the field was empty now. John felt a tightening in his chest as panic set in. He took a deep breath in and exhaled slowly.

'Do you remember him or not? Alfie. His name's Alfie.'

The coach was looking alarmed now. 'I remember seeing him playing but, I'm sorry, I don't remember when he left.'

The coach was saying something else, but his voice became muffled as if John was sinking under water.

He began walking quickly towards the car park.

'*Alfie!*' he yelled.

He was still holding his coffee cup, but threw it onto the grass.

'*Alfie!*'

Cars were driving out and back to the warmth of their homes, children strapped safely inside.

He looked in the direction of the lake and an image of his son's body, face-down in the water, flashed before him. He ran towards it, but it was deserted. He raced back to the car park.

The last few cars were leaving.

He sprinted out onto the main road, and looked up and down the paths, praying to see his little boy aimlessly walking on his own. No child in sight, so he ran back to the carpark. His SUV was the only vehicle there now.

Panic consumed him, and his breathing became laboured.

'*Oh, Jesus Christ. Where are you, Alfie?*'

Every second that passed filled him further with dread. He went back to the football pitches, scanning the horizon and out towards the distant fields. His heart pounded hard in his chest, and he felt like he was having a heart attack. He gripped his coat, bent forward and fell onto his knees.

'*Alfie!*' he roared across the fields, ending in almost a dying gasp.

The four swans momentarily ruffled their wings at his roar, but then wrapped themselves tighter against each other, none of them daring to glance up or be witness to the scene.

At the edge of the football pitch where Alfie had played, John spotted a white label crunched up on the ground. He scrambled to his feet and hurried towards it. He snatched it up and with both hands unfolded the sticky white paper.

*He* had written the single word on it – *Alfie*.

# Four Days Later

# Wednesday

# 18 December

# Chapter 1

'I really don't think that's a gun he's holding, Mr. Kayani,' Detective Sergeant Darcy Doyle said, leaning forward towards the black-and-white video monitor.

'Look closer,' he told her. 'When I was a boy in Pakistan, I saw many, many guns. And that, Lady Detective, is a gun.'

He was standing behind her, squinting at the computer's monitor. Darcy turned her head to look at him. She thought he might be the oldest man she had ever seen. He had a bald brown head with tiny wisps of white curly hair that she imagined might blow away if she breathed too heavily on them. In contrast, his long white beard looked like a theatre prop that seemed to match his peculiarly large ears and bulbous nose, and his skin was not dissimilar to an old leather football. His eyes, however, glistened with a sharpness that made her doubt her own ability to detect the gun in the assailant's hand. She turned back to the monitor and she too squinted.

The film played again, frame by frame.

'There!' he exclaimed, pointing a bony finger at the screen. 'You see it now?'

Darcy paused it again and leaned in further.

'I'm not so sure, Mr. Kayani. I'm sorry. It just looks like a ... a ... a phone.'

Mr. Kayani threw his skinny arms into the air.

'Have you ever even seen a real gun, Lady Detective?'

'Yes, Mr. Kayani. I have.'

Darcy straightened up and stretched her back.

Mr. Kayani was the owner of the local corner shop in the Liberties in Dublin, Darcy's local corner shop. He had been having a spate of small robberies and she had, much to her regret, promised she would do something about it. Giving him her mobile number had also been, she realised now, a bad idea.

'He's just a kid robbing some junk,' she said, turning back to the screen.

'I promise you, I do not sell any junk.'

'Yes, I'm sorry, Mr. Kayani. I didn't mean that. I meant some sweets and chocolates.'

'Then what are you going to do about *these bloody little scumbags*? This is my seventh time to be robbed this year.'

Whenever Mr. Kayani swore, his accent shifted from Pakistani to thick inner-city Dublin.

Darcy scanned the rest of the room. They were in the back of the shop, a heavy black curtain separating them from the main shop area. The walls were decorated with photos of his family, both in Ireland and in Pakistan, a movie poster of *The Quiet Man* with Maureen O'Hara hoisted up in the arms of John Wayne and a large map of Pakistan.

Darcy spotted another security monitor attached to the wall beside the curtain. She walked over to it.

'When did this happen?' she asked him. On the screen was a black-and-white film of a man with a hoodie covering his face, pointing a gun at the young cashier girl as she emptied the till. 'Now *that* is most definitely a gun, Mr. Kayani.'

'*Ya Rab! That is now! Not a replay! Ameera! My granddaughter!*' He grabbed the curtain.

Darcy pulled his hand off the curtain and used her body to shove him behind her. She peeked out through the side of the curtain. The hooded man was grabbing the cash from the girl and stuffing it into his pockets.

'*Stay back*,' she whispered to Kayani, reaching inside her jacket to unholster her service pistol. She pointed it down and to the side.

'*Ameera*,' she heard Mr. Kayani say to himself.

She flung back the curtain and pointed her gun at the criminal.

'*Armed Gardaí!*' she yelled. '*Drop your weapon and get on the floor!*'

He turned his head towards her. There was a scarf covering the lower part of his face and she could see more shock in his eyes than fear.

'*Drop it now!*' she screamed at him.

He twisted his entire body in a fraction of a second and, like a greyhound out of a trap, darted for the door. Darcy followed him through the line of sight of her gun, but she wasn't prepared to shoot anyone in the back for some petty cash from a till.

She raced after him, crashing into a shelf of canned products, which stopped her dead. The man bolted out of the shop and turned right, pushing people out of his way.

Darcy grabbed a tin of peas off the shelf and raced after him. A daily runner, she closed in on him quickly.

She saw him turn onto Meath Street, holstered her gun and pulled the radio off her belt.

'Urgent assistance! I'm in pursuit of an armed suspect heading along Meath Street on foot!'

'Roger that, Doyle,' a response came back. 'Will send a unit to you now.'

Darcy stuck the radio back onto her belt, gripped the tin of peas in her other hand and pushed herself to run faster.

At the top of Meath Street, she could hear him panting heavily ahead of her. His hoodie had flapped back off his head and, when he glanced back at her, she saw the scarf had loosened and she thought she recognised his face.

He was pushing people out of his way, but his initial adrenaline-fuelled burst of energy was fading. He was slowing down. Darcy raised the tin of peas above her head.

He turned his head again. He locked eyes with her, and only at the last moment did he see the tin hurtling towards him. He made half an effort to avoid it but failed and the impact of the tin slamming into his back sent him crashing to the ground.

Darcy slowed and walked the remaining few metres.

'*Me fuckin' ribs!*' he cried out. '*You've broken them, yeh mad bitch!*'

'You'll be grand,' she told him, grabbing his right arm and twisting it behind his back.

'*Ah, fuckin' hell!*' he screamed. '*That hurts!*'

She grabbed his other arm and pulled it back to meet the first. Her cuffs were tucked into her belt – she pulled them out and clicked them shut around his wrists. Then she searched inside his jacket and pulled out the small handgun.

'It's a fake,' he told her. 'I wasn't goin' to shoot anyone.'

Darcy lifted his head up and looked at his face.

'Stephen Byrne? Are you not supposed to be in prison?'

'Good behaviour,' he told her, still panting for breath. 'I got out early for Christmas.'

Darcy stood up, twisted him around onto his back and looked down at him.

'Didn't I stand up for you in front of the judge?' she said, then bent down and picked up the tin of peas. 'You gave him some sad story about your family. You also promised him the good citizens of Dublin would be free from your petty crimes in future.'

'I never said anything about Paki bastards, did I?' he scoffed.

She rolled the tin of peas in her hand and then let it drop onto his chest.

'*Oops!*' she said.

'Police brutality,' he gasped, wincing. 'I need witnesses.' A small crowd was forming around them. 'Are you lot watchin' this?'

'Shut the fuck up, Byrne,' Darcy said.

'I want me solicitor. This is harassment.'

Her phone buzzed in her pocket.

'Is that your bird callin' you?' he said. 'Are you a lezzer?'

'*Shut up!*' she said, taking the phone out of her pocket. She looked at the number, took a deep breath and answered.

'Yes, Chief,' she said.

'Where is he?'

'Who?'

'Don't play games with me, Doyle.'

'I'm just on my way to pick him up, Chief. I think he said he was going to hit the gym this morning.'

'Mick Kelly doesn't even know how to spell the word *gym*,' Chief O'Riordan told her.

'*I want me fuckin' solicitor!*' Byrne called out.

Darcy used her foot to push his arms further up his back. He let out a scream.

'What was that?' O'Riordan demanded.

'Nothing, Chief,' she said. 'I'm on my way now to get him.'

There was silence for a few moments on the other end of the line. She could hear her boss breathing.

'Chief?' she said.

'There's been a body found,' he said, his voice more serious now. 'Looks like that missing little boy.'

'Ah, fuck.'

'Ah fuck is right. Get Kelly and get over there. I'll text you the location.'

'Yes, Chief.'

'And Doyle. If the two of you aren't on the scene in the next hour, it's not your case anymore. Understood?'

Darcy was about to reply, but the phone went dead.

She was still holding the phone when a marked Garda car pulled up and two uniforms got out.

'Well, if it isn't Byrne, ya little fucker!' one of them said in a strong Kerry accent. 'I heard you got out two days ago. Haven't you been a busy lad?'

'Yeah, I have, yeah!' Byrne spat at him. 'I been busy ridin' your missus when you're on duty.'

The Garda's face flushed and he even raised his foot to kick Byrne, but his older colleague held him back.

'Lads,' Doyle said, holding out the replica gun to them, 'can you take care of this one? I've got to go.'

'What about the report?' the older one said.

'It's all yours,' she told him, and bent down to remove her handcuffs from Byrne. 'He was robbing Mr. Kayani's shop. There's CCTV footage.'

'*That Paki bastard!*' Byrne yelled. '*Takin' our jobs!*'

'You've never even had a job.' Darcy sighed and stepped over him.

The older Garda shook his head as the other reached down and yanked Byrne up off the path.

# Chapter 2

Irena Novak had come to Ireland from Croatia at the suggestion of her son and his wife. The plan had been that she would stay with them and mind her two beautiful grandchildren while they were at work. Then her daughter-in-law lost her job and at the same time, in Irena's opinion anyway, also lost her manners, her hospitality and quite possibly her mind.

Rather than cause a rift between her son and his wife, she left their house and found a place of her own. The thought of having to move away from her grandchildren and back to Croatia and to her job as a guide for English-speaking tourists was unbearable. She was, perhaps, one of the few people in the world who looked on the walls of Dubrovnik and felt nothing but exhaustion. Her husband, a secondary-school teacher, had died suddenly, five years earlier, and despite herself she had grown fond of Dublin with its quirky ways and its quirky people.

Her one-bedroom apartment was cosy, and her part-time job as an office administrator for a small construction company provided her with a decent enough living to afford her a happy, if sometimes lonely life. It wasn't that she lacked male attention, despite her age, but she was reluctant to plunge into the complications of a new relationship.

Irena was sitting in her kitchen sipping her second cup of chamomile tea that day when the doorbell rang. She went and checked the spyhole before opening the door.

'I'm really sorry to disturb you, Irena,' Darcy said. 'He's not here, is he?'

Irena smiled and, with a wave of her hand, invited Darcy in.

Darcy walked over to the couch where Detective Inspector Mick Kelly lay face up, loud vibrating snores emitting from his open mouth. His shoes had been removed and one of his socks had a hole in it, a big toe with a large nail poking out. His jacket had flopped open, and his SIG Sauer P226 service pistol was visible.

Darcy thought how one incriminating photo sent in to their Chief, at the National Bureau of Criminal Investigation on the fifth floor of Harcourt Street, would have him fired before lunchtime.

'Sorry about this, Irena,' Darcy said, turning to her. 'I promise I'll have a word with him.'

'It's OK, Darcy. I heard him singing at about two o'clock this morning and when I went outside he was asleep in the hall. What else could I do? Mr. Jones had come out of his apartment too and helped me get him in here.'

'You're very kind, Irena.'

'Mick is a very nice man. He just needs to stop drinking. That is all.'

'Yes,' Darcy agreed, shifting her focus back to Mick. 'That is all.'

The last time Darcy had woken him in this state, he'd jumped up so fast that she'd thought he was going to attack her.

Through the door into the kitchen she spotted a sweeping-brush leaning against the wall.

'Can I borrow your sweeping brush?' she asked Irena.

Irena nodded, looking puzzled.

Darcy fetched the brush and then, from as far back as she could, she prodded Mick in the chest with the end of the brush handle. Nothing happened. She tried again, harder this time. Mick stopped snoring for a moment but then resumed, louder than before.

Darcy looked at her watch. It was already thirty minutes since the Chief had called her. She poked Mick harder in the ribs.

He let out a yelp and jumped up, grabbing the end of the handle of the brush.

'Jesus, what the fuck?' he mumbled.

Darcy turned back to Irena and they both smiled.

'That worked anyway.'

Darcy came out of the small petrol station a few minutes from Mick's apartment, carrying two cups of coffee. She slowed her pace as she approached the car and looked in at him through the open window. His head was tilted back on the headrest and his eyes were closed. She felt like tipping the full contents of the cups onto his lap.

She placed one of the cups on the roof of the car and opened the passenger door.

'*Hey!*' she yelled at him.

Mick startled awake.

'Drink this.'

Mick took the cup from her and stared at it before taking a sip. He winced at the taste and spat the coffee onto the ground beside the car. '*Fucking hell!*' he said.

'Hey,' Darcy said, 'that was probably mine. It's soya milk.'

He looked down at the cup. 'Sorry about that.'

Shaking her head, she took the second cup off the roof and handed it to him before slamming the door shut. She walked around, got in the driver's side and started the car. She drove back into the traffic, glancing in his direction every now and again. He ignored her. Eventually, he took out a packet of cigarettes and placed one in his mouth, but he knew better than to light it in her car.

'You want to talk about it?' she said.

They had already worked together for a few months, but she had never seen him look so ... she searched for the right word ... despondent. She reminded herself how little she really knew about Detective Inspector Mick Kelly. Because of his talent and ingenuity, which she had observed in their last case together, she always ignored the rumours about him and had even defended his character. But her doubts were beginning to grow, and her patience to dwindle.

'You've been missing for *three days!*' she said. It came out angrier than she'd intended.

'So what?' he replied, not looking at her.

'*So what?* So, I'm the one who had to cover for you. I'm the one who's been lying to the Chief for you.'

'I never asked you to,' he said flatly. 'You're not my mother.'

She hit the brakes, pulled the car in to the side of the road and switched off her engine. The cars behind her beeped.

'You're one-hundred-percent right, Mick,' she told him. 'I'm not your fucking mother. I'm your partner. And that means you're supposed to be mine too. But do you know what? If that doesn't suit you then that's fine with me. *You can get the fuck out of the car!*'

Mick let out a sigh, but he still didn't turn to face her. 'I fell off the wagon.'

'Really?' she said. 'And here's me having to use all of my detective skills to figure that one out.'

Mick chanced a look in her direction and then focused on his coffee.

'Anything else?' she asked.

He looked at her again. 'Sorry?'

'For fuck's sake, Mick.' She looked at her watch.

She pulled back out into the traffic and then into the bus lane, overtaking the long queue of cars.

There was a minute's silence before Mick asked, 'Where are we going?'

Darcy focused on the road for a few moments before replying. 'They've found a body. Looks like it's the boy.'

Mick had seen the news reports over the last few days of mixed sobriety. He'd watched the parents' anguish on TV in a pub the previous evening.

He took another sip of his coffee. 'How do I look?'

'Like shit,' she told him. 'So, basically, no different than usual.'

Out of the corner of her eye, she saw him smile, or maybe it was a grimace.

'What's the story with you and Irena?'

'What?'

'She's a good-looking woman.'

Silence.

'Bit of a Sharon Stone vibe from her. Is that your type?'

'What the fuck are you talking about, Doyle?'

'Never mind,' she said when she saw the perplexed look on his face.

# Chapter 3

The body of the little boy lay where an early-morning hiker had spotted him behind a stack of recently felled trees. The red blanket in which he'd been wrapped had caught the hiker's attention, and curiosity got the better of him. The hiking route was not one of the more popular trails in the Dublin Mountains as it allowed for very few views of the city below, and it was well known that the branches of the tall Noble pine trees held on to every rain shower for days and then randomly dropped them onto the passing hikers below.

After calling 999, the hiker, a man in his fifties, had stayed with the little boy. He had only stopped crying when emergency services arrived, and they had arrived in their dozens. Local Gardaí at first, followed quickly by an ambulance, a fire engine and even a team from Mountain Rescue.

Dr. Phoebe Pepple had arrived at the scene almost an hour before. Born of an Irish mother and a Nigerian father in a diverse and happy home, she had excelled in her studies and had been offered a job immediately by Forensic Science Ireland upon completion of her degree at University College Dublin, over a decade ago. She had requested to go back into the field, so she'd been given the opportunity to study Crime Scene Investigation and had then taken a role with the Technical Bureau.

She and her team had erected a white tent over the body, more to preserve the scene than to protect the privacy of the boy from the public and reporters that would undoubtedly show up in droves.

She exited the tent, removed her mask and looked up at the darkening clouds on the horizon. A single crow cawed loudly from the top of a distant branch. Rain had been forecast for the afternoon. A full and immediate inspection of the area was vital, but she had already prepared her initial findings for the investigators. She looked down towards the dirt road and saw Darcy's old car pulling in behind the other vehicles.

Because of the emergency vehicles' indiscriminate parking and her own somewhat late arrival, Darcy had no choice but to park quite a distance from the main activity of the crime scene. She saw the white suits of forensics as they examined and photographed the area and spotted one of the crime scene investigators looking down at them.

'Dr. Pepple is already here,' she told Mick.

She began to walk up the hill, Mick following behind her, his head down. A young, uniformed Garda lifted the tape to let them through.

Darcy looked over at the group of Emergency Response Unit officers, the armed division of the Gardaí. One of them was staring at her — Jamie, her ex-something-or-other. 'Captain America', Mick always called him. He was easy to spot as he always seemed to be wearing a uniform one or two sizes too small, to emphasise his physique earned from hours of sweat and toil in the gym every day. She smiled brightly and waved. She hadn't seen him in over a month, not since she'd told him to stop calling and texting her late into the night whenever he got drunk.

He kept eye contact with her for a moment, then turned away and said something to one of his colleagues who then looked over his shoulder at her and laughed.

Darcy turned away to hide the anger that surged through her and continued the climb.

'Glad you could both join us,' Dr. Pepple said when they'd reached the top.

'Morning, Fifi,' Darcy said.

'Is it him?' Mick asked her.

'Never one for the small talk, Mick,' she replied.

'Well?'

'Most likely. But I don't know yet.'

'What can you tell us, Fifi?' Darcy asked.

Dr. Pepple looked over at the tent before replying. 'Matches the boy's description, age, hair. Hard to argue with the probability factor on this one. We'll need to do a DNA test, of course, or maybe we can get dental records if he has any, but it doesn't look good for the Scanlans.'

'Eye colour?' Darcy asked.

'You'll see for yourself.'

Darcy looked over at the tent. A shiver ran down her spine, but she turned back to Dr. Pepple.

'Any indications of how he died?' she asked.

'Not yet. Even with the blanket around him, he's been left out in the elements so, besides the cold and the rain, he's been picked at by every bird and curious little creature on this hill. The poor little chap.'

'Time of death?' Mick asked, brushing away any sentimentality.

'Again, it's just a best guess at this stage,' she said. 'More than a few days, anyway.'

'How long exactly has the Scanlan kid been missing?' Mick asked Darcy.

'Since Sunday morning. So, four days.'

It was only Darcy's second murder case, and she steadied her nerves for the scene she was about to face inside the white tent. When she had first been asked to join the National Bureau of Criminal Investigation, she had imagined it would be a lot more fast-paced. Indeed, there were many times when she almost looked back at her years in Domestic Violence through rose-tinted glasses.

After the success of her first case with her new partner, the famous, or was it infamous, Detective Inspector Mick Kelly, they had returned to more run-of-the-mill cases. Even Dublin's gangland seemed to be on hiatus in the run-up to Christmas. Damien 'Diablo' Dunne had fled to Dubai after the third attempt on his life. Two months before, Darcy had been the one to hand-deliver to him a GIM — Garda Information Message — form which advised him that his life was under threat. Apparently, he had finally taken the hint. Since then, the streets had quietened to a more manageable level. Word on the street was that there was little appetite for a return to the tit-for-tat killings that had seemed unending only six months before.

Over the past idle months Darcy had watched Mick slowly lose his focus and, without a 'big case' to hold his attention, the demons of booze had taken their hold on him again. At first Darcy had tried to cover for his absence, but the Chief was no fool, and she knew a day of reckoning was upon them both.

A colleague and a friend had warned her when she had first teamed up with the elusive 'Columbo Kelly', as he had once been known, that if Kelly were to fall from grace she should make sure she was standing well back, or else she'd be going down with him. With Mick's recent drink binges, those words had been ringing in her ears.

Perhaps this case would be his saving grace, she thought. But it came at a price. And that price lay inside the tent.

Darcy shivered when she stepped inside. The air seemed even colder. In the centre was the body of the little boy. His face was tilted towards the roof of the tent, his eye sockets dark and empty, and where his eyes should have been there were only shadows. The birds had been efficient. He looked taller than Darcy imagined a four-year-old would be. The red blanket he had been wrapped up in had been opened to allow Dr. Pepple to examine him, and Darcy fought the urge to grab the blanket and cover him up again.

She watched Mick scrutinising every inch of the space before approaching the boy and bending down over him. He then straightened up so that Darcy could see too. Her first thought upon seeing the boy's small face was that he would have made a handsome man, if he had lived, and she knew it was a strange first impression.

There were scratches on his cheek, and she wondered if these had been made by the killer or the animals Dr. Pepple had mentioned. She felt a deep sadness well up inside her at the thought of him here alone for days and nights, but she stopped it when it reached her throat and forced it back down inside her. She would have to deal with it later on her own.

The shape of the boy's face was similar to the images of Alfie Scanlan in the TV news reports. She tried to imagine his face with blue eyes full of life and spirit, and not the hollowness that looked upwards as if able to see through the roof of the tent and into the sky beyond. His blond locks were matted and partially stuck to his face, but his hair was the only part of him that still looked alive. There would have to be a formal identification from the parents, but Dr. Pepple was right: it didn't look good for the Scanlans.

Mick let out a deep sigh and, then, as if soothing a sad but living child, he patted the boy on the shoulder. Perhaps, Darcy thought, Mick was thinking of his own son at this time, like most parents would.

She had no children of her own, but in her second foster home there had been a playground in the park facing the housing estate where a child had fallen and died years before. A commemorative plaque had been screwed into a bench in his memory, and she remembered seeing parents read it and holding their own children more closely.

Outside the tent, in contrast, it felt almost balmy. Darcy breathed in the air and looked up at the enormous grey clouds above. The rain was coming. But, in Dublin, the rain was always coming.

The phone buzzed in her pocket. She looked at the screen and showed it to Mick before she answered it.

'Chief.'

'Are you at the scene?'

'Yes, Chief.'

'Is it our missing boy?'

'We don't know yet, sir. DNA and bloods will take a little time. We need to get him off this mountain and into Whitehall for the autopsy.'

'Jesus Christ, Doyle. Is it him or not?'

She hesitated and looked back at the white tent. 'He matches the physical characteristics.'

'Get the body to Whitehall. I'll organise the parents to meet you. They can ID the boy, and we'll take it from there.'

'We should really wait for –'

*'Just do it.'*

Darcy looked over at Mick. He was kneeling, examining the ground outside the tent.

'I'm escalating this case from a missing person to a murder enquiry,' Chief O'Riordan told her. 'It's your case now.'

# Chapter 4

Darcy drove across the Father Mathew Bridge and pulled in to the side of the Brazen Head pub. She switched off the engine. Beside her, Mick was already leafing through Alfie Scanlan's file. After leaving the crime scene, she had driven back into the city and picked up the file from HQ, hoping they could find something in it that the Missing Persons detectives had missed.

'You see anything?' she asked Mick.

'Not really,' he told her without lifting his eyes. 'It's well researched. All the bases are covered, as they say. He was taken from a sports pitch on Saturday morning. The lake was dredged near where he was playing football, and the search intensified after that. The kid may have known the abductor as there were no signs of a struggle. Plus, none of the parents spotted anyone unusual hanging about that they didn't know anyway. No CCTV. Might possibly be a bit of luck on the abductor's part rather than pre-planning. A quick snatch-and-grab maybe.'

'The lads said they interviewed all relatives, neighbours and friends,' Darcy said. 'Went over every minute of the boy's weekly routine. Hauled in every suspect and convicted sex offender in the city. Nothing.'

Mick pursed his lips.

'What is it?' Darcy asked.

'I keep going back to that Montessori Alfie went to. There's something ... I don't know ...'

'Go on.'

Mick shrugged. 'It's just that one of the teachers ... there's something off about her.'

He turned back some pages in the report.

'Rachel Robinson. She just seems a little too evasive with the officers. Like she was hiding something. I'd like to ask her the same questions and see how different her answers would be this time.'

'Or exactly the same.'

'Precisely.'

'Well then, that's where we'll begin,' Darcy said, starting the car. 'When I got the file from the Missing Persons detective, I asked him where he thought we should begin. He told me the same thing you just did. Though he sounded like he fancied her, to be honest.'

She looked up and down the road and then joined the cars heading back along the quays.

Little Steps Montessori was located in a housing estate in Rathfarnham, a quiet suburban part of the city. It was the last unit in a row of businesses that included a butcher's, a newsagent's and a post office that had a queue stretching out onto the path. Darcy looked at the people in the post-office queue, none of whom looked in her direction. Each wore an expression telling that they'd rather be anywhere but there.

She rang the bell of the Montessori.

'Hi,' a female voice said over the intercom. 'Who is it?'

'Hello,' Darcy replied. 'Gardaí. I wonder if we could have a word?'

There was silence.

'OK. Come in, but I was just about to close.'

There was another pause and then a buzzer rang that released the lock on the door.

Inside, there was one large room, which was filled with children's chairs and tables and whose walls were covered with colourful paintings and pictures about the weather and the planets. A woman, perhaps in her early thirties, was stacking chairs onto the tables.

'Are you Rachel Robinson?' Darcy asked, holding out her ID.

'That's me,' she replied, without stopping her stacking.

She was attractive, with long red hair, an oval face, and big blue eyes. She wore a short tight skirt with black tights which Darcy felt wasn't very child friendly.

'I'm Detective Sergeant Darcy Doyle and this is my colleague, Detective Inspector Mick Kelly. We only want a few minutes of your time, Ms. Robinson.'

'Yes, that's fine. Please call me Rachel.'

'What's your official role here exactly, Rachel?' Darcy asked.

Rachel paused in her work 'The title seems to change every year, whenever a new Department of Education committee is formed, but I suppose you could just call me a Montessori assistant.' She began to stack again. 'Sorry — I'm afraid I'm under a bit of pressure to finish tidying up. Our cleaner, the poor woman, has been off for a couple of weeks, and I have to leave soon. It's been so crazy here the last few days. Stressful, you know? We're all so very worried about Alfie.'

'Yes, I'm sure it's been very tough for you all here,' Darcy said.

'It has. He was a lovely boy,' she said, and stopped tidying up. 'Always ready with a big smile and those big blue eyes. And he was a kind boy. He was ...' She paused and began to cry, covering her face with both hands.

Neither Darcy nor Mick said or did anything.

'I'm sorry,' she said, sniffling. 'We've had a lot of media attention, and it's been very stressful.'

'I'm sure it has, Ms. Robinson,' Darcy said. 'But I'm afraid it's going to get a bit worse.'

'What do you mean?' she asked.

'They've found a body.'

'*Oh God. Alfie?*'

'We're not sure yet, but it doesn't look good.'

Rachel leaned back against one of the tables.

Mick walked over to her, ripped off a sheet of paper from a paper roll and handed it to her to wipe her eyes. He waited until she had composed herself. When he spoke, his tone was one of compassion but firmness.

'Is there anything at all you can tell us that might help our investigation, Rachel?'

'I'm sorry. I've already told the other detectives everything I know.'

Darcy noticed that this time she didn't look up at Mick when she spoke. Mick's instincts were proving right again. They needed to keep digging until something began to show.

Mick's phone beeped. He took it out of his jacket pocket, read it and then showed the screen to Darcy. It was a message from the Chief.

**Scanlans arriving at 3pm in Whitehall to identify body. Be there.**

Darcy nodded.

'Is there anything you'd like to tell us, Rachel, before we go?' she asked.

Rachel's watery blue eyes found Darcy, but she shook her head.

# Chapter 5

On the top step of the State Pathologist's mortuary, a hundred-year-old building in Whitehall on the northside of the city, Darcy and Mick were standing on either side of Chief Superintendent Glenn O'Riordan. They hadn't chosen to stand as if they were his bodyguards, but the Chief had instructed them to be on either side of him.

Whatever was about to happen, Darcy thought, the Chief didn't want to get the full blame for this one.

Uniformed Gardaí stood around the entrance below them, ramrod straight in the presence of the Chief. In contrast, Mick had his hands in his pockets and was leaning against a concrete pillar. If it weren't such a solemn occasion, Darcy would have punched him. There were also a few journalists, four or five photographers and a small group of members of the public. It was supposed to have been a closed affair but, as always, the press had been tipped off.

A Garda car turned onto the street, escorting an SUV marked *Scanlan's Construction*. Both the Garda car and the SUV pulled in and parked alongside the kerb. The uniforms rushed to the opening doors and assisted the grieving parents through the small crowd. The traffic had stopped at the junction, the drivers peering out at the scene before them, which had become eerily quiet except for the rapid clicks from photographers' cameras.

John and Valerie Scanlan climbed the steps like two old pilgrims reaching the top of Croagh Patrick. Chief O'Riordan descended to greet them halfway, helping Valerie the remaining distance and opening the heavy wooden door for her. John Scanlan followed with Darcy and Mick, and several uniformed officers fell in behind.

In the ornate hall, with its brass fixtures and original plaster features, Deputy State Pathologist Dr. Catherine Daly stood waiting for her visitors, an assistant on either side.

She shook hands with the Scanlans.

'I have everything prepared for you,' she said. 'Please come this way.'

She gently took Valerie by the elbow and led the way into the building.

Inside the small theatre, Darcy saw the single trolley that held the body of the little boy, a crisp white sheet covering him. Fluorescent lights from above reflected off it so that the sheet gave the impression it glowed, as if the source of light filling the room was coming from the child.

Valerie began to weep. John went to her and placed his arms around her. With the side of her head tucked into his chest, he stepped forward slowly as if pushing her towards the table.

There was no need for words. No need for instructions. Everyone knew what they were there for, and everyone wanted it to be over. For days the Scanlans had hoped and prayed this moment would never come, and now they took the last few steps, every heart-breaking moment of every day leading to this point.

Catherine placed her hand on the corner of the white sheet. She waited for the couple to be close enough to see, so close that there could be no doubt.

John and Valerie Scanlan looked down at the outline of the little boy's face, the hollow of his sunken eyes, nose and lips pushing upwards under the sheet.

Catherine removed the top section of the sheet, revealing the face of the child. A thin strip of cloth covered his eyelids.

Valerie convulsed into tears. She sank to her knees, and John knelt and held on to her as Catherine placed the sheet back over the boy's head.

Next to her, Darcy heard a sigh of relief leave the Chief and felt him move away. There was a shuffling of feet as everyone else slowly left, allowing the Scanlans some privacy. Only Darcy, Mick and Catherine stayed.

Valerie was still on her knees in tears, her husband kneeling beside her, tending to her.

He turned towards Catherine.

Darcy watched as he shook his head.

'That's not him,' he said. 'That's not our Alfie.'

# Chapter 6

The top step acted as a makeshift platform for Chief O'Riordan as the band of journalists stood looking up at him. Several microphones were placed close to his face as he stared out onto Griffith Avenue. A camera flashed and he jumped slightly. No matter who had stood beside him earlier, he was now on his own.

'I can confirm that the body found today is that of a young boy,' he told the journalists. 'I can also confirm that the body is not that of Alfie Scanlan. We have no positive identification at this stage.'

After a slight pause, several questions were thrown to him at once so that they sounded like one single cacophony of noise.

'The missing person case concerning Alfie Scanlan is still open and under active investigation,' he continued. 'Results of the post-mortem will dictate our course of action and if we will be pursuing a murder enquiry. That's all I have today.'

In a small act of solidarity, Darcy and Mick followed Chief O'Riordan to his car and then watched him leave.

The lift doors pinged open, and Mick stepped into the corridor of his apartment building. As he stood at his door, holding the key in his hand, his neighbour's door opened slowly.

Irena Novak stepped into the hall holding a rolling pin that was speckled with flour.

'Is that to beat me up with?' he asked.

She looked down at her hands, unsure what he meant.

'Sorry about this morning,' Mick tried again.

'Would you like to come in for some coffee?'

'No, I'm ... I'm exhausted, to be honest. It's been a long day. A rough day, you know?'

'Is that poor little boy the case you're working on?' she asked.

He didn't reply for a moment, but then nodded. 'Thanks, anyway. I'm all coffee'd out, if you know what I mean?'

She nodded. 'Goodnight then, Mick.'

She went back inside and closed the door.

He looked at the closed door, unsure whether he'd said the right thing, the wrong thing, too much, or more likely not enough. With women, that's how Mick always felt.

It was perhaps the first time in about five days he had looked at his apartment fully sober. It did not make for a pretty picture. His stomach grumbled. He looked down at it protruding so far that he couldn't see his shoes. He scratched it. Such a fat and full thing, he thought, and yet it still wanted more. The greedy bastard.

He walked over to his CD player with the long shelf next to it bearing rows of CDs which were mostly male artists. Hidden behind one of the rows were three CDs and he chose one. He cracked open the CD cover and slid the shiny disc into the player.

Celine Dion's voice filled the apartment. He closed his eyes and stood there for a moment. Calm came over him, as it always did, as her melodies and powerful vocals uplifted him from his earthly chaos. Recently, he had heard one of her songs on the radio in Irena's apartment. The next day he had bought three of her CDs and he now played them almost every evening when he got home.

He walked into the kitchen and looked at the counter. There was a kettle, a toaster, a ripped-open box of Lyons tea bags and an empty bottle of cheap whiskey with perhaps the dregs of half a glass at its bottom. Mick stared at it as if it held all the power in the world. At least all the power to redeem or destroy.

He lifted the bottle up and unscrewed its cap. He smelt its contents. It smelt like the perfume of a long-lost distant lover. Without thinking about it, or rather before he had time to think about it, he poured it down the sink.

He knew he should eat something, but the effort of cooking or even ordering takeaway food was enough to stave off his appetite so he walked back into the living room. The city lights lit his apartment. He opened the window and took out his cigarettes. He cupped one in his hands and lit it, inhaling deeply as if it were his first of the day. Even though he lived alone, his son would sometimes come to visit, so he never smoked in his apartment. Officially, anyway.

It was a moment for him to think about things, to sort all the shit out in his head, but his head felt like an overflowing glass, and now all he wanted was a little sleep. He inhaled the tobacco deep into his lungs a few more times and then squashed out the tip of the cigarette before dropping it into the car park below and shutting the window.

He'd promised himself he'd take a shower when he got home and now, as he stepped into his bedroom, he promised himself that he would take a shower in the morning. He removed his jacket and laid it across the empty side of his bed. He unclipped his sidearm, checked its safety was on and then put it in the top drawer of his bedside locker. He sat on the bed, took off his shoes and socks, his trousers, and placed them all on top of his jacket.

He slid his bulk under the covers of his bed and felt the cool sheets grip him like an icy hug. Then he thought about what he always thought about the last thing at night – his son Michael and his daughter Lucy. He tried to imagine what they would be doing right now at that moment and then he didn't notice the cold anymore. He only noticed the silence and the cold sweat that was forming on his face.

He looked up at the ceiling and tried to focus on the lyrics of the old Celine Dion track as it conjured up memories of the past, but he knew there would be little sleep for him tonight.

Darcy lived at the centre of a line of nine little houses, mirrored on all four sides, making up a square, where the residents perpetually vied and fought for parking spaces like food rations in the Gulag. There was an arched opening that allowed only one car at a time to enter or exit. It was already dark and cold, but the lights from the tinsel-decorated windows reflected out onto the cobblestones, emitting a warm lustre into the air. Through the windows, Christmas trees dressed in multi-coloured lights added a magic to the secluded neighbourhood that would fail to move only those who bore the coldest of hearts. More than once, when driving into the square, Darcy thought the image reminded her of an old TV Christmas ad, almost too perfect to be real.

Her home was a small one-storey one-bedroom house in a traditional working-class area called the Liberties. The auctioneer had used words like 'quaint' and 'cute' and 'surprisingly large for its size' whatever that meant but, either way, Darcy thought it was perfect. She lived alone and there was more than enough space for her, her stuff and her thoughts.

She broke up some instant noodles into a bowl, poured water from the tap over them and then stuck it in the microwave for five minutes as she went to take a shower. She ate as she dried herself and was surprised by her hunger. Then she gulped down a glass of cold orange juice as it was the only cold liquid she had in the fridge.

Her breath was visible in the icy air when she left the house. The people of Dublin were all chatter about the possibility of a white Christmas, the first in over twenty years. Bookmakers were taking bets and children in schools barely spoke of anything else.

Darcy welcomed the warmth of the foyer as she entered the Mater Private Hospital on Eccles Street. Its decor of pastel-coloured furnishings, ornately framed paintings of 19th century upper-class Dublin, and thick carpeted floors had been designed to imitate the opulence and serenity of a five-star hotel. All feigned serenity was shattered, Darcy felt, by the aroma of artificial lavender soap and lemon-scented cleaning products, which failed to camouflage the bitter antiseptic smell common to all hospitals throughout the world, one that all too often secreted a generic sense of pain and hopelessness.

There was only one porter who worked the night shift after eight, and he had raised his eyes at the sound of the automatic doors opening, but when he saw Darcy, he gave her a familiar nod and returned to the sports section of his newspaper.

Darcy took the lift to the rehabilitation ward on the third floor. Her shoes squeaked along the sparkling clean corridor until she came to

Room 332. She inhaled sharply through her nose, exhaled through her mouth, and then knocked lightly twice and entered the room without waiting for a reply.

There was a small desk lamp illuminating the corner, but most of the room was lit by the orange streetlights from the window. On the bed, her boyfriend and colleague Seán Murphy lay staring out at the orange glow. By now almost all his medical equipment had been detached and removed. Only the cannula drip on the back of his hand gave any indication of the intense medical attention he had received in the previous three months.

Seán had been working undercover and assisting Darcy on a case when he had been shot. Most of the damage had been done by a single bullet to his spinal cord just above his hips. The surgeons had been pessimistic at first but, to their surprise, Seán had survived the operation when they'd removed the bullet and stabilised the spine with plates. Once he'd been transferred from ICU, he had worked hard in rehab on his core and upper-body strength. However, he had been made aware from the first day that he would never walk again.

Nowadays, he could dress himself, albeit slowly, with the help of his crutches, but still needed assistance in other areas of his life like showering.

As usual, Darcy forced herself to use a more cheerful tone than she actually felt.

'Good evening, you. And how are you feeling today?' she asked him, and kissed him on the cheek.

She then busied herself with her usual routine of tidying the room, fluffing his pillow and rearranging the cards from well-wishers, which were fewer now. She noticed a full cup of tea on his bedside table and, when she touched it, it was cold.

'I really must get a kettle in here for you,' she said. 'I'll make you a proper cup of tea next time I come in. Although how you drink your tea so strong and then are able to sleep ...'

It was only then she realised he had not moved or said anything. She looked at him and saw that he was still staring out the window.

'Seán? Are you OK? Is everything OK?'

He didn't reply.

'Seán? Will I get the nurse?'

He shook his head.

'What is it then?'

'They told me I can leave.'

A big grin crossed her face. 'That's wonderful!' She bent down and kissed him on the lips. 'That's great news, Seán. When? When can you leave?'

Seán shrugged. 'Whenever I want to, I guess.'

'So why the long face?' she asked and ran her hand down the side of his cheek.

'I don't know. I'm sorry.'

Darcy looked behind her for the chair and then dragged it to the side of the bed. She sat down, reached out and took his hand in hers.

'Do you remember what that doctor told you at the start of all this?' she said. 'Months ago. Because I do. He said that everyone, your family, your friends, would tell you that getting home and leaving here was the finishing line and they would treat it as such, but that you would feel differently about it. Do you remember that?'

She gently stroked the back of his hand and Seán let out a deep sigh as if he'd been holding his breath.

'He told you, he told us, that after months of being in here, in this room, with the hum of the machines and the antiseptic smell and the rhythm of the nurses coming and going, you would grow to feel that this room was almost like home to you, and with the safety and security that that brings. And you might not see leaving here as the victory that some others might. But that it was the start of something new — new challenges, new things to learn, new mistakes, new failures and new victories.'

Darcy felt so sorry for him, but she knew she couldn't express that emotion to him.

'It'll take time,' she told him. 'You're strong. We're strong. We'll get there.'

'I know. I'm sorry. I'm struggling every day not to feel sorry for myself.'

He looked up at her and they made proper eye contact for the first time.

'My parents called in earlier,' he told her. 'They've offered to take me, of course, but to be honest I think I'd rather take my chances in the rehabilitation centre in Cabinteely.'

'But it's Christmas next week!'

Seán laughed. 'What's that got to do with anything?'

'I know I'm no Mrs Christmas myself, but you can't spend Christmas in a rehab centre.'

'I just can't face my mum and dad. Going back to my old bedroom, my mum fussing over me about every little thing. I know they mean well, but who needs that? Give me the rehab centre any day.'

She stood up, turned and walked to the window. Frost was already forming on the cars below, reflecting the bright, cold moon that shone down from a cloudless sky. She surprised herself at how quickly she made the decision.

'You'll move in with me so,' she told him. It wasn't a question.

Seán didn't say anything.

'It's the only way. I'll call the doctors tomorrow and make the arrangements.'

'Look, Darcy,' he said, 'I appreciate the offer, don't get me wrong. But I think the rehab centre really is the best place for me.'

'Have you ever been to one of those centres? Trust me, it wouldn't be the best place for you. I can take you there for your sessions. The job will support us, they've already been very supportive of you. I know my place is small, but it's mostly open plan. Everything is on one floor — the bathroom, the kitchen, the bedroom. The place was practically built for a wheelchair.'

'I'm not so sure, Darcy. I know how much, or I should say, how little, actual time you'll have for me. I need help getting in and out of the shower although I'm getting faster at dressing myself. I can't ask that of you.'

'And who would shower you if you went to your parents?'

'I'd be provided with a Home Support Carer for two hours every day. In the mornings, I think.'

'So rather than the carer going to your parents' house, why can't they come to my house when I go to work?'

Seán just stared at her and Darcy knew he couldn't think of anything to contradict her.

'Darcy,' he said, softer this time, 'I know we've grown closer in the time I've been here. But to move in? Share a bed? Are we ready for that?'

'We'll find out, won't we? And if I find out you are beginning to annoy the shit out of me, I promise to dump you at the door of the Rehab Centre. Even if it's on Christmas Day.'

She held out her hand for him to shake. He placed his hand in hers.

'And if I find you unbearable,' he smiled, 'and I ask you to drop me at the Rehab Centre, then you promise to do that also?'

'Agreed,' she said.

And then he gently pulled her arm closer to him, and she bent down and kissed him on the lips.

# Thursday

# 19 December

# Chapter 7

The James Joyce Martello Tower stood in stoic silence as Niamh jumped feet first into the sea, the bitterly cold water jolting through her body like an electric shock. Although her daily routine for the last five years, it still caught her breath every time. She cried out a self-congratulatory *whoop* as she swam and smiled up at the empty rocks and pier of the small harbour known throughout Dublin as 'The Forty Foot', though the reason why was lost in the mists of time. It was still dark, but the reflections from the street lights flickered along the crests of the gentle waves as they drifted in to shore. There were never many fellow swimmers at six in the morning and today there were none. She put that down to it being a particularly cold morning, even for December.

Although respected by both her colleagues and patients in the Urology Department of St. Vincent's Hospital, where she had worked for ten years, she knew they all thought her ritual swim put her in the slightly crazy category. It didn't help her case either that she never bothered dyeing her greying hair, or that she cycled to work and didn't own a car, or that, rather than two weeks at a Spanish resort for her annual holiday, she instead went on yoga retreats in India.

She didn't mind, really, what they thought of her. Soon, she would be retired, and she would be as forgotten in the hospital as a library book that had never been returned.

She swam briskly, her eyes darting from side to side. For six consecutive mornings she had seen a seal popping his head above the water as she swam. She had hoped that one of these mornings it would come close enough for her to run her hand along its back. But maybe this morning was too cold even for a seal.

'Do you think it's possible to befriend a seal?' she had asked the urology consultant yesterday who had stared at her for several moments before returning to a medical chart without dignifying her question with a reply.

She felt a thud at her legs and her heart skipped a beat. The seal had returned. She stopped swimming and tread water. Afraid to frighten it away, she didn't turn around or make any sudden movements. It bumped off her again, closer this time. To encourage it, she inched her arm back and caressed its skin.

It felt smoother than she'd imagined it would. As it drifted up beside her, she dared to turn her head and face it.

The corpse's face and body drifted by her and Niamh stared into its glassy dead eyes. She felt her insides curl up and her heart stop. She could not move, her brain trying to come to grips with the dead body floating inches from her.

A cry pushed up from her, but no sound came out. It lodged in her throat, preventing her from breathing. Then panic set in and she splashed chaotically at the water, the white foam of the sea bubbling all around her.

She kicked and flailed her arms until she eventually moved in the direction of the pier. Her elbows and knees knocked off the ancient stone and ripped open her skin, but it wouldn't be until much later that she'd even notice the pain. Clambering up the steps, she didn't stop until she reached the pier wall where she had left her bag and clothes. She gulped in the air and tried to control the initial hysteria she had felt. Her whole body began to shake.

Her medical training and professionalism kicked in as her heart rate calmed somewhat. She reached into her bag and pulled out a towel and threw it over her shoulders, then she searched in the bag's pockets for her iPhone. She slid her finger along the screen to unlock it, but it didn't open.

She dropped her iPhone and rubbed her hands along the towel to remove the slick seawater deposits. She rubbed and rubbed as her eyes rested on the dead body, its face staring up into the early morning heavens, the torso bobbing gently up and down, disturbing the reflection of the lights on the crests of the waves, as if waiting patiently to be rescued.

# Chapter 8

Darcy parked along the side wall of the James Joyce Martello tower in Sandycove. She looked down at the waves lapping against the boulders, their gentleness belying the icy depths below the surface.

'It's just a quick look, that's all,' Mick told her.

'You think it's more than a drowning?'

'I don't know. Something in the way the report described the body ...'

An image of the little boy's dead body bobbing in the sea popped into her head and she shuddered.

'Where are Burns and Kane anyway?' she asked, shaking the thought away. 'They're the ones supposed to be here. Most likely tucked up in bed.'

'Yeah, side by side.'

Darcy laughed.

'Come on then,' she told him before opening the door. 'Get your game face on.'

Mick smiled at that one and zipped up his jacket to his chin before getting out. The northern wind scurried along the surface of the Irish Sea and threw an ice-cold misty breeze at them. All the warmth from their twenty-minute drive vanished immediately.

Darcy looked over towards the Forty Foot swimming area and saw two members of the Garda Sub-Aqua Team climbing up the metal ladder and out of the water. A closed body bag was already laid out on the small pier. Two ambulances had reversed down towards the water's edge.

'Looks like we beat forensics this time,' Darcy said.

'So maybe it's not true after all,' Mick told her.

'What's not true?'

'Dr. Pepple. They say she never sleeps.'

'I can believe that.'

Inside the first ambulance, a woman sat with a shiny foil blanket wrapped around her, sipping from a cup. She was being consoled by a female paramedic. Another member of the ambulance crew stood outside. Darcy approached him, her ID already in her hand.

'Good morning. You think it's OK if we have a word with her?' she asked him.

He shrugged. 'She's fine, Detective,' he told her. 'Just a little shocked, that's all.'

Darcy kept her ID in her hand and walked up to the open door of the ambulance.

'Hi,' she said. Both women turned to her. 'I'm Detective Sergeant Darcy Doyle and this is Detective Inspector Mick Kelly. Niamh, isn't it?'

Niamh nodded.

'Do you mind if we have a quick word?' Darcy directed her question towards the paramedic, and she took the hint and stood up to leave.

'I'm just outside if you need me,' the paramedic assured Niamh.

Darcy climbed in and sat opposite Niamh as Mick waited at the entrance.

'That's a terrible shock you're after getting,' Darcy said.

Niamh nodded.

'Would you mind going over what exactly happened this morning?'

'I'll do my best,' Niamh said.

'Thank you. Try to include everything, even things that you feel may be irrelevant.'

'OK.'

At the start of a recent case, Darcy had mentioned to Mick that there was someone she thought could be a potential suspect. Mick had laughed at her. 'At the start of every investigation,' he'd told her, 'everyone is a potential suspect.' She doubted that this could apply to this severely shocked woman — and one who had called the emergency services. Still, she might have observed something significant.

She listened without interruption to Niamh's account of events. She smiled and nodded and allowed her to talk. After Niamh had finished, Darcy still didn't speak. Sometimes witnesses were uncomfortable with the silence and filled it with information they would have been better off keeping to themselves.

This time, however, Niamh just stared at Darcy, as if unsure whether she was supposed to say something else.

'We'll let you get on your way so,' Darcy told her. 'If we need anything further, we'll get in touch. I have all your details here. Is that OK?'

'Yes, yes, of course,' Niamh told her.

Darcy put out her hand and Niamh shook it. Her hand was still icy cold.

Mick was already halfway down the pier when Darcy stepped down from the ambulance.

That man has no patience, she thought to herself and followed him. Two uniformed Gardaí from the local station stood side by side rubbing their hands to stay warm.

'Alright, lads?' Mick greeted them.

'Sir,' they both mumbled.

Darcy walked over to the zipped-up body bag. In Templemore Garda College she had been shown the different stages of decomposition that a body suffers when submerged underwater for long periods. Photographs of half-eaten faces with hollow eye sockets and bloated bodies had been displayed on the monitors.

'Open it,' Mick told her.

She studied Mick's face and suddenly had the thought that he already knew who was inside. She braced herself, bent down and unzipped the bag.

At first, it was the near-perfect condition of the face that surprised her. Then she looked more carefully.

'*Holy fuck!*' she said. She looked up at Mick. 'Isn't that …?'

'Yeah,' Mick agreed. 'Rachel Robinson. From the Montessori. That's who she looks like anyway. Any ID on her?'

Darcy continued to unzip the bag, revealing more of the body, and then she stopped. She turned her head and looked up at Mick.

'Is that what I think it is?' Darcy asked him.

'Yep. Gunshot wound. Better call the Chief.'

'There has to be a connection, Chief,' Darcy said into the mobile phone. 'It can't be a coincidence.'

Twenty minutes after Darcy had ID'd the body, Detectives Kevin Burns and Paul Kane had shown up. They both stood close to her in an attempt to intimidate her into passing the case over to them. They already had a boatload of cases to attend to but, the way they saw it, anything to put Doyle back in her box would be considered a win.

'That missing boy is your priority, Doyle,' the Chief's voice came down the line. 'We can't afford any distractions from that. Give the case to Burns.'

'It is *not* a distraction, sir,' she told him. 'There has to be a link. We spoke to this woman just eighteen hours ago and today she shows up in the sea with a gunshot hole. That's *not* a coincidence.'

There was silence at the end of the line. Darcy turned away from Kane and Burns. She could smell Kane's aftershave which was strong enough to even block out the smell of the sea. She turned on him quickly and placed her hand firmly on his chest. She pressed the mobile phone against her jacket to block the microphone.

'Don't even fucking try to bully me, Kane,' she said into his face. 'I'm warning you. *Back the fuck away.*'

Then she turned, moved a little distance away and held the phone up to her ear again.

'Look, Chief,' she said, 'this murder of Rachel Robinson has to tie in with Alfie missing. I just know it. And I know it'll lead us on the right path to finding the boy. Whether he's dead or alive.'

She could picture her boss sitting in his office with the glass door so he could look out at his detectives at work.

'Alright,' he said with a sigh. 'It's yours. I have a meeting this afternoon with the Commissioner. He can smell blood like a shark and if this thing doesn't start to make sense, then my head's on the chopping block.'

'Yes, sir. I understand, sir.'

'I don't think you do, Detective. But if you need any motivation for a quick solve then think about this. If I get the boot from NBCI then the position falls to the most senior man in our department. You know who that is?'

'No, sir.'

'Burns.'

Darcy turned and saw Burns staring at her as if he could hear everything the chief was saying.

'I understand now, sir.'

'Good,' the Chief told her, and he hung up.

'Give me that phone,' Burns called out, walking towards her. 'I want to talk to him.'

'Well, he doesn't want to talk to you,' she told him, pocketing her phone. 'He says you can go back to bed and leave this one to the professionals.'

Darcy turned away from him but Burns grabbed her by the shoulder.

'*You're not one of us*,' he said, his face close to hers. '*And you never will be.*'

'One of you? What's that? A misogynistic arsehole? Now get your hands off me.'

Burns kept his hand on her. 'Never forget,' he said, 'that you're only here because you've got a pair of tits.'

Darcy swept her left arm to the side and dislodged his grip on her and with her right arm she shoved him hard in the chest. Burns almost lifted off the ground as he stumbled backwards. Kane put his hand out to steady his colleague but Burns slapped it away.

There was silence on the pier as everyone collectively held their breath. Darcy looked over at Mick. He shook his head at her.

The two uniformed Gardaí were smiling but changed their expressions when Burns turned around.

Without saying another word, he stormed off back up the pier to his car, with Kane, like a lapdog, scuttling after him.

Within the hour, Rachel's body had been removed to Whitehall for a post-mortem. At the crime scene, Dr. Phoebe Pepple had confirmed the victim had died from a single gunshot wound to the chest. Two fingers on the right hand had also been shot off, which she put down to a defensive wound.

Darcy stared at the spot on the pier where Rachel's body had lain. She put away her notebook and looked around for Mick. She spotted him among some rocks overlooking the area. His head was bent down as if he were searching for a lost pair of glasses.

She climbed the slippery boulders over to him.

'What are you doing?' she asked him.

'Turn around and look.'

She did and could see the expanse of the coast all the way into Dun Laoghaire.

'Nice view. Even on a freezing day like this,' she said. 'But again, Mick, what are you doing up here?'

'I've walked by here a hundred times in the evenings with Michael. I'd collect him from his mother in Dalkey, and we'd drive into Blackrock and then walk along here. It has the best views, as you can see.'

'And?' she asked, trying not to show her impatience.

'I've never walked along here without seeing someone up in this spot. Young fellas smoking or lovers taking advantage of the privacy. I think these boulders are smooth because so many Dubliners' arses have sat on them for generations. Notice the way it's sheltered, the way it isn't as cold up here?'

'I'm listening.'

'I took a chance that there may have been someone up here last night,' he said. 'Nice view of the pier from here as well.'

They stared at each other for a moment.

'You found something, didn't you?' she said.

Mick held out his hand. In it was a white handkerchief. He unfolded it.

'What is it? A joint?'

'It's more than just a joint. It's a very special type of joint you rarely see.'

Darcy raised her eyebrows at him but didn't reply. Mick gently folded the handkerchief back around the joint and put it in his pocket.

'Have you ever smoked that stuff?' he asked her.

'A couple of times as a teenager,' she admitted. 'When I was out with some friends.'

'And did you or any of your friends ever throw a half-smoked joint away?'

'Never.'

'Of course not. Who doesn't finish a joint right down to the butt? No one would leave it except for good reason. So, what do you make of that?'

Darcy didn't say anything for a moment. 'Someone was in this spot, last night,' she said then. She looked back towards the pier. 'They didn't want to be seen, so they stubbed it out and then forgot about it.'

'How do you know it was last night? Maybe that's been here for a few days.'

She shook her head. 'Because you found it straight away. Someone else would have found it too if it was here for even a day. Whoever smoked this was the last person up here. Until you arrived.'

'Good. I'll see if Dr. Pepple can get any prints off it,' he told her and began to climb back down to the pier.

'Hey, Mick! I'm sorry I lost it with Burns!'

He looked up at her. 'I hear the station has you odds-on favourite ahead of me now.'

'On what?'

'On being fired before me,' he said and grinned at her.

Darcy watched him descending the giant boulders awkwardly in his crumpled suit and allowed herself a smile as she knew he couldn't see her.

# Chapter 9

On the NBCI's fifth floor, in Harcourt Street Garda Station, they had set up an incident room for Darcy. Mick trailed in behind her. The room's tables and chairs were arranged as if it were a classroom. A weak afternoon sun provided most of the light through three grubby windows that looked down onto a car park below. Someone, in a moment of festivity, had stuck a three-foot Christmas tree in the corner, but had obviously abandoned the project as its scrawny branches were bare of any baubles or tinsel.

Six uniformed Gardaí, who had been hauled in to do the donkey work and assist in the case, squirmed uncomfortably in their seats. Two of the Gardaí, Garda Aoife Farrell and Garda Eoin Flanagan, sat at the front. They had both worked with Darcy before, so assumed a self-appointed, if somewhat misguided, seniority in the room. Darcy and Mick stood at the top and the six officers sat looking up at them like fledging college students waiting on a lecture.

On the wall were two large corkboards. One of them had already been adorned with photos from the crime scene. Also attached, by coloured thumbtacks, were maps of the area, and a holiday photograph of the Scanlans with their son, Alfie, all three smiling, with the sea and a bright blue sky in the background. Beside it, in stark contrast, was a photo of the dead boy. His face was pale and still, a thick black line obscuring where his eyes had once been.

Even so, the similarity between the unidentified dead boy and Alfie was obvious to everyone: approximately the same age, same fine blond hair. Even the shape of their jaws and button noses were similar. Alfie was smiling with his parents, but Darcy found it disturbingly easy to imagine the dead boy with the same perky laugh.

Darcy held back a little, waiting on Mick to direct the investigation, but he indicated for her to begin. In their previous major case Mick had been very much the leader, but now he was allowing her to take the lead. She wondered if perhaps he was simply too weary to proceed or if he was finally gaining confidence in her ability to lead her own investigation. Maybe it was both. She looked down at the six expectant faces and hoped that her nervousness did not show on her own face.

'First of all,' she began, 'apologies that you had to wait around half the day for us. As I'm sure you've already been told, a body was recovered from the Forty Foot in Sandycove this morning. Although it's only a preliminary identification, Detective Kelly and I have ID'd her as Rachel Robinson, one of the assistants who worked in Alfie's Montessori.'

She paused to make sure she had their full attention.

'As you can imagine, we find it hard to believe there isn't a connection between the disappearance of Alfie and the death of his teacher Rachel.'

Darcy looked behind her at the corkboard full of photographs and information.

'Good job on the board, Aoife. I appreciate you doing that, thanks.'

Aoife nodded but kept a stern face. Darcy saw Eoin sliding his leg under the table and tapping his foot off hers.

'Our job at this moment,' Darcy continued, holding up three fingers, 'is threefold. Number one, find Alfie Scanlan. Number two, find the identity of the dead boy and the circumstances in which he died. And number three, find out who shot Rachel Robinson, and why.'

She smiled at them for the first time.

'What could be easier than that?'

They all returned her smile.

Darcy turned to Mick. 'Anything to add?'

He straightened up.

'We should assume that Alfie Scanlan is still alive,' he told them. 'Much of the media has given him little chance. I want you to treat this case as if he is alive. Is that understood?'

They all nodded.

'Are there any questions before we hand out your tasks?' Darcy asked.

'It's hard to believe that no one has reported the dead boy as missing,' Aoife said. 'Is it possible he's from out of the State?'

'Good point. We're checking with the UK Missing Persons Unit at present. Europol and INTERPOL have also been contacted.'

'Surely an identical boy turning up dead doesn't bode well for Alfie Scanlan's chances?' someone else asked.

'I told you we're not making that assumption,' Mick told him, 'and I'm not expecting you to either.'

'Yes, sir.'

'Anyone else?'

Darcy saw Eoin look to his left and right before asking, 'Do you think we could be looking at another serial killer?'

It was a question Darcy had been expecting, although she'd thought she'd have to face it in front of the press. Eoin had worked with her before on a previous serial-killer case, hence the use of the word 'another'.

'We can't answer that yet, Eoin.' She tried to think of something else to say as the room stayed silent.

Mick spoke up. 'OK then, when you're given a task for the case, don't just perform your duty and tick a box. Think about what you're doing and think about how it connects to everything else. OK?'

There were mumblings of 'Yes' and 'Yes, sir'.

Darcy took out her notebook and flipped it open.

'Aoife, I want you to go to Rachel's apartment. It's one of those new apartment blocks along the Liffey somewhere. Get her exact address from PULSE. We'll be there later.'

'How will I get in?'

'Ask the manager or whoever's in charge of the building. Use a bit of muscle if you have to.'

'Take one of the lads with you,' Mick told her.

'I'll go,' Eoin volunteered.

'No, you won't,' Darcy said. 'I need you to start on the IT stuff — her social media presence, texts on her phone, medical records, bank-account details. All that juicy stuff. Also was she in a relationship or were there any exes?'

'And check out G-Tube for any unusual similarities over the last couple of weeks,' Mick suggested. 'You never know, this may not have been his first outing.' G-Tube was the term used by Gardaí to describe all the captured CCTV footage of crimes committed throughout the country. Whenever an officer had a few spare minutes, they could watch the videos in the hope they'd recognise a suspect and assist another station with a solve.

Eoin lowered his head.

'If you had wanted to go knocking down doors,' Darcy asked him, 'then why did you bother learning all the techy stuff?'

Eoin had no answer for that.

Darcy moved on. 'You two,' she said, pointing at the male and female Gardaí sitting at the end. 'Door-to-door. Businesses close to the Montessori and her apartment neighbours. Did anyone notice any visitors? Or anyone hanging around? You know the drill. Now, who's left?'

The remaining Garda, who Darcy reckoned looked about fourteen years-old, put his hand up.

'There's a helpline number going up today,' she told him. 'I need you to man it. There'll be a lot of shite. Most of it, in fact, but you might get something. You can never tell with these things. Record everything.'

'Yes, sir,' he said. 'I mean ma'am.' He shifted in his seat and took his eyes off her.

Darcy stared at him, enjoying his uneasiness.

Mick spoke up and put the guy out of his misery. 'Detective Doyle and myself are heading down to talk to the State Pathologist. She has her initial results for the boy on the mountain.' He looked at his watch. 'We'll meet again here this time tomorrow. Do you all have our phone numbers? Get them off Aoife or Eoin if you don't. And switch numbers with each other as well.'

He paused for a moment to make sure he still had their full attention.

'Whatever the fate of Alfie Scanlan, it won't be from lack of trying on our part that we don't find him. Do your best and let's get this kid home to his parents before Christmas. OK?'

Darcy was about to walk out the front entrance of Harcourt Street when Mick grabbed her by the elbow and pulled her to one side.

A Garda motorcycle had pulled up outside the building and a black Mercedes drove in behind. The driver of the Mercedes was a uniformed Garda and he jumped out and opened the back door. Garda Commissioner Donal McMahon stepped out, straightening his jacket. His shiny cap had gold ivy trimmings along its brim, and on the front was a large orange badge, like a miner's light that seemed to illuminate his way as he walked.

He climbed the steps of Harcourt Street as if he were a conqueror returning to Rome.

'Now that the missing boy is all over the media, he probably sees it as an opportunity to get his face on the evening news,' Mick said from behind Darcy. 'Self-righteous arsehole.'

'Aren't they all?' she asked.

'No. I've seen some good ones. Commissioners who are on our side and are ready to jump to our defence when it's called for. McMahon's only interest is pleasing the politicians who appointed him and, of course, anything for his own benefit. I'd say he hates our GRA and AGSI unions more than he does the gangsters. He'd also destroy your whole career rather than allow a blemish on his own. We'd come a long way from the misogynist and bigoted organisation of my rookie days. That's until he took over.'

They both stood and watched Commissioner McMahon enter the building as his uniformed assistant scurried after him. When the desk sergeant looked up from his newspaper, the colour drained from his face. Unsure exactly what he should do, he jumped up from his sitting position and stood to attention. The commissioner walked by, ignoring him, and went straight to the lifts. His uniformed assistant managed to jump ahead of him and press the button.

When they had entered the lift and the doors had closed, Mick and Darcy walked back to the main exit. She watched his body relax and the anger drain slowly from his face.

'You know,' she said, 'for a man with a reputation for being a bit of a hard case, I've never seen you so scared before.'

'I am not afraid of him,' Mick said, taking out a cigarette from its packet.

'That's not what it looked like from where I was standing.'

'I was only protecting you,' he said.

Behind them, they heard the lift doors ping open.

'*Oh shite! He's back!*' Darcy gasped.

Mick pulled the cigarette quickly from his mouth and looked over at the empty lift.

She smiled at him, and he put the cigarette back between his lips.

'Alright,' he said, as he walked out the front door. 'I'll give you that one.'

'You'll have to explain that to me, please, Dr. Daly.'

'Of course. And remember, Darcy, please call me Catherine.'

So far Dr. Daly had ignored Mick. Their first meeting in a previous case had found him in a foul mood, and she had not as yet happened upon the better side of him.

'Let me show you,' Catherine said and removed the sheet from the top half of the boy's body.

In her peripheral vision, Darcy saw Mick draw back slightly. She knew that in his thirty-year career he had seen dozens of dead bodies, some in horrific conditions, and like all cops he had become desensitised to the shocking sight of a corpse. It gave her some solace, however, although she wasn't sure why, that the sight of a child's body could still trigger a revulsion that even a veteran like her partner could not dismiss too easily.

'It might be of some consolation for his parents, whoever they might be,' Catherine told them, 'that Joey shows no sign of any sexual or physical abuse.'

'Wait a second,' Darcy said. 'Has the boy been identified?'

'No, not as far as I know.'

'You just called him "Joey".'

'Well, we couldn't keep referring to him as "the boy", could we?'

Darcy thought about this for a second but couldn't think of a reason to disagree with her. She looked down at Catherine bent over the body as she used her pen to point out various bruises and lacerations.

'Now look here,' she continued, 'all along his right-hand side.'

'They look like bruise marks to me,' Mick said.

'Fifi, I mean Dr. Pepple, mentioned possible animal interference while he was lying on the mountain,' Darcy said.

'I know how thorough Dr. Pepple is,' Catherine said. 'And she's right. But my findings are also based on an autopsy. It would be impossible for anyone, even her, to guess at hypernatraemia at a crime scene.'

'Hyper ...?' Mick asked.

'Hypernatraemia. Basically, it's a high concentration of sodium in the body. Initially its symptoms are nausea, weakness or light-headedness, but if allowed to continue untreated then matters can get quite severe.'

'How severe?'

With her open palm, Dr. Daly indicated the body beside her.

'Sodium?' Darcy asked. 'You *do* mean salt?'

'Yes.'

'But why would it be allowed to continue untreated, Dr. Daly? I mean, Catherine,' Darcy asked.

'I'm afraid that's for you and your partner to find out, Darcy. What I can tell you is that I've seen the symptoms before, but it's usually in the elderly who live alone. Not a child.'

They all stood in silence, looking at the boy's face, each imagining the ordeal he must have suffered. Having named the boy seemed to have added to the poignancy.

'How do you diagnose hypernatrim ...?' Mick asked.

'Hyper-nat-raem-ia,' Catherine said slowly, happy to correct him. 'The sodium levels in Joey's blood were through the roof. Unfortunately, it can take weeks for the full toxicology reports to come back, and at this time of year it may not be till February, but I'm sure they'll confirm my findings.'

'Well, Catherine –' Darcy began.

'There's one more thing,' Catherine said, cutting her off.

'Yes?'

'It's not backed by any scientific analysis as yet, and I hate to go out on a limb, but take a look at this.'

She stepped behind the boy's head and, as if prising open a cracked coconut in two, she removed the top half of the boy's skull, exposing his brain. It made a loud suction noise.

'*Jesus Christ!*' Mick said.

Darcy felt her lunch rise into her throat. Beside her, Mick took a step back.

'What?' Catherine asked, oblivious to the cause of their distress, then looked down at the brain and the separated skull in her hands. 'Oh, sorry. I should have warned you. My bad, as the kids say.'

'*Just get on with it*,' Mick said roughly.

'Right, then. If you look here,' she said and placed her finger along the edge of the brain and the skull, 'there's an unusual swelling that couldn't have been caused by hypernatraemia. If anything, it should be the opposite. You see, the brain adapts to the high levels of sodium, and it shrinks.'

Darcy dared herself to lean forward and look closer.

'And this has, what? Swollen up?' she asked.

'Precisely,' Catherine said and gently placed the skull back into position.

'So, what could cause that?' Mick asked her.

'Overcompensation, would be my guess.'

'Meaning?'

'Meaning, Joey was given too little water over a long period or too much sodium, and then a correction was made. But it was too much. A hospital would have slowly administered him IV fluids, and that would have helped with any dehydration. But Joey was suddenly given too much, and it had the opposite effect. Cerebral oedema occurred, resulting in his death.'

'So, he had too little water but then was given too much?' Darcy said.

'Exactly. The high levels of sodium in his blood would have caused him severe dehydration and vomiting but it was the overcompensation of water that killed Joey. The high sodium levels in his blood would have shrunk his brain, but then as the excessive water rushed into his brain cells, it caused the swelling. Eventually, the salt in his blood would have put him in a coma, but perhaps someone tried to help him and that was what killed him. Maybe he was killed by kindness? Either way, he didn't have much of a chance. The poor little guy.'

# Chapter 10

A robin landed in the middle of Frank 'The Face' Kavanagh's lawn and began violently pecking between the blades of grass. Frank watched it for a few moments and was about to turn away when he saw the neighbour's cat, a large tabby, crouched down and inching its way in the grass behind. So focused on its meagre pickings, the robin was unaware of the imminent danger lurking behind it. A simple tap on the glass would have alerted the robin and spoiled the cat's lunch, but Frank let the drama between the assailant and its prey continue to its natural and inevitable conclusion.

The cat pounced, and Frank knocked back the last of his espresso as the tabby stood over its kill, picking feathers from its teeth.

He scanned the rest of his manicured and landscaped back garden. A dull pain, which had not quite manifested into a full-blown migraine, festered just below the surface of his forehead. He rubbed the area with the tips of his fingers as if trying to scratch under his skin. Overseeing the financial statements to all his properties and investments was not a task he enjoyed.

Twenty years ago, he had diverted the majority of his substantial resources into legitimate businesses, imagining he would be able to sit back and watch his portfolio grow. He had been surprised at the number of tax-free loopholes that the corporate world enjoyed. Investing money in pension plans, mutual funds, and offshore private holding companies to capitalise on tax-avoidance schemes was, if he had to be honest, wholly criminal.

In his younger years, when he operated his drug enterprise, it had been a simple supply-and-demand import business where each link in the chain received their cut of the profits. In the corporate world, however, it seemed to be all about squeezing the man below you in order to maximise profit for the fat cat at the top.

But Frank was no crusader. Who was he not to exploit every penny for what it was worth?

There was a knock on the door, and it opened to reveal Frank's main muscle man and sidekick, Tony.

'Excuse me, Boss,' he said. 'There's a woman at the gate asking for you.'

'What does she want?' Frank asked.

'No idea, Boss,' Tony said.

'Didn't you ask her?'

'No, Boss.'

'Right. Does she have a name?'

'Yes, Boss.'

'Jesus Christ, Tony, it's like talking to a fucking vending machine! What's her name?'

Tony took out a piece of paper from his pocket and read aloud.

'Ella Brunelle.'

Frank felt as if someone had just walked over his grave. Without thinking about it, he walked over to his bar and took down a bottle of whiskey. Tony watched him.

'Will I get rid of her, Boss?'

Frank poured himself a small measure and drank it in one go. 'No,' he said, his voice gentler now. 'Bring her in.'

'Both of them?'

'Both?'

'There's a girl with her.'

'For fuck sake, Tony! Bring them both in.'

Frank poured himself another and drank it back.

Ella Brunelle was still every bit the beautiful woman that Frank had known almost twenty years before. Her hair was shorter now, but it suited her strong features and made her even more beautiful than he remembered her.

She walked up to him and kissed him on both cheeks. Her eyes were still the colour of dark chocolate but there was a tiredness behind them that had not been there before.

'Frank,' she said.

He closed his eyes and, with that single word in her French accent, all the years seemed to fall away.

'Ella,' he replied.

She stood to the side, and he saw the teenage girl behind her. She was so like Ella sixteen years ago that it took his breath away. She gave him a shy and sad look, but she didn't have the eyes of her mother. Her eyes were a shade of blue like the sky on a rare cloudless winter's day in Dublin.

'This is Chloe,' Ella said.

'It's very nice to meet you, Chloe,' Frank said with a nod.

Ella touched Chloe's arm with the affection of a mother and said something to her in French. Chloe looked around and, seeing the sofa that faced out into the back garden, she went and sat there. Neither Frank nor Ella's eyes had left her.

Once she was seated, Frank noticed Ella looking around the large open-plan room. Few people failed to hide their admiration for its size. Apart from the enormous sofa and armchairs looking out onto the back garden, and the generously stocked bar, there was another space with an L-shaped couch, two matching armchairs and a dark mahogany coffee table in front of a 50-inch TV.

Ella walked to the TV area, the furthest point in the room away from Chloe and sat down.

'Can I get you a coffee or a tea?' Frank asked her.

'A glass of water is fine,' Ella said. 'Thank you.'

'What about you, Chloe? You fancy something to drink?' Frank called over, but the girl's head didn't budge.

When Frank looked back at Ella, she shook her head. 'She's fine.'

'So how long exactly has it been since we were going out?' Frank asked as he stepped behind the bar and poured her a glass of water, topping it up with some ice cubes.

She smiled, but it was awkward, as if her mouth had not made that expression in a while.

'Seventeen years. Almost two decades.'

Frank let out a whistle. 'You're making me feel like an old grey man now, Ella.'

'You *are* an old grey man. But still the handsomest man I know.'

'I somehow doubt that. So, first things first. What's this about? Money?'

'Always straight to the point. No bullshit. It was one of the reasons I loved you.'

'So, it *is* about money?' he said as he walked back to her. He placed the glass in front of her and sat down on one of the armchairs.

'No. You have provided more than enough for us throughout the years. Do you really think that I raised your daughter by myself to come here now and ask you for more money?'

Frank shook his head and glanced over at Chloe again. She had her back to them, her attention on the garden. '*Hmm*,' he said and tilted his head.

'What is it? Is it a shock to see her so big now?' Ella asked him.

'No, it's not that. Kids grow up. We get old. Our parents die. Then we die. That's how it works. Or at least that's how it's supposed to work.'

'What is it then?'

'Her eyes,' Frank said. 'They're bluer than I remember when I first saw her.'

'I've sent you photos.'

'Yes, yes, I know but it's just ... Seeing her this close. She reminds me of my mother. True Kavanagh blue eyes.'

'That girl has more of Rosie Kavanagh in her than you know.'

Frank picked up on the slight rebuff in her tone. 'Meaning?'

Ella shrugged. 'Your mother was a unique woman, Frank.'

He didn't want their conversation to slip into an argument, so he let it go. He took another mouthful of whiskey, and she sipped from her glass.

The silence in the room grew, and Frank didn't feel uncomfortable in allowing it to linger.

'So, is she the reason, I mean, the real reason you walked out on me?'

'Come on, Frank. You know the reason. I didn't want to be a gangster's wife. But you're right, I guess. As soon as I found out I was pregnant, my mind was made up. Of course, I knew your claim of owning an import business was a charade. I wasn't that gullible. Even back then. But I was that much in love, and you should never underestimate the power of a woman's denial.'

'So, one evening I go out to meet some guy in a pub about a deal,' Frank said, 'and when I come back, you're gone. No note. No goodbye.'

'I did say goodbye. Before you left for your meeting. You just didn't hear it.'

Frank was listening to her, but he had turned his attention back to Chloe. Why was he feeling so emotional about something that had happened and been resolved so long ago?

Almost two decades ago, and just after their breakup, Ella had moved back to France. She had often dreamed of returning to Dublin with Chloe, but her mother became ill and Ella could not act on her dream, instead caring for her mother during the years of her degeneration. However, every year for two weeks, during Chloe's school holidays, they had come to Dublin to enjoy the city and meet up with old friends. Her friends had married and had children Chloe enjoyed playing with through the years and improving her English. But on one of those early summer visits, when Chloe was perhaps three or four, they had been walking down Grafton Street, hand in hand, when she had spotted Frank walking towards her. He'd taken one look at her and the little French girl with blue eyes and he'd understood everything. She'd been genuinely surprised by his lack of resentment. A month later, she received a cheque for €4,000, and every month after that. Over the years, she'd sent some photos of Chloe to him by SMS, but she had never seen him again. Until today.

When Chloe was fourteen, Ella's mother had finally died, and she inherited the house. Within the year, she had sold the house and she and Chloe had moved back to Dublin. For her own reasons, Ella had not informed Frank of her return.

Frank stood up and went back to his bar. He poured himself another whiskey. Ella watched him. He sat back down in front of her.

'OK, then. We'll leave aside how much you hurt me at that time. And we'll leave aside your having a baby without telling me. We're all grownups here,' Frank said and looked over once more at Chloe. 'So back to my original question, what is this about?'

Any playfulness fell from Ella's face. She reached for her water but didn't pick it up. 'Can I have one of them?' she asked, nodding at his glass. 'No ice.'

Frank walked back to the bar and poured her a good measure of whiskey. He brought it back, and handed it to her. She drank half of it straight away. She kept the glass in her hand, glanced over again at Chloe and then faced Frank.

'I'm sorry now that I didn't tell you we had come back to Dublin.'

'It is what it is. Tell me what happened.'

'It was during the summer. Last year. Just after her sixteenth birthday. She had a boyfriend, Sam, from her school. I had met him only once. I didn't like him. He was one year older than her and too full of himself, as they say, but sometimes love can force good girls to make bad decisions, *n'est-ce pas*?'

She looked into his blue eyes, and he held her gaze but said nothing.

'He was a bit stand-offish,' she continued, 'but he was just a kid. A teenage boy. I had just started a new job on the French desk in Accenture, and I was very busy with that, so Chloe was not my primary focus, but she should have been. She told me she was going to his house to watch a movie or something. She only remembers fragments of what happened after that. He put something in her drink. We think it was Rohypnol. She remembers two other boys arriving, and all three of them standing over her, and then being carried upstairs and ...'

Ella took a drink from her whiskey. Her knuckles were white around the glass.

Frank waited, staring at her intently.

'You can imagine the rest. Each boy *used* her. They took turns and they laughed. All the time they laughed. When Chloe came home, she went to her room and I didn't see her. She told me the next morning she was ill, but I made her go to school. All I knew at that time was that she became sick and stopped eating. I took her to the doctor, and they diagnosed anorexia. It was only after two months, when I found her in the bathroom with cuts on her arms, that I began to really question her. I eventually discovered the truth. I took Chloe with me, and we went to the police. They treated us well and they were gathering evidence in order to make arrests.'

Ella stared at the empty glass as if the words to finish her story were inside the glass. She didn't look up at Frank.

'One night three men came to my house. They pushed their way inside. They dragged me by the hair into the sitting room and they put a gun into my mouth. They told me that if I didn't drop the charges against Sam Gallagher and the two other boys then they would come back another night when I was asleep in my bed. I had no choice. The police tried to persuade me to change my mind but I would not. I was too afraid. Afraid for me and afraid for Chloe. She has no one except me.'

Ella put the glass on the coffee table and joined her hands together as if in prayer.

'*Sam Gallagher?*' Frank said.

Ella raised her head and nodded.

'*Jimmy Gallagher's son?*' Frank said.

'Grandson.'

'Of course.'

Frank stood up. He still held his own glass, his fingers wrapped around it tightly. Jimmy Gallagher was one of the biggest criminals in Dublin. Like Frank, he had been in the game a long time.

Frank always put his own longevity in crime down to three things — his indirect involvement in anything illegal, the huge sums in taxes he paid each year and his negotiating skills with the other crime families. Jimmy Gallagher could put his own success down to one simple thing — his cruelty and ruthlessness that instilled fear in everyone who had the misfortune of coming into contact with him.

Frank walked around the table and sat beside Ella. She was perfectly still, and she looked as if she were made of stone.

'So, what do you want from me?' he asked her.

If he had any doubt about the answer, it vanished when she turned and looked him in the eyes. Those chocolate-brown eyes were now the colour of darkness, but she said nothing. There was no need.

Frank took a deep breath and let it out slowly. He did not want to go to war with Jimmy Gallagher. But blood was blood and, with that in mind, he stood up and went to Chloe. She was looking out at the garden and, even when he crouched down in front of her, she did not break her focus. Frank looked around to see what had her attention, and he saw the tall leafless silver birch trees, their branches swaying in the wind as if dancing to some melancholic tune that only they could hear.

He turned back to her, and took both her hands in his.

'And you, Chloe,' he whispered to her, 'what do you want?'

She withdrew her attention from the tree and looked into Frank's own blue eyes, a mirror image of her own.

She squeezed his hands and said, 'I want them to suffer. I want them to know pain. And I want my revenge.'

Frank could feel the tips of her nails digging into his skin.

'*Vengeance, papa. Je veux ma vengeance.*'

Frank and Ella continued to talk as the shadows grew longer in the garden and the leaves of the evergreen plants turned black. Their conversation switched to older times, and simpler times. They wondered why life got more complicated the older they got, like the branches of a tree as they stretched out and grew and intertwined with one another. They sipped on their whiskies slowly, old familiarities returning easily to them. The memories of their summer love affair in Dublin all those years ago brought a lightness to Ella's mood, until she reflected that it was doomed to fail from the first kiss.

At some point, Frank had got up to refill their glasses and, noticing Chloe was asleep on the sofa, he had placed a woollen throw over her.

Eventually, Ella looked at her watch.

'My God!' she said. 'I should go.'

'Why don't you stay for something to eat?' Frank said. 'I'll order in.'

'No, I must go. I already feel a little woozy,' she put a hand to her head, 'and I ...'

Frank noticed her blush.

'What is it?' he asked, smiling. 'A man?'

'No, no, nothing like that. I should be so lucky. I see a psychotherapist once a week.'

'Does it help?'

'Very much, yes.'

'You think it would be good for me too?'

'No offence, Frank. But any psychotherapist you go to would probably end up needing their own psychotherapist. You need a priest, not a shrink.'

Ella rose and went over to Chloe.

'Chloe? Chloe?' She reached down and shook her gently.

'She OK?'

'She suffers from insomnia. Then sometimes she crashes and it's impossible to wake her.' She shook her shoulder again. '*Chloe!*'

'I tell you what,' Frank said. 'Why don't you leave her here? You have my number. Text me when you're home, and I'll make sure she gets home safe. Let her sleep for now.'

'I don't know ...'

'Look, I'll have one of the lads drop you off wherever you need to go now, and you can give me a buzz when you're finished.'

Ella bit her lip and looked down at her sleeping daughter. She seemed so peaceful.

'She'll be safe here,' Frank said. 'I promise.'

'OK,' Ella agreed.

She typed as Frank walked to the door and opened it.

'*Lurch!*' he called out.

A few moments later, the tallest, thinnest and whitest man Ella had ever seen came into the room.

'Have one of the lads drive Ella to wherever she needs to go,' Frank told him.

Lurch stepped to the side to allow Ella to leave.

She went onto her tiptoes and kissed Frank on each cheek.

'Call me anytime if she needs me,' she told him.

'I promise,' he said and then he watched her leave, with Lurch close behind her.

When they were gone, Frank went back to Chloe and crouched down in front of her. He looked closely at her face, that beautiful face so much like her mother's when he was so young and foolish that he actually thought he could turn away from the life he led. And then one day she was gone. And so too were all his dreams and his wishes, and he buried them inside himself and hid them from the world and from himself.

A wisp of her hair had fallen in front of her face, and Frank reached out and gently placed it back. An image of those boys, those bastards, using her as she lay unconscious like this, flashed into his mind, and the rage welled up in him. His hands curled into fists, but he resisted the urge to slam them onto the table. He left out a long slow breath and relaxed his grip.

To go after Jimmy Gallagher's grandson would be suicidal for anyone. But Frank Kavanagh wasn't just anyone. He didn't want to go to war with Jimmy Gallagher. But he also couldn't not act.

Frank didn't see Lurch standing beside him, and he didn't hear him, but he knew he was there. He stood up, his eyes never leaving Chloe's face.

'Get me the Estonian,' Frank said.

# Chapter 11

'*Shit, shit, shit!*' Darcy cursed as she slammed on the brakes outside her house. She pulled into a neighbour's space and got out.

'I'm so sorry I'm late, I'm so sorry,' she said as she approached the ambulance that was parked at her door.

Two medics and Seán Murphy were sitting in the back, Seán in his wheelchair, a small suitcase on his lap.

One of the medics stood up.

'I'm really sorry,' Darcy repeated.

The medic pushed Seán out onto the ramp and then lowered it slowly. It made a buzzing hydraulic sound, and no one said anything as it descended, the electronic sound echoing through the square.

The medic handed Darcy Seán's two crutches.

'Alright, mate, that's you done,' the second medic said to Seán as he slammed the back doors shut. 'Best of luck with everything.'

'I appreciate all your help, lads,' Seán said.

'See you, buddy!' the first medic called out and waved.

'Thank you!' Darcy shouted, but they both ignored her and climbed into their cabin.

The ambulance drove off. She stood the two crutches up against her car.

'I'm sorry, Seán. I really am. I should have got you a spare key. I never thought of it. I've been working on that missing boy's case, and it's ... well, you know.'

Seán let out a deep breath. 'I know, Darcy. It's OK. Can you help me inside, please?'

She leaned over the wheelchair, inserted the key into her front door and opened it. As she pushed him through the doorway, the right wheel hit off the door frame and the wheelchair came to a sudden stop.

'Sorry,' Darcy apologised and then, more gently this time, pushed his chair through the open door.

She had planned on having the place bright and warm for him and some food ready to be served, but the visit to the State Pathologist had gone on longer than she'd hoped. The one-liners she'd conjured up in her head to break the ice for Seán's arrival now seemed inappropriate.

She ran around the house, switching on lights and turning up the heating. Then back outside where she grabbed the two crutches leaning up against her car. She paused for a moment, stood, closed her eyes and breathed in the cool air of the square. It filled her lungs and she exhaled slowly, the fog of air disappearing in the silence of the night as she opened her eyes again.

'Can I take your case?' she asked when she got back, indicating the suitcase.

He nodded.

'I'll put it on my ... on the bed for you,' she told him.

When she came back from the bedroom, he was still in his wheelchair. He looked so out of place in the middle of the room.

He stared up at her, and she held his gaze.

'What?' he asked her.

'I'm so happy that you're here.'

He smiled. A real smile.

'Anyway,' she clapped her hands, unsure why she did, 'how about some food? I had planned on cooking something, but it's getting a bit late now.'

'I'm fine. I wouldn't mind a change of clothes, to be honest. Get that hospital smell off me.'

'Of course. Do you need help?'

'No, I can manage,'

'*Em* ... how about I pop out and get us some chips and a burger? There's that local chipper we like.'

'Sure,' Seán said.

'I left the crutches by the bathroom door, OK? I've also left some extra towels and blankets for you on the bed.' She took two steps towards the door, but then turned back to him.

'Are you sure you can manage on your own?'

'I'm fine, honestly,' he said and began to wheel his chair towards the bedroom.

'Did you organise the home carer for tomorrow?'

'It's all sorted, thanks. She'll be here at ten.'

'She?'

'Yes. Her name's Gabriela, I'm told. She'll be here for two hours.'

'Gabriela, is it? Sounds Brazilian or Spanish. *Hmm* ... perhaps I'll pop by in the morning unannounced ... just to see if she's up to scratch?'

'Grow up,' he told her.

She threw him a smile and then stepped out into the cold air, closing the door behind her. The bang of the door echoed throughout the square. She leaned her back against the door and inhaled a deep breath, and then watched the fog of condensation appear and then disappear as she exhaled.

Her car was parked two spaces up and she walked to it and got in. There was still a little heat inside and she allowed herself to be consumed by the silence for a few moments. She thought of Seán inside her house bumping around and trying to change his clothes.

For a moment her thoughts turned to regret. She felt as if she were trapped in her car and that some stranger had suddenly taken over her house and pushed her out. She shook her head and forced out those feelings. She was the one who had offered, hadn't she? Besides, she was in love with this man. Wasn't she?

She was about to start the car when there was an abrupt downpour of rain. The noise was thunderous as it lashed off the roof of the car, and blocked her view from every window, cocooning her inside.

Darcy leaned back again into her seat and watched and listened and waited for it to end.

Mick had just stepped into the Church of Assumption in Dalkey village when the downpour began behind him.

'Can I help you?' the lady sitting at a table in the porch asked him.

There was a man standing at the entrance to the church, his arms folded. He stared at Mick.

It was an unfortunate side-effect to being a Garda or a policeman in any country, as Mick was well aware. Sometimes dealing with those on the bottom rung of society left their mark on you. Just like a farmer – you can't handle manure all day without smelling a little bit like shit.

Although, not having showered or changed his clothes for two days coupled with a bad dose of the DTs wasn't doing him any favours either.

'I'm here for the concert,' he told the woman.

'You're very late. It's already halfway through.'

Mick looked past her into the church. He could feel the heat and hear the singing from the boys and girls of Assumpta Secondary school.

'Is everything OK, Deirdre?' the man said, having come over to get a closer look at Mick.

'Everything's fine,' Mick assured him. 'I'm here to listen to my son. Michael. Michael Kelly.'

The man shook his head and straightened himself up. 'There's no Michael Kelly in our school,' he said.

They both stared at Mick.

He put his hand to his forehead. 'Sorry,' he said. 'Michael Quigley.'

His ex-wife Marion had registered their son under her maiden name. Another little passive-aggressive jab at him. She was a master of it at this stage.

The man and the woman looked at each other. Technically there was nothing to stop them from barring the entry of this man in front of them.

The man eventually shrugged. The woman turned back to Mick.

'It's ten euro,' she told him.

Mick could have argued that since it was already half over he should only have to pay five, but he wasn't about to push his luck.

With his right hand, he swung his jacket open and reached into his back pocket to take out his wallet, letting them both catch a good glimpse of his sidearm. The woman leaned back in her chair and the man took a step back.

Mick took ten euro from his wallet and handed it to her.

'You have a gun,' she told him, as if he were unaware of the fact.

'Oh, sorry about that,' he told her, unfolding his wallet and showing her his ID. 'Detective Inspector Mick Kelly.'

Her hand reached out and took the ten-euro note. Neither she nor the man spoke, so after a moment Mick made his way past them and into the church.

On the altar were two young teenage boys singing 'Rudolph the Red-Nosed Reindeer' while a tall man leaned over a piano keyboard like a praying mantis, accompanying them. Ripples of laughter echoed off the ceiling. It was a large church but a small school, so all of the parents had managed to fit into the first five rows. Although Michael had Down syndrome, he attended a mainstream school. It was a private school whose fees were paid solely by Mick's ex-wife.

'Expensive and exclusivity applies as much to schools as it does to jewellery,' she had once told him. 'Smaller is always better.'

'Are you talking about the school now or that new boyfriend of yours?' Mick had replied.

Nevertheless, he couldn't help but appreciate the fact that Michael's school fees afforded him the opportunity to share a teacher with the small number of boys and girls now present. Normal schools in Ireland could have up to thirty children in a single classroom.

He spotted Marion's short blonde hair on the last row, and then he smiled at the back of the figure sitting next to her. Despite his wife's hairdresser's astronomical charges, her daughter's natural-blonde hair made hers look unmistakably fake. His daughter Lucy must have come home for Christmas from her boarding school in England. He couldn't imagine what that school must be costing, and he had never asked.

He and Lucy had a very cold relationship since his divorce from her mother, but Mick was unsure exactly why. He could make a good guess though. Previous heated arguments between them had been exacerbated by the geographical distance, and Mick had tired of the petty arguments and the sour goodbyes before not seeing her again for several months.

She had only one more year to go at school, and he'd heard she wanted to come back to Dublin for college next year. He had decided some years ago to be patient and to wait until she was a little older and back in Dublin and not as easily influenced by her mother's acerbic tongue, before attempting to rekindle their relationship.

The audience clapped as the two boys left the altar, and a lady strode on to announce the next act. Three boys and three girls walked confidently on and turned to face the audience. The second boy was Michael and Mick was already smiling with pride and elation.

The pianist began again, and a chorus of 'Silent Night' filled the church.

*'Silent night,*
*Holy night,*
*All is calm,*
*All is bright ...'*

Mick continued to beam with pride until the song came to an end. A huge round of applause erupted in the auditorium and Mick joined in, clapping the fastest and the hardest. The group walked off stage, and Mick then caught sight of his wife staring at him.

He nodded at her, a nod that said everything and nothing. He watched his wife lean towards his daughter and whisper something in her ear. He stood up and began to make his way towards the end of the pew to say hello to Lucy.

His daughter's head turned slowly, and she made eye contact with him. He stopped. Like all cops, Mick was a good reader of people's eyes. 'You can tell a lot about people,' he had once told Darcy, 'from looking into their eyes and then down at their shoes.'

After a moment, Lucy turned away from him and faced the altar. His ex-wife shrugged at Mick and her mouth offered him a sympathetic and pitying smile. Any thawing of his heart for her froze again.

# Friday

# 20 December

# Chapter 12

For the first time, in so long she couldn't remember how long, Darcy lay in bed and heard the seven o'clock chime on her watch. She had decided not to run at her usual time of six o'clock. Despite feeling the twitches of protest from her legs, like a pair of dogs wanting their morning walk, she forced them to rest still.

Beside her, Seán slept. She couldn't claim to have slept with enough men to make her an expert, but he was undoubtedly the quietest sleeping man with whom she had ever shared a bed. Being paralysed from the waist down also made him so still that at times she found herself checking the rise and fall of the sheets covering his chest.

She couldn't help being startled when he suddenly opened his eyes.

'What are you staring at?' he asked.

'What?'

'Are you checking that I'm still alive?'

'What? No! Of course not!'

But by now he was smiling. And she relaxed too. She propped herself up onto an elbow and looked down at him. He turned his face back towards the ceiling.

'I know what you're thinking,' he said.

'No, you don't.'

'You're thinking about how everything inside my body can work normally, my heart, my lungs, my stomach, and yet I cannot even twitch my big toe.'

Darcy said nothing.

'It's OK,' he told her. 'That's what I thought about for weeks, lying in the hospital, staring up at the ceiling.'

'And now? What are you thinking about now?'

A smile spread across his face. 'I'm thinking about the last time I looked up at the ceiling here in your bedroom. I'm thinking about the fun we used to have in this bed.'

'Typical man,' she laughed. 'It wasn't just the sex, you know. I remember we used to talk for hours about nothing at all. I remember calling in sick and then popping out to buy coffee and fresh croissants and coming back to bed. I remember us lying together in silence listening to each other's breath until one of us fell back asleep.'

'*Nah*. I don't remember any of that.'

'Well, we did,' she said and slapped him lightly on the chest. 'I remember one night when we ordered Chinese takeaway and ... oh, my God!'

'What?' he said.

'Your ... I mean you ...'

Seán followed her eyes and saw the mound in the middle of the bed.

'My, my,' Darcy said. 'It looks like some parts of you don't appear to have any mobility difficulty.'

'Oh, Jesus!' Seán pulled a pillow from under his head and covered himself. 'It seems to have a mind of its own these days.'

'It must have been the thought of that Chinese takeaway,' Darcy said, smiling.

'At least I'm with you. Sometimes I'd be getting examined by the nurses and ...'

'And I don't suppose any of the nurses ever gave you a *helping hand*?'

'They were very obliging in the ward, but they weren't that obliging. Especially the Sisters of Charity.'

Darcy laughed. She sat up in the bed. 'Well, maybe I could 'oblige'?'

She leaned down and kissed him on the lips and with her right hand she removed the pillow from the sheets.

A bus blew its horn at Darcy as she nipped in front of it and drove up the bus lane on Cork Street. She would have preferred to stay at home today, to cater to Seán's every need and to somehow normalise this new situation for them both. But for now that was impossible. It will take time, she told herself for the hundredth time. It will take time.

Her phone buzzed, and she answered without looking at the screen.

'Detective Doyle? It's Eoin Flanagan.'

'You're in early.'

'We've got some new info.'

'Go ahead.'

'I've printed out her bank details from all her accounts for you, and I've left them on your desk.'

'She had more than one?'

'Several, in fact. I've left her medical records on your desk too.'

'I don't suppose she ever had a child?'

'No, nothing came up about her having a child. But, more importantly, we've managed to find her ex-boyfriend. According to a statement she once submitted, it appears he has a bit of a violent history. Numerous arrests. GBH.'

Darcy could hear Eoin clicking buttons on his computer before he continued.

'He was on a methadone treatment programme up until recently but lately has gone off the radar.'

A black BMW tried to cut in front of Darcy and she blasted on her horn. The driver gave her the finger, but she ignored him.

'Good work, Eoin,' she told him. 'Will you call Mick and let him know, please?'

'He's here already.'

Jesus, Darcy thought to herself, doesn't anyone sleep anymore?

'I'm on my way now.'

'Just to let you know,' Eoin said, his voice a little lower this time, 'Mick wants to raid the ex-boyfriend's house this morning, but the Chief told him to call ERU to assist. They're on their way now.'

'OK, thanks for the heads-up, Eoin,' she said and disconnected.

Her ex-love-interest Jamie would no doubt be there. *Shit*. The last thing she wanted was any personal stuff interfering with this case.

With her mind on the meeting ahead, she failed to see the young female Garda who had jumped out into the bus lane, her arm outstretched in front of her. Darcy slammed on the brakes and stopped only just in time.

The young Garda strolled around to the driver's side of the car, preparing to give Darcy a lecture and a ticket for illegally driving in the bus lane.

'I'm sure your enthusiasm is appreciated,' Darcy told her, holding up her ID. 'But a traffic ticket isn't worth losing your life over.'

The incident room was full of bodies by the time Darcy arrived. There was a swarm of uniformed and fully armed ERU officers standing on one side of the room, chatting and sipping from paper takeaway cups. Most of the ERU officers carried either a SIG Sauer P226 or a Walther P99 as a sidearm, but there were also Heckler & Koch MP7 assault rifles on display. A heavy-set officer who must have weighed well over 100 kilos had a Remington Model 870 shotgun slung over his back. He was so big that the shotgun looked like a toy.

Darcy felt the energy in the room had changed from last time. It was an energy of testosterone and machismo that she didn't like. But it was a necessity that she could appreciate. Walking into any situation, with the potential threat of being shot at, required a special kind of personality. Having spent some time with Jamie, she understood that personality. At least she thought she did.

She spotted Jamie talking to five of his colleagues. He looked good, she had to give him that, and his colleagues obviously had the highest respect for him. They saw themselves as an elite unit and, in many ways, they were, but despite Jamie's assumptions they were not superior to her own team.

Mick stood in the opposite corner, and she made her way over to him

'Morning,' she said to everyone and then indicated the ERU. 'Mick, is it too late to suggest we try to go talk to the guy first?'

'It's not our call,' he replied. 'The Chief reckons if this man's our killer, and at the moment he's our prime suspect, then we go in fully prepared. And that means fully armed.'

Darcy shrugged.

'Besides,' he whispered, 'if our man starts taking potshots, I don't want to be first in the queue, do you?'

He went and leaned into the group of uniformed Gardaí, and they all leaned in too like a rugby scrum.

'Are we doing this or not?' Jamie asked in a loud voice, appearing beside them like a giant. They all looked up at him like children caught smoking by a teacher.

'OK,' Mick said and walked to the top of the room.

Jamie didn't make eye contact with Darcy, so Darcy assumed he was going to be cold and yet professional with her. That suited her fine. She took her place beside Mick at the top of the room, facing everyone.

'For some of you who weren't here,' Mick began, 'I'll give you a quick rundown as to who we're after, and why.'

'We don't care about why,' the large ERU officer with the shotgun said. 'We only care about who.'

Some of his colleagues chuckled.

'Well, then,' Mick told him without a pause, 'if you'd care to wait outside, I'll call you when we're finished.'

He locked eyes with the big man and neither seemed about to give way.

'Dave!' Jamie called to his colleague.

The officer shrugged.

'Anyway,' Mick continued, 'our man's name is Kevin Brennan. He's had several previous convictions, all drug-related. One serious GBH. As you may know, his ex-girlfriend Rachel Robinson was pulled out of the Forty Foot yesterday with a gunshot wound in her chest. His methadone clinic said he hasn't been seen for nearly two weeks, so we'll assume he's back using. In the last few years, he'd sorted himself out and had been holding down a job in a warehouse for a furniture company, but he's been AWOL from them too. It's important, though, that we try to detain the suspect unharmed. He could be the key to finding Alfie. Brennan's last known address is Balwood Flats.'

'That's a kip of a place,' one of the ERU officers said.

'Like most areas, it has its bad element,' Mick told him. 'But our problem doesn't lie in the area, it's the flat's location that'll give us the most headaches. It's on the sixth floor. Don't be surprised if you get up there before me.'

Mick wanted this guy alive and his attempt at humour was in order to bring down the tension in the room. He wanted the ERU there as a precaution, not to go in guns blazing.

'Garda Flanagan here,' Mick continued, 'came across a complaint on Brennan's PULSE file that was made two weeks ago by our man against the victim, Rachel. It was also around that time that he stopped showing up for work.'

'Wait. *He* made a complaint against *her*?' one of the uniforms on his team asked.

'Yes, that's right,' Mick told him. 'Eoin, do you have that recording?'

Eoin took out his phone and pressed some buttons. He placed it face up on a table, close enough for everyone to hear it.

'This was what I got from the phone records in Pearse Street Station,' Eoin said, his voice unnaturally squeaky. He pressed play and increased the volume to maximum.

*'Pearse Street,'* said a male voice.

*'It's my son.'*

*'Your son? What's happened to him?'*

*'He's missing. I was with him last week and now he's gone.'*

*'Gone? What do you mean by "gone"?'*

*'He's not there. He's gone. He's missing.'*

*'What's your name, sir?'*

*'Kevin.'*

*'Kevin what?'*

*'Kevin Brennan.'*

*'What's your address?'*

*'He doesn't live with me.'*

*'How old is your son, Mr. Brennan?'*

*'He's four.'*

*'So who does he live with? Your partner?'*

*'Yeah, my ex. I went round there to collect him. I always take him on Sundays. We go to the park or a film and then to Burger King.'*

*'And she doesn't know where he is?'*

*'No.'*

*'Has he run away?'*

*'No.'*

*'Can I speak with your ex, please, Mr. Brennan?'*

*'She's not here.'*

*'Where is she?'*

*'She's in her own place.'*

*'Where your son lives?'*

*'Yeah, but he's not there anymore. He's gone. I pushed my way past her at the door and looked in her apartment and he wasn't there. He wasn't ...'*

*'Mr. Brennan? Are you still there?'*

*'There was nothing belonging to him in the place. No toys, no pictures. He was gone. It's like he's vanished.'*

*'What did your partner, your ex, say?'*

*'She's talking shite. It's not true.'*

*'Mr. Brennan? What did she say?'*

*'She said it's all in my imagination. She said he never existed.'*

*'Sorry? What did you say — that last bit?'*

*'She said he never existed.'*

*'I see. Give me your details. I'll send a car around now.'*

Eoin pressed a button on his phone.

There was silence in the incident room for a few moments.

Then Darcy asked, 'Didn't they investigate it?'

'They did,' Eoin answered. 'Unfortunately, it was his word against hers. She was an employee in a successful Montessori in Rathfarnham. He was an ex-junkie in Balwood Flats. She told them he'd been harassing her, and they cautioned him not to contact her again.'

'And what about his supposed son?' Darcy asked.

'She told them there was never any boy. Kevin Brennan admitted to never having been inside her place before, so couldn't one hundred-per-cent say he'd ever seen any evidence of the boy's life in the apartment.'

'Sorry. How does this all tie in with the missing Alfie?' Jamie asked.

'Hopefully, we'll find some answers to that today from Kevin Brennan,' Mick said.

As they all filed out, Eoin sidled up to Darcy.

'*Em*, Detective Doyle,' he said, his voice barely audible.

She stopped and faced him.

'Can I, *em*,' he muttered. 'Can I come too?'

He reminded Darcy so much of a little boy asking for permission to come along with the adults that she couldn't help but laugh.

Eoin's face flushed, and she instantly regretted it.

'Sorry,' she said. 'Yes, of course, Eoin. You helped get this lead more than anyone. So come if you want to.'

He nodded enthusiastically.

'But remember,' she said, 'let the big boys go in first. In spite of their bravado, it's a tough job and they do it well. You can never tell what's going to be behind that door. Now, let's go.'

# Chapter 13

Eoin sat in the back of Darcy's car, Mick being in front, and watched the two ERU black Audi Q7's weave in and out of the traffic ahead of them. Darcy followed them perfectly as if attached by an invisible chain. Sirens blared and blue lights flashed as all other road users did their best to get out of the way. Eoin could feel his heart racing, but the frenzy of the high-speed drive through Dublin's streets was not the only reason.

Darcy was so focused on the road that it gave him an opportunity to watch her. For the hundredth time he told himself that he didn't stand a chance with her. He knew she had history with the head guy from the ERU but had also heard she'd been in a relationship with the undercover detective in hospital who got shot. It had taken Eoin quite a while to uncover that information about her. Any whiff of his interest in her would lead to certain mockery and ridicule from the guys at the station.

He leaned forward in the back seat to watch her more closely. It wasn't just her looks that made her attractive – she was also the toughest woman he had ever met.

'I can barely keep up with them,' Darcy said, having to raise her voice above the roar of the engine. 'Remind me to put in for a new vehicle in the New Year.'

'There's nothing wrong with this baby,' Mick said, patting the dash as if petting a tired old dog. 'Anywhere you go in this car, you know what people are thinking about you?'

'Loser?'

Mick laughed. 'No, they're not thinking anything. That's the point. You blend in.'

Darcy gave him a sideways glance.

'What do *you* think, Eoin?' she asked as she hit the brakes and chose a lower gear. The engine disagreed with her choice and cried out in protest. 'Keep or change?'

'I think it's always good to have a change, Darcy. I mean Detective Doyle.'

Mick looked back at him.

'Well, at least, I mean, I think it's seen better days.'

'You see,' Darcy said. 'Eoin agrees with me.'

'I've seen better days,' Mick said to Eoin. 'You think I should be replaced too?'

Eoin felt panic rising. Darcy smiled when she looked in the mirror and saw his face.

'Don't mind him, Eoin,' she said. 'You and I will go car-shopping in the New Year, OK?'

'Yeah, I'd love that,' Eoin said but then regretted it as he spotted a smile on Mick's face.

There was silence for the rest of the journey.

'You ever been to one of these before, Eoin?' Darcy asked as they turned in to the block of flats.

'No, I haven't.' Eoin looked up at the towering buildings that surrounded them. They were each seven storeys high, and looked down on a communal area that held the remnants of a playground, a burnt-out car and two shopping trolleys. Some kids were bouncing on the roof of the car, preferring its entertainment value over the fragmented playground.

'Well, remember,' Darcy said, 'stay at the back and let the pros do the heavy lifting, OK?'

Eoin nodded.

The two SUVs slowed down in front of them, the doors opening even before they had come to a complete stop. Three Garda cars stopped behind Darcy's. None of the children moved or ran away at the sight of the heavily armed officers.

Eoin made eye contact with one of the little girls as he got out of the car. He smiled at her, and she stretched out her arm towards him and shaped her hand into a gun.

The ERU officers, all wearing black face masks, ran for the stairs. One of them at the front was carrying a red, metal battering ram. None of them shouted or even spoke, contrary to what Eoin imagined they would do. He had read somewhere that tactical teams like the ERU shout both to intimidate their targets and embolden themselves.

Darcy and Eoin walked past the closed and graffitied lift doors and began to climb the stairwell. Above him, Eoin could hear the boots of the others charging up the stairs. It sounded like gunfire echoing off the walls.

They were halfway up when they heard the battering ram being slammed into the door. It took two goes before they heard the door smash open.

*'Armed Gardaí! Hands in the air! Armed Gardaí! Don't move!'*

As their shouts ricocheted off the walls and windows, some residents came out onto their balconies to gawk at the commotion.

After only a few moments, the commands ceased. By then Darcy and Eoin had reached the sixth floor. Both of their faces were flushed and their breath was coming short. They both gaped when they saw Mick standing at the top of the stairs waiting for them.

'Didn't know you had wings, sir,' Eoin said.

'There are two types of people in the world,' Mick told him. 'Those who make assumptions and walk by perfectly working lifts, and those who don't.'

Still wearing a black face mask with only his eyes visible, Jamie stepped out of the flat and into the corridor. He saw Darcy and signalled for her to come forward.

She went inside.

Mick reached into his jacket pocket, pulled out four blue latex gloves and handed two to Eoin. 'Put these on.'

Mick let Eoin enter the flat first, but as soon as Eoin took a step inside he put his hand up to his face and turned back around.

Mick put out his arm and stopped Eoin from going back outside.

'It won't be the last time you smell that,' he told him. 'You don't have to get used to it, but you do have to learn to live with it.'

Eoin kept his hand over his mouth and nose and followed Mick inside. The curtains were drawn, and the lights were off. The air was rancid as if meat had been left out to decay in the sun. Eoin forced down the gag reflex he felt in his throat.

The hall opened into a room with a television on one side and an old brown sofa on the other. The remains of a microwaved meal and several empty cans of beer were on the coffee table.

'*In here, Mick!*' Darcy called.

The flat was small with only one bedroom. They went inside and saw the corpse on the bed. He was an emaciated white man, possibly in his thirties. A tourniquet made by a belt was half-open on his left arm, an empty syringe still resting in his right hand.

Darcy looked down at him, her hand covering her mouth and nose. 'It seems every time we get a lead in this case, a door slams in our faces,' she said behind her hand.

Mick went over to the window and with a single blue latex finger pulled back the curtains slightly. Light streamed into the room as he peered across the balcony and down at the cars below.

'I'll call forensics,' he said without turning around.

'*What the fuck!*' Darcy said.

Mick turned around to her. 'What is it?'

'Open the curtains wider.'

She reached down for the small, framed photograph on the man's bedside locker and picked it up. Mick looked closer as she held it up to the light. The photo was of Kevin Brennen holding a little blond boy in his arms, a set of swings in the background.

'*What the actual fuck!*' Darcy said.

'Jesus, that's him!' Mick said. 'That's Joey from the morgue.'

# Chapter 14

Frank Kavanagh sat in the passenger seat of his Land Rover in a large car park that was overlooked by an almost twenty-metre-high billboard. On the billboard was the smiling face of Barry Boyle, the very man who had asked Frank to 'pop by for a bit of a heart-to-heart'.

'**Barry's Beds**' the sign read, and under Barry's enormous fat face was his quote and guarantee: '*My beds will help you sleep better than a box of sleeping pills.*'

Barry Boyle was five years older than Frank, but they had grown up together in the late sixties in the working-class streets of Crumlin. During Frank's teenage years, they'd drifted apart, each choosing a different career path. Barry picked up a guitar and joined a show band. Frank picked up a crowbar and joined a crime gang.

Barry tried to get Frank to join his band, not because Frank was particularly musically talented (neither was Barry for that matter), but Frank had the looks. 'You're the spitting image of that Pierce Brosnan fella,' Frank had often been told and Barry knew with Frank on stage the girls would flock to see the Barry Boyle Showband. But Frank earned more in a single night as a criminal than Barry earned in a month touring the country as a singer.

Barry did manage to achieve a modicum of success, touring with big stars like Dickie Rock and Brendan Bowyer, and at one point looked like he was about to hit the big time, but eighties pop music took over and the appeal of showbands suddenly became old-fashioned and obsolete.

Barry was so caught up in his own self-adulation that he didn't see the dark clouds on the horizon in the form of Wham, Duran Duran and Rick Astley. Despite the impending downturn in showband popularity, Barry took a big gamble. He hired out several large stadiums and went on a nationwide tour. Ticket sales were horrendous, and Barry went bankrupt before the tour even ended.

It was then he turned to his long-time friend Frank Kavanagh and borrowed the thousands he needed to stave off the debt collectors. By then Frank had moved up the ranks in the criminal hierarchy and a few thousand was pocket-change to him, even in the eighties. In fact, too much cash was becoming a headache. Frank saw an opportunity in his friend's regrettable failings as a musician. Barry had something that Frank didn't have, and even with all his money he couldn't buy — a clean record.

Even before CAB – the Criminal Assets Bureau – had been set up to monitor and retrieve profits from criminal activity, it was hard for Frank to launder any significant amounts of his rapidly rising cash stock. He had already opened a couple of strip clubs, a car wash and a video arcade to convert his criminal cash into 'clean' cash, but he wanted to explore other legitimate businesses. Frank wanted the holidays, the cars, the clothes, the houses and all the trappings of a wealthy businessman, but he didn't want the cops to be able to walk up at any time and take it all away from him.

So, when Frank was given a contact name for a man who could import beds and mattresses from the Far East, he rented a warehouse and called his old mate to front the business. He even let him put his name on the front. Little did Frank know at the time that Barry's Beds would go on to open sixteen warehouse stores around the country, making Barry Boyle a household name and a mini-celebrity in his own right. Something, ironically, that show business had failed to give him.

'I know he's your mate and all that,' Frank's driver, Tony, said, 'but I can't stand this fucker.'

'You can make lots of new things, Tony,' Frank told him, 'but you can't make old friends.'

They both continued to stare up at the large billboard with Barry's face on it.

'Look at the state of his fucking head!' Frank said.

On the poster, Barry had thick black hair the colour of coal, his teeth shone as if torchlight was reflecting off them and his skin was bronzed like tanned leather from years of lying under a sunbed in a spare room at his enormous house in Ballsbridge. Some people thought his image was a caricature until they met him in person. Although only a B-list celebrity at best, Barry squeezed every ounce of notoriety he could from his status.

Frank climbed out of the Land Rover and Tony followed him.

'Why are you coming here to him?' Tony asked as they walked towards the entrance. 'Out of respect, shouldn't he be coming to you?'

'Look, having Barry Boyle turn up at my house I might as well advertise that this is my business. There's too many cops always driving by my gaff. Nosey fuckers. And, let's face it, Barry isn't exactly what you would call inconspicuous.'

As if to make his point, they both looked up at the billboard one more time before entering the store.

The shop was one single large room. Dozens of beds lay facing each other, their headboards back-to-back with long aisles running the length of the shop. The place reminded Frank of a cemetery.

They made their way past the sales staff and through the door marked STAFF ONLY. Barry's office was at the end of the corridor and Frank walked in without knocking.

The room was dark and had its blinds pulled down. It took a moment for Frank to make out Barry sitting in a large black leather chair behind a desk, his head leaning back, and his eyes closed. He sat up quickly when the door opened.

'*What the fuck!*' he shouted.

When he saw who was standing in his office, his hands went to his crotch and he zipped himself up.

'Get out!' he ordered, and a woman, who couldn't have been more than twenty years old and was wearing an orange shirt with '*Barry's Beds – I'm here to help*' written on the back, stood up from under his desk.

'*I told you to lock the fucking door!*' he shouted as she scurried out of the office.

Frank and Tony turned and watched her leave, and then Tony closed the door. The lock clicked loudly and then Tony stood with his back to the door.

'Sorry about that, Frank,' Barry apologised, as he smoothed down his thick black hair. 'Just breaking in some new staff members, if you know what I mean. Didn't think you'd be here this early.'

'The early bird and all that. Besides, I couldn't give a shit who's blowing you, Barry. As long as it doesn't interfere with business, you can write down 'decent blow job' as a job requirement for all I care.'

Barry laughed nervously and came out from behind his desk. He opened the blinds on the two windows and light poured into the office from the car park outside. Frank could see his Land Rover. Barry put his hand out for Frank to shake but Frank kept his hands by his sides and looked down at the outstretched hand.

'Fair enough, I suppose,' Barry said and took back the offer of a handshake. 'That's sort of what I wanted to talk to you about, Frank.'

He walked over to a tall cabinet in the corner and opened its doors. Inside were several bottles of whiskey, vodka and a collection of crystal glasses.

'Fancy a drink?' he asked.

Frank shook his head.

'What about you, Tony?'

Tony looked at him but said nothing.

'Do you mind if I have one?' he asked Frank.

He was stalling, and Frank knew it. He was beginning to think that whatever Barry had to say was a lot worse than he had imagined. But as much as Frank wanted him to hurry up so they could leave, he allowed Barry to pour himself a drink and return to his chair. There was a pile of the morning newspapers on the desk and Frank noticed Barry's eyes resting on them as he sat down.

'Please, Frank, sit down,' Barry said, indicating the chair in front of him. 'You're making me nervous, and this is hard enough as it is.'

Without saying anything, Frank sat down. He crossed his legs and placed his hands on his lap like a priest awaiting a confession. Behind Barry was a large poster of the world. It had coloured tacks pinned into various international cities — some in North America, most of the capitals in Europe and a couple in Australia. Frank wondered what they represented as the furthest west or east that Barry's Beds operated was Ballina and Ballymun.

Barry took one of the newspapers and handed it to Frank. He took it and read the headlines. As he read, Barry drank his whiskey.

'This has nothing to do with me,' Frank said. 'So, I'm guessing it has something to do with you?'

'It's that woman, Rachel. The Montessori teacher.'

'Yeah, I get that. Again, though, what's it got to do with me?'

'Here's the thing, Frank. I met her about four years ago in a nightclub. We then met up a few times after that. Then the stupid bitch got herself pregnant. I told her I'd pay for the abortion and everything, but she said she wanted to keep it. When I said to her that I didn't want to have anything to do with some kid, she was fine with that.'

'But?' Frank said.

Frank had heard hundreds of these stories and there was always a 'but' somewhere in the middle.

'You're right. There was a *but*. She told me she wanted financial support. She didn't say she'd tell Joan or anything, but I couldn't take a chance.'

'You honestly think Joan doesn't know about you messing around all these years? Joan is a smart woman. Smarter than you, anyway. But the only thing she gives a toss about is you paying off her credit-card bill every month. So, you fuck around, and she spends around but *"East is East and West is West and never the twain shall meet"*. The perfect relationship, you might say.'

Barry seemed to sink further into his chair.

'How much? Frank asked.

'A grand.'

'A month?'

'Yeah.'

Frank looked down at Rachel's face on the front of the paper.

'That must be the most expensive ride you've ever had,' he told Barry. 'Hope it was worth it.'

Barry didn't say anything.

'So again, Barry,' Frank asked. 'What the fuck's this got to do with me?'

'Well, what if they find a connection between her and me?'

'And how would they do that? It's not like you were taking the bleeding kid to the park every Sunday.'

'No, of course not.'

'Then what?'

'The money.'

'The money? How could the cops trace the money to you? They can only do that if ...'

Barry's head sank lower.

'Tell me you paid her in cash.'

Barry said nothing.

'You fucking eejit.'

Frank stood up and looked at Tony, then turned back to Barry.

'You transferred a grand every month into her account from your own account?'

'No, it's not that bad. I'm not that stupid.'

'*How stupid are you then?*'

'I had her down in the books. You know, as an employee.'

'*You stupid fucking prick!*'

The venom in Frank's voice made the colour drain from Barry's face.

'So, when they look at her bank account, they're going to see your company as her employer?'

'I know that, Frank, but I'll just say she worked here on the weekends. That'll explain the grand.'

Frank thought about this, pacing the room.

'There's something else,' Barry said meekly.

Frank stopped walking and stared at him.

'About a month ago she came to me with an offer to end the payments. Said she wanted to emigrate with the little lad and needed cash to set herself up. She said if I paid her fifty grand that she'd never get in touch with me again.'

'You didn't pay her, did you?' Frank asked.

'No. I told Joan everything though. We had a massive fight. I'm still sleeping in the spare room, but she said not to pay her. And, also, that I should tell you.'

'She's got a bigger pair of balls than you, your missus. I should have set her up in business all those years ago instead of you.'

Frank picked up one of the newspapers again and stared at Rachel. Any problems with this girl or any problems that were coming his way were not going to be solved in this office today.

'How'd you know the kid was yours?' Frank asked Barry. 'Or even if she had a kid?'

'She showed me the scans and then photos of the young fella. A boy. Lovely little blond fella, he was. Luke she called him.'

'Luke?' Frank asked. 'Why Luke? Was that her idea?'

Barry shrugged. 'Well, not mine.'

'So, a red-haired woman and a dark-haired man have a blond little boy. Does that not strike you as somewhat odd?'

Barry looked down at the newspaper again as if searching for an answer. When he heard the click of the door unlocking, he looked up, but Frank and Tony were leaving.

'You recognise that girl in there?' Frank asked Tony when they were back in the Land Rover.

'Which one? The one that was blowing him?' Tony shook his head.

'She's Charlie Cooney's young one.'

'Anita?'

'Yeah, that's her name.'

'I haven't seen his daughter since she was going to school,' Tony said. 'If Charlie knew what she was up to, he'd come down here and put a hole in Barry the size of that fucking billboard.'

'I'm not so sure,' Frank said. 'From what I hear, she's as bat-shit crazy as her dad.'

One of the reasons Frank had survived as a crime boss for so long in a career that generally lasted about the same time as that of a pope and whose tenure had the same abrupt ending, was that Frank was always prepared to walk away. Whether it was family, friends, or heaven forbid, money, Frank would always choose to walk rather than fight for the remaining chips on the table. Everyone knew that, and that's what made him so dangerous.

Frank sat for a moment, looking up at the billboard, and wondered if it was perhaps time to call it quits on Barry's Beds.

# Chapter 15

Darcy stood at the front door of the flat and watched Mick light a fresh cigarette using the remainder of his previous one. He was leaning forward over the balcony, watching the activity below.

She joined him and watched as more emergency vehicles arrived. A press crew, who must have been tipped off, she figured, was setting up at the entrance to the block of flats.

'*It never rains but it pours*,' she said.

'Something like that, alright.' Mick took another deep drag from his cigarette. 'Any luck on a suicide note?'

'You still think it's a suicide?'

'Hard to know with junkies. Could have been an accidental OD, but I doubt it.'

'I took a photo of that little boy in the frame with my phone and sent it to Dr. Pepple and Dr. Catherine Daly. Just to get a second opinion, but there's no doubt in my mind anyway that the kid in the photo in there is the same one that's lying in Whitehall morgue.'

Mick nodded, deep in thought.

'So that means the voice recording to Pearse Street Station from him was correct,' Darcy said. 'Rachel Robinson was lying. There was a boy in her apartment and Kevin Brennen was the father. Or at least assumed he was the father. Right?'

Mick grunted.

She studied his face. 'How are you holding up?'

He turned away from her. 'It's funny,' he said. 'When I'm dealing with all this shit, I don't feel like a drink, and yet it's all this shit that'll make me need one later.'

Darcy didn't reply.

'It's like I'm on a merry-go-round — but everything's OK. It's only when I stop going round and round and I actually get off that I start to feel ... groggy. It's the damnedest thing.'

Darcy felt like she wanted to push him further but was afraid of crossing the line.

'You know, if you ever wanted to talk about it properly ...' she finally said.

'With you?'

'No, not me. I mean someone ... professional.'

'What? You think I need a shrink or something?'

'No, I'm not saying that.'

Darcy's phone beeped in her pocket.

'What then?' Mick asked and crushed out his cigarette with his foot.

*Damn it*, she thought. 'Forget about it,' she told Mick. 'Sorry. I didn't mean ... I don't know what I meant.'

She took her phone out and looked at the screen.

'It's Dr. Daly.' She held up the phone to him.

*OMG!!! That's defo him. :-(*

'Jesus,' Mick said, 'where did she get her medical degree? In a fucking lucky bag?'

Darcy looked below them and saw Phoebe Pepple getting out of her car.

'I'm going back inside,' she told Mick. 'I'll have one more look before Fifi throws me out.'

She put on a fresh pair of latex gloves and went back into the flat with her hand over her mouth, preferring the scent of talcum powder and latex over the rotting stench of Kevin Brennan.

In the bedroom, Eoin was slowly closing a drawer.

'Anything?' she asked him from behind her gloved hand.

'Just socks and jocks.'

'OK,' she said. 'The Tech Bureau's on their way up. Better go wait outside.'

Darcy looked around the bedroom when Eoin was gone, surveying everything except for the body on the bed. She knew better than to stare too long at a decaying corpse because if you did, then when you closed your eyes at night, that's all you would see.

Kevin Brennan didn't appear to be much of a reader as there were no books or even magazines in the place. She didn't imagine either that there'd be any last will and testament by the recently deceased. She was simply going through the motions for Mick. She felt he was clutching at straws and desperate for a lead. She'd seen other detectives do that — wish so hard for a clue that the whole case became distorted.

The kitchen and living room were all one area. The smell of cigarette smoke permeated everything: the grubby furniture, the stained curtains, the greasy walls. Even with the odour of a dead body to contend with, the stink of nicotine was still very much present. This flat didn't need a spring clean, it needed everything stripped out and burnt.

The only thing recently added to the place was a two-foot Christmas tree standing in the corner with its lights unplugged, a pathetic attempt to bring a splash of joy into an otherwise depressing space, like the child's drawing of a stick family that was lying on a coffee table in front of the television. She had no doubt who the tree was for and who had drawn the picture. The same boy on the side of the cold mountain who had been picked at by wild animals for days.

In her adolescent years as she was shuffled from one foster family to another, she had once stayed in a place like this. It had only lasted a week. Her foster 'dad' had come home drunk one night, and he had tried it on with his wife. She wasn't having any of it and threw him out of their bed. On his way from the bedroom to the couch, he had found his way into the fourteen-year-old foster girl's room. Luckily for Darcy, she had been awake at the time, smoking a cigarette and staring out at the glow from the neighbouring flats across the complex.

She remembered the sour stench of alcohol from his breath as he tried to placate her with slurred comments about her figure being 'mature for her age'. She had tried to ignore him, warning him to leave her alone as she stubbed out the cigarette into a plant pot on the windowsill. The moment he had slid his hand up her leg, instinct had taken over, and she had struck out with her elbow, catching him square in the face.

His screams shot through the flat. Blood poured between his fingers as he clutched his broken nose. His wife came charging into the room. *"The little bitch hit me!"* he had roared. Darcy darted from the room as his wife rained down slaps onto her.

She hadn't bothered to try and tell her version of events to the foster agency when they came to collect her the next day. She knew from experience it was a waste of breath.

'You want to know why I always get to the crime scene first?' a voice asked, startling Darcy from her thoughts.

Phoebe was standing beside her, dressed from head to toe in white overalls, her face covered with a breathable mask showing only her dark eyes.

'I've heard what you detectives say about me,' Phoebe said. 'Thinking I sit in my car waiting for a crime to happen so that I can get here first.'

'I've never heard anyone say that about you,' Darcy lied.

'Well, be that as it may, the reason I'm always first is because when I'm not first, this happens. How long have you been walking around contaminating my crime scene?'

'What did you think of that photo of the boy? Is he our boy?'

'Looks like him,' Phoebe said. 'But all you white people look the same to me.'

'*Come on, Doyle, let's go!*' Mick shouted from the hallway. He was all business again. Any signs of his melancholic mood were gone.

'I wonder where he's in a rush to all of a sudden,' Darcy said.

'I got a match on those prints from the joint Mick found on the rocks,' Phoebe explained.

'Who is it?'

'A teacher from a secondary school — Brian Meany,' Phoebe said. 'He was on our system for some minor offences when he was a teenager. Must have cleaned his act up to become a schoolteacher. There was a second set of prints, but there's no match for them.'

'It's the last day of school before the Christmas holidays,' Mick told Darcy, entering the flat. 'So, if we don't go get him at work now, we'll be chasing him into the New Year.'

Darcy looked at the drawing of the stick family one more time. They were all holding hands with a bright yellow sun behind them. The drawing bothered her as much as it made her sad.

She remembered a drawing she had once made herself, of herself with some large fictional family, holding hands with both parents who existed only in her imagination, with brothers and sisters filling the page. She remembered one of her earliest memories and the happiness of holding hands with her father, as much as she recalled the heartbreak when he let go. She felt like a kindred spirit to the little boy, knowing that he would never hold the hands of his mother and father again. Or his ... Darcy looked closer at the drawing.

'I wonder who the other woman is?'

'What?'

'The little boy drew himself holding hands with a man and a woman,' Darcy said, bending down and tracing her gloved finger along the figures, without touching the paper. 'But there's another woman, then the man and the boy. Why would he draw *two* women? Rachel would be one. But who's the other?'

Phoebe moved closer to her.

'Assuming our boy drew this picture,' Darcy said, looking up at Phoebe, 'you might be able to get a quick fingerprint match to the body in the morgue.'

'OK, good,' Phoebe said, taking out a clear evidence bag. Using a tweezers, she picked up the page at the corner.

As she lifted it, Mick came to stand beside Darcy. 'Are we going?'

'Just a sec,' she said, staring down at the coffee table. 'There's a handwritten note here. It was under that drawing.'

Phoebe placed the drawing into the evidence bag and then took out another. Using the tweezers again, she picked up the handwritten page and placed it in the second clear evidence bag. She handed the bag to Darcy.

Mick and Phoebe listened as she read.

'*Dear Luke – In a few years you probably won't remember me but, whenever I collected you, it was the highlight of my week. The only thing I enjoyed in my life. To be honest, you were the only bit of good I had to look forward to. I didn't have a great life, to be honest. I wasn't very good in school and all that. I fell in with the wrong crowd, as my ma says, and I'd probably never have been able to provide for you or look after you properly. Not the way you deserved anyways. I hope whoever gets to look after you, that he's good to you though – that you get a good da. I hope he plays with you the way I did. And that he gets you proper toys, not the crappy ones I got you. And I hope he's proud of you the way I am. You were the brightest thing that ever happened to me and, now that you're gone, the darkness has come back, and I just haven't got the strength in me to fight it again. I've had a shitty life anyway so it's not like I'm really going to miss that much. It doesn't matter anyway. No one's going to miss me. Except my ma. Sorry, Ma. Goodbye, Luke. I wish I had just one more day with you. See ya, buddy.*'

# Chapter 16

It was lunchtime when they set off for the school. Most businesses were already closing, many not returning until the New Year. Even with Darcy's blatant disregard for the rules of the road, it would take wings on the roof of her unmarked car, not blue lights and sirens, to make any progress in the traffic.

'So can we assume now that Kevin Brennan is linked to the dead boy on the mountain, who we can now call Luke?' Darcy asked Mick.

'We can assume anything,' he told her. 'But let's get the facts straight first.'

'OK. Luke is the dead boy. We'll need that confirmed, but let's take it as read for now. So, Kevin Brennan was his father, and if not his actual father he at least thought he was. He also believed that Rachel was Luke's mother.'

'Yes, because Rachel told him so.'

Darcy squeezed her car between a stationary bus and a truck that was turning right.

'Nothing came up in her medical records about her having a child,' she said, 'so we can say he wasn't Rachel's. She did have a miscarriage some five years ago, but we'll come back to that later. But Brennan was convinced he was the kid's father.'

'And he reported the boy missing before Luke died. That's important.'

Darcy hit the brakes hard, and Mick jerked forward in his seat.

'Sorry,' she said and drove on. 'Rachel was pretending that Luke was Kevin Brennen's son. Luke dies so obviously he can't see him anymore. He knocks on her door, and she denies Luke ever existed. She knew it was her word against his. Closed case.'

'So, what did she need from Kevin when Luke was alive?' Mick asked.

'Drugs? Money? A free babysitter?'

'Not drugs. If Kevin was holding down a job, then she must have been hitting him for cash. Then the poor kid dies, and she doesn't need him anymore.'

'If that's the case then Rachel was one cold-hearted bitch to let him suffer like that. We have to rule him out as a suspect for Rachel's murder though, as he obviously died before she did,' Darcy said.

'Besides, a junkie doesn't get a gun and shoot you beside the sea. A junkie gets an iron bar and bludgeons you to death as he's robbing your pockets.'

Darcy tapped the wheel with her fingers. 'Pass me my phone, please,' she said.

'I'll call,' Mick said and took out her phone. 'You're going to get us killed.'

'Give Eoin a buzz. Find out if there was any progress made on the bank-account details for Rachel and tell him to check Kevin's account as well. And tell him he needs to get answers today or the banks'll be closed till God knows when.'

'He'll get it done. That fella would jump through a flaming hoop for you,' Mick said as the phone dialled. 'You know he has the hots for you, don't you?'

'Who?' Darcy asked.

'Hi, Darcy,' an overly enthusiastic voice came over the phone. 'I mean Detective Doyle. How can I help you?'

Mick winked at Darcy.

'That's all I need,' she said.

According to the Department of Education, Blassfin Secondary School was noteworthy for two things. It had the highest turnover of teachers in Ireland, the average length of stay being sixteen months. And it had the lowest percentage of pupils who, after they'd left school at eighteen, continued into further education.

Darcy and Mick followed Geraldine, the school secretary, to Brian Meany's office in the corner of the building. It was only after they had threatened her with obstructing a case that she eventually agreed to assist them in locating Meany. Darcy had met her type before, gatekeepers for big institutions who considered themselves at the top of the food chain when really they were at the bottom. As in the past, the only effective way to deal with them was to out-bully them. She marched ahead of them while they elbowed each other like two kids being brought to the principal's office.

The corridor was adorned with Christmas decorations that looked like they had been taken out of storage and dusted down every year for the past twenty years. The intention behind them was one of tradition,

Darcy assumed, but they emitted only a sense of tattiness. She had never seen decorations make a place look even more drab than it already was.

Geraldine knocked and stood by the door, but Mick reached around her and pressed down the handle, not willing to wait for a reply. Darcy squeezed by her and entered the office behind Mick.

'I beg your pardon!' Geraldine protested.

The man sitting behind the desk was younger than Darcy had expected. His carelessly styled lush dark hair and boyish good looks gave him the appearance of a university student rather than that of a teacher. He had fumbled with the keyboard for a moment as soon as Mick opened the door and had then, despite it not facing them, casually reached for the monitor and switched it off.

'I apologise for the intrusion, Mr. Meany,' Geraldine blurted, but Darcy already had her ID out and was holding it out for Meany to see.

'That's OK, Ger,' Meany said, raising his hand in the air. 'I can manage, thank you.'

Darcy walked to the door and held it open. A pithy quip popped into her head, but she bit her tongue.

With a face as if she were sucking on a mouthful of sour gooseberries, Geraldine left, and Darcy couldn't help but shut the door with a bang behind her.

It was a windowless office painted the same colour as the rest of the school, a sort of institutional yellow that probably originated from leftover buckets of a large government job. Darcy looked around as Mick made the introductions. There was nothing personal hanging on the walls or on Meany's desk, a sign of impermanence. Faded pages that were curled at the corners were stuck on a notice board that took up most of one wall. She spotted a letter from the Department of Health about vaccinations that was dated four years before. The room smelt of recycled air, dust and gloom. Her gaze settled on the seated man, and she instantly disliked him.

'You know why we're here,' Mick said. It was a statement not a question and a tactic that he liked to use to fish for information. Often the interviewee admitted to crimes that weren't the reason they were there, but Meany was too smart for that.

'I have no idea why you're here, Detectives. Perhaps you'd care to enlighten me.'

'Approximately two days ago,' Mick continued, 'you left the scene of a crime in Sandycove.'

'Sandycove? In this weather?'

'That didn't sound like a denial to me.'

'Mr. Meany, did you witness the murder of Rachel Robinson?' Darcy asked.

'Who?'

'Who?' Mick laughed. 'Have you been living under a rock for the last two days?'

'Yes. That's exactly what it feels like in here.'

'A woman was shot on Wednesday night and a joint with your fingerprints was found at the scene. Can you explain that, please?'

'So, am I being arrested for possession?'

'No,' Mick told him.

'Well then, until I am officially under arrest, I have nothing further to say.'

'Are you single, Mr. Meany?' Darcy asked.

'Why? Is that a crime now as well?'

'I'll assume you're single since you're not wearing a wedding ring.'

'Not that it's any of your business but, yes, I am single.'

'I think what my colleague is getting at,' Mick said, 'is why a single man, such as yourself, would choose a place like Sandycove on a freezing cold night to meet up with anyone.'

The smile left Meany's face, and he looked down at his keyboard as if searching for something.

'Someone's wife perhaps?' Darcy said.

'Or someone's daughter?' Mick added.

Meany switched his monitor back on.

'I still have a lot to do before school closes for the Christmas holidays. If you don't mind seeing yourselves out? I'm sure you can find your way. You are detectives after all.'

'What is your problem, Meany?' Mick said.

'*My problem?*' Meany shouted, standing up. '*What is your problem? You want to arrest me for smoking a joint? Is that it?*'

'Because there's a little boy in the morgue, a woman shot dead, and you know something, and you're not telling us.'

Meany sat back down and made a conscious effort to control his emotions.

'I have nothing further to say,' he told them in a calmer voice.

Quietly, Darcy asked, 'Who do the second set of fingerprints on the joint belong to?'

For the slightest moment, the expression on Meany's face changed, and he looked up at Darcy. He caught himself and looked away again. This time he said nothing.

A loud bell rang out and echoed along the corridors. Outside there was the noise of doors being opened and voices trying to be heard over each other.

'Whatever you're up to,' Mick said, quieter this time. 'I hope you know what you're doing. And who you're dealing with.'

Mick opened the door and the noisy babble of teenagers poured in.

Meany turned his attention back to his computer.

'You planning a trip?' Darcy asked him. It was a hunch. She had spotted a travel brochure for Australia on his desk, and it was perhaps the only thing up-to-date in the office.

Meany glanced at the brochure.

'I'm thinking of emigrating, actually,' he told them. 'Getting out of this poxy country.'

'In the middle of a school year?' Darcy asked.

'I didn't say I was doing it now, did I?'

'You didn't say you weren't,' she said.

Meany's eyes went back to the screen, and he didn't take them off again until Mick and Darcy had left the room and closed the door behind them.

They paused in the corridor and streams of boys and girls in blue school uniforms flowed past them, the excitement of school closing for the holidays in just a few hours showing in their faces.

'What's he up to?' Mick asked.

'He sounds like a man with a plan to me,' Darcy said.

'Even though he's a so-called respectable schoolteacher now, you can still get the smell of criminal off him.'

'I know what you mean. I think he ...'

Mick looked at Darcy. 'What?'

'Down the corridor on the right-hand side, against the wall.'

Mick took his phone out of his pocket and held it up at the same time as he glanced down the corridor. A girl, about sixteen or seventeen years old and wearing heavy makeup, was standing with her back to the wall. She was biting her nails and throwing furtive looks at them both. Everyone in the corridor was moving in one direction or another — only she stood still.

'What you reckon?' Mick asked.

'It'd be a long shot,' Darcy said, 'but I'd like to see if her prints are a match to the ones on our joint.'

'Now that would be a bit of a stretch, but I could do with a bit of a stretch.'

'She's on the move.'

'Well, reel her in then. I'll meet you outside.'

Darcy walked quickly down the corridor after the girl. The girl looked over her shoulder and when she saw Darcy following, her pace increased as she headed for the school's exit. She turned a corner and Darcy lost sight of her, but by the time Darcy had her back in her sights the girl had ploughed straight into three guys coming in her direction.

'Watch where you're going, love!' one of them said and pushed her back.

'Unless you were trying to bump into us,' one of the boys said, looking her up and down.

The three boys formed a semicircle around her, their eyes taking in her body.

Darcy stepped in front of the girl. 'Fuck off, the lot of you!' she told them, and they lowered their heads and walked away.

Darcy took the girl by the arm and led her to a quiet area away from the front door.

She looked at Darcy. 'You're a copper, aren't you?'

'It's OK, it's OK,' Darcy reassured her. 'I'm not here to cause you any trouble. I'm Detective Darcy Doyle. Are you OK?'

'What do you want from me?'

'What's your name?' Darcy asked her.

'I have to tell you my name, don't I? I mean if a Garda asks me?'

'Technically, yes, you do — but if you'd rather not for now, that's OK.'

She thought about that before answering. 'Sophie Ryan.'

'OK, Sophie. We're not here for you. You don't have to worry.'

'So why were you in Brian's ... Mr. Meany's office?'

'You know why we're here, Sophie? Don't you?'

Darcy held her breath and said nothing until finally Sophie gave a few small nods.

'Like I said, it's OK. You're not in trouble,' Darcy assured her.

'It's about the other night, isn't it?'

Darcy nodded.

'I told him we should have just reported it.'

'We just want to hear your side of the story, that's all.'

'*Excuse me*,' Geraldine, the school secretary, interrupted. 'You have no right to speak to that child unless an adult or a teacher is present.'

Darcy ignored her, but Sophie was already turning away.

'Sophie!' Darcy said.

'Back to class, young lady,' Geraldine instructed, and Sophie was quickly swallowed up in the river of blue uniforms going by.

Darcy let out a deep sigh and clenched her fist.

'*You stupid cretin!*' she said.

Geraldine stood back in shock. 'What did you call me?'

Darcy walked towards the exit before she did something she'd regret.

'I'm going to report you for this!' Geraldine called after her. 'Do you hear me?'

But Darcy was already gone.

# Chapter 17

The Ryanair flight from Strasbourg touched down at Dublin airport a few minutes ahead of schedule. Oskar Hallik looked out at the grey sky and the grey concrete that blended into each other in the distance. The terminal looked distorted through the raindrops on his window. He leaned back in his chair and unbuckled his safety belt.

He had left Tallinn in his native Estonia very early that morning on a Lufthansa flight to Frankfurt in Germany. From there he had paid cash (too much cash in his opinion) for the direct flight to Strasbourg and then from there on to Dublin. In each of the airports he had left through the main exit and had taken a taxi drive around the city for twenty minutes before returning.

He sat up in his chair and looked back down the rows of seats. No one looked in his direction. He turned around and took out three passports from inside his jacket and chose the French one. The other two, German and Russian, he concealed in a secret compartment behind the lining of his hand luggage. He spoke each of the languages of the passports but still struggled at English. At sixty years of age, he was resigned to never mastering the nuances of this ubiquitous language.

As the plane taxied to the terminal, he switched on his phone, and the local telecom carrier gave him a signal. The date written on the display was December 20th. It was his father's birthday, and by sheer coincidence the same date that he had shot him in the stomach and watched him slowly die. Oskar allowed himself a few moments to think about his father. Was it an age thing, he wondered. Like most people, the older he got and the less time he had to look forward, the more time he spent looking back.

His father, Hugo Hallik, was born in 1920, and during World War Two had been a member of the Forest Brothers, a resistance movement against the Soviet occupation of Estonia during and after the war. With the help of the British, he continued the fight against the Soviet Union, alongside his fellow partisan soldiers until Stalin's death in 1953.

When he returned to his family home in the harbour district of Kalamaja in Tallinn, he met and married a local girl named Polina. She died giving birth to their only child, Oskar. Barely coping after ten years of war, Polina's death broke what was left of Hugo's spirit. Oskar was often left to fend for himself and even as a young boy would sleep rough on the streets and go missing from home for several days, not that his alcoholic father ever noticed.

Under Soviet occupation, life was tough for everyone, but for some it was unbearable. A good day for Oskar was being hungry and belittled. A bad day was being hungry and beaten. Several times into his teenage years, his father beat him so much that he thought he had killed his son. After that, he would not go near Oskar for months. But then the boy would do or say something or look a certain way, and the memory of his wife or his years spent as a Forest Brother partisan would consume him in anger and revenge. Oskar should have died as another statistic in a Cold War era but he survived because, as soon as he was old enough, he left. It wasn't a clear decision he had fully thought through. One day, he just simply never returned home again.

There was only one route for Oskar: crime. And Oskar took to it very well.

He rose through the ranks of the ethnic Estonian Mafia by displaying ruthless cruelty for his enemies, mostly competing Russian gangs, and was rewarded lavishly with money, drugs and a pick of girls from their human-trafficking operations. Even at twenty-five years of age, he was favoured to lead the entire organisation until one night in a bar a Soviet soldier took a dislike to Oskar's apparent privileged status among the staff and the girls.

Despite gentle and then stronger verbal warnings to back off, the soldier continued his tirade against Oskar. With so many witnesses, Oskar's authority could not be questioned by a mere foot soldier. When the soldier smashed a bottle off a table and lunged at him, Oskar stepped to the side and drove his fist into his throat. It was a lucky, or rather unlucky, punch and the soldier's trachea was crushed by the blow.

As the soldier lay gagging for breath on the floor, his hands around his own throat, Oskar turned back to the bar and finished his drink. Everyone else ran.

He was given a fifteen-year sentence in a high-security prison in the Kolyma region that had once served as a gulag camp under Stalin. His term was reduced in 1991 under Gorbachev's perestroika policy, and he was set free and sent home to Estonia.

He avoided his hometown of Kalamaja for two years until he used the port to bring in a consignment of cocaine from Helsinki. The operation went well, but before he left he paid a visit to his family home.

The house was in darkness when he walked inside, the only light coming from the moon through the grubby windows and dusty curtains. A figure, asleep, was hunched over the kitchen table, with an empty bottle of cheap vodka lying on its side. Although a man in his seventies now, his father heard the footsteps and raised himself up.

Oskar looked at this weak, old figure and wondered where the great and powerful Hugo Hallik had gone.

'What the fuck do you want?' Hugo asked his son.

'Nothing from you, *kallis isa*,' Oskar said.

Oskar looked around the grubby kitchen where a mother he had never met had once cooked, and a father whom he had always hated had beaten him.

'Then I ask something of you,' his father said. 'I can see in your eyes that your soul has been damned, and that it is too late for you. Just like me.'

'We are not the same.'

Hugo laughed. It sounded like his lungs would collapse from the effort.

'No, we are not the same,' his father told him. 'I fought for my country. I fought for freedom for our people. You can walk the streets of my beautiful Tallinn because of men like me.'

Oskar said nothing but instead spat on the floor of the kitchen.

'And you,' his father continued, 'what do you fight for? Money and power. No, Oskar, we are more different than you could possibly imagine.'

Oskar shrugged, suddenly bored by this old man, and he turned to go.

'*No, wait!*' Hugo called out.

Oskar stopped.

'I ask the blackness of your heart for only one thing. Before you leave your home and are gone forever.'

Hugo stood up, holding the side of the table to support himself. The empty bottle fell onto the floor but didn't smash.

'What do you want?' Oskar asked.

Hugo's hands were shaking as he undid his scruffy old coat and opened his shirt, revealing a torso of grey skin and protruding ribs.

'I ask for compassion,' he said.

Oskar looked into his father's eyes, the same chilling blue eyes that faced him in the mirror every morning, and he understood. He nodded and his father closed his eyes.

His mouth had formed the start of the word '*Polina*' when the bullet entered his stomach. He fell back onto the kitchen floor. Oskar watched his chest continue to rise and fall, each time taking a little bit longer and becoming more shallow.

A bullet to the gut is a horrible way to die. If you're lucky, you can bleed out in minutes. Unlucky shots can take hours of pain before an inevitable death. Hugo Hallik was lucky. The bullet severed several arteries, and he instantly began to bleed profusely.

He opened his mouth, wheezing in and out. Later Oskar would wonder why he did not step forward and finish him off with a quick death. Perhaps, he thought, his father was right after all. Oskar Hallik truly had no soul.

Years passed, and younger and more vicious men came to replace him as leader. Even after Estonia's independence, Russian crime bosses refused to leave. Oskar survived several assassination attempts before finding himself back in jail with a ten-year sentence. Today he couldn't even remember which crime they had finally pinned on him.

When he was released, in his fifties, his income did not match his lifestyle, so now he found himself with a €50,000 loan that had to be paid back. Oskar had wondered about the coincidence that the payment for this Dublin job was the exact sum he had to repay, but when he tried to think about it too much it gave him an unbearable headache.

The pilot's voice broke him from his memories, as the plane came to a halt at the terminal. He waited as he didn't want to be first at the immigration but also didn't want to be last. He found a family of seven and slipped in beside them as they queued with their passports. The immigration officer was still smiling at a little girl holding up her Irish passport when Oskar held up his own. The officer saw the EU passport and waved him through.

In most places in the world, a cop will recognise another cop or a criminal, even if the cop is off duty or the criminal is having a drink in a bar. But a criminal can do the same.

When Oskar's stare met Tony's searching eyes in Arrivals, the men held each other's gaze for a moment.

Tony stepped forward and put out his hand. 'Tony,' he said.

Oskar shook it and nodded and followed him out to Frank Kavanagh's waiting Land Rover.

# Chapter 18

'We'll come back in the morning, Mick, I promise,' Darcy said. Her toes felt like they were frozen solid, and she could see her breath even inside the car. 'I think we could both do with a bit of kip. Plus ...' She paused for a moment.

'I know,' he said. 'You've someone waiting for you. What do you say we go back in to the parents and get them to phone her again? She has to come home sometime.'

Darcy looked at him from the corners of her eyes. Even in the darkness she could feel how restless he was, a reflection of her own impatience to find answers.

He stared intensely at the front door to Sophie Ryan's house, willing her to walk up to the driveway.

'Fuck you anyway, Sophie!' Mick said.

Darcy started the car. 'I'll drop you home.'

Darcy stopped outside Mick's apartment block.

'Tell Seán I said hello,' Mick said, and opened the car door.

'I will, thanks. You should come by and visit him.'

Mick paused for a second.

'Yeah, I'll do that, I promise,' he said and got out of the car.

He walked towards the building's entrance. He didn't hear Darcy drive off, so he knew she was watching him. Only when the main door of his apartment block was opened did he hear her drive away.

Mick's flat was in a nondescript building on a nondescript road. It was not supposed to conjure up thoughts of misery or depression the moment Mick walked through the door. He walked into the kitchen, opened the fridge door, looked inside and then closed it again.

He had just planted himself down onto the sofa and picked up the remote control when there was a knock on the door. He was tempted to ignore it, but the knock came again. He let out an audible groan as he got up and placed his eye against the spy hole. Irena, his neighbour, was holding a bowl covered with a tea towel in both her hands. The thought of leaving her standing there crossed his mind, but he didn't have the heart for it.

'Irena,' he said when he'd opened the door.

'Michael,' she replied, matching his tone. 'I heard you come in and thought perhaps ...'

She let the bowl in her hands finish her sentence.

'That's very thoughtful of you, Irena.'

She shrugged. 'It's nothing. Only leftovers.'

Mick looked down at the bowl.

'Hungarian goulash,' she said, as if answering a question.

'I thought you were Croatian?'

'I am Croatian,' she said.

'Oh, I see.' Although what he saw was unclear.

She held the bowl out further in front of her, and an image of Oliver Twist ran through his head.

He took it from her. 'Thanks.'

She looked over his shoulder into his apartment, and Mick looked behind him. When Irena didn't say anything after he'd turned back to her, he finally gave in.

'Would you like to come in?'

She smiled, took the bowl back from him, and stepped inside. Mick glanced up and down the corridor before closing the door, by which time she had already disappeared into his kitchen.

'Do you have a pot?' she called in to him.

'Should be one in there. But I've a microwave if that's of any use.'

'Microwaves!' she tutted as if she were saying the words 'Nuclear Radiation'.

Mick stood for a few moments unsure whether to follow her in but then decided to let her manage on her own and went back to the couch. He turned the television on, all the time listening to the clank of pots and pans in the background.

He scanned the news channels for anything new on Alfie Scanlan. More than once in the past, Mick had heard new information from the evening news about a case he'd been working on. Today however, the news was full of the usual government scandals and social crises.

'Ready when you are!' Irena said, walking back into the living room.

Mick reached over and cleared some books and an ashtray to make a clear space on his coffee table. Only when the expected dinner didn't arrive did he look around at the kitchen. Irena was seated at the small table there, opposite a place set for him.

He lumbered to his feet.

When he'd sat down, he wondered if he'd ever sat at this table before. Since he'd moved into this apartment, dinners normally consisted of a takeaway brought home or delivered or a few cans of beer till the hunger left him. The only reason he had so many pots and cutlery was because they were left by the previous tenant.

He looked down at the bowl of food. Steam was rising from it.

'Looks lovely,' he told her. 'Smells lovely too.'

'Yes, it is one of my specialties. My mother taught me this. *She* was Hungarian.'

'Oh really? I didn't know that,' Mick said and then realised what a stupid thing it was to say, as how the fuck could he have known this titbit of information about a woman he barely knew anyway?

Irena watched him as he took a spoonful and tasted it.

'Delicious,' he told her, sounding like a host from a television cooking show.

'I thought perhaps a little too much salt, no?'

'No, no. Not at all,' he told her and took another spoonful as if to prove it.

He took another few spoonfuls but her watching him was starting to freak him out, so he put his spoon down.

'Listen, Irena,' he said. 'There's something I want to talk to you about.'

'Yes.'

'Well, it's not so much to talk to you about – it's more just to, well, I suppose to apologise.'

'Apologise? For what?'

'You know, for coming home a little worse for wear sometimes. I mean, for me being in a bit of a state and you helping me home or back to your place. I'm trying to say sorry.'

'There is no need for an apology,' she told him.

'OK, well then, if not sorry, then at least thanks.'

Irena didn't try to make out that it was nothing or ask him any prying questions. She simply said, 'It's OK,' and Mick was very grateful for that.

After his confession or apology, Mick became less self-conscious around her and picked up the spoon again. He ate in silence as she watched him. To Mick, she seemed to derive a certain satisfaction in having someone eat and enjoy her food, at least that's what he told himself as he slurped his way through the remainder of the stew.

# Chapter 19

Darcy was two minutes from home when her phone rang. She looked at the screen and pulled in to the side of the road. A car horn blared at her as it passed. The phone continued to ring in her hand as she stared at the screen. **M** for **Mother**. Resisting the urge to let it go to voicemail, she pressed the green button and held the phone to her ear. She let out an audible sigh and listened.

'Darcy? Are you there?'

'I'm here.'

'Darcy?'

'I said I'm here.'

'Where are you, Darcy?'

'I'm on my way home.'

'Can you come by, hun?'

Darcy held the phone away from her and let out a deep breath.

'Darcy? Are you still there?'

She was tired, plus an image of Seán sitting in his wheelchair waiting for her popped into her head. She held the phone back up to her ear.

'It's been a long day, but I'll come by for ten minutes.'

'Really?' her mother said.

'Ten minutes. That's it.'

'Ah, you're a sweetheart. And would you pick me up twenty John Player Blue, hun? I'm dying for a smoke.'

Darcy closed the phone without saying anything else.

Darcy parked her car outside her mother's house. It was the same home she had been taken from by Child Protection Services when she was just seven years old. With an absentee gang leader for a father and a junkie for a mother, she was truly a child living on the margins of society. So why, whenever she looked back on those first seven years of her life, did she remember them as among her happiest?

The front door was painted black and stood in the middle of a street of houses with no numbers or names on display. In the house to the left of her mother's, there were four cars parked in a garden that had parking space for only one. The house on the right was boarded up with wooden sheets of cheap wood over its windows. A scrambler motorbike belched along the street, its underage driver not wearing a helmet. It pulled along a shopping trolley with another child sitting inside who screamed with laughter.

Her mother's small front garden was empty of any rubbish and the grass was as neat and trimmed as a soldier's haircut. She could see the front door was slightly ajar, which was normally not a good policy in this neighbourhood but when that door had an association with the infamous Frank 'The Face' Kavanagh, it might well have been the door to a bank's vault.

Darcy stepped into the hall and closed the door behind her. She made her way into the living room where she found her mother sitting in her armchair.

'Kettle's just boiled if you fancy a cuppa,' her mother said.

In the kitchen area, steam rose from the spout of the kettle, a half-eaten sandwich sat on a plate and the neck of an empty bottle of vodka poked out of the recycling bin.

Placing the packet of cigarettes on a small table beside her mother, Darcy stood back, deciding not to sit.

'You been drinking again?'

'It helps me sleep.'

'Does it?'

'Not really.'

Darcy looked around the room. Nothing had changed since her last visit a few months before — the same pile of paperback novels against her chair, the same half-filled ashtray that perfumed the room like a nicotine potpourri, the same dimly lit lamps that made the room appear in a constant sunset at every hour of the day, the same walking stick within her reach.

Darcy's eyes continued to the sofa where she had hidden when her mother lay unconscious on the floor with a needle stuck in her arm. Hidden until she was led away by the hand of a female Garda. Darcy had spent too many hours and too many nights lying awake wondering where she would be if she had let go of that hand. She longed to destroy forever that part of her that wished she had simply just stayed.

Her mother's wheezing voice broke her thoughts. 'What's it like looking at my house through the eyes of the filth?'

Darcy stiffened for a moment but then forced herself to relax. Her mother saw the sudden tension, smiled and rewarded herself with another cigarette.

'Why did you phone and ask for me to come over?' Darcy said. 'To insult me? I can get that in the streets outside that front door.'

'Ashamed of where you come from?'

'I didn't say that.'

'Think you're better than us now?'

Darcy sighed and forced herself to look into her mother's eyes.

'You remind me so much of your father in the old days,' her mother said.

'Believe me, I'm nothing like him.'

'Oh, I know that,' her mother told her, making it sound like a put-down. 'I meant your looks. I was pretty too once, you know.'

Darcy remembered back to the attention her mother would get from men, and how she had loved that attention.

'I could have had my pick of the boys,' her mother said.

'Why didn't you then? I never remember you with anyone.'

Her mother laughed. 'Cause I was damaged goods, wasn't I?'

'Damaged?'

'You think any man would go near me after I had a child with Frank Kavanagh? You must be joking. I was the Crown Jewels, a bloke who fancied me once told me. He could look, but he could never touch.' She took a long drag from her cigarette, blew the smoke in front of her and stared at it as if looking into the past. 'I remember it, that time I mean, before you went away, as being so lonely. Night after night in front of that poxy little telly once you'd gone to bed.'

'It's funny,' Darcy told her. 'I don't remember any quiet nights by the fire reading bedtime stories. I only remember loud music and drink and drugs.'

'Once you were old enough to reach the milk in the fridge, and the cereal in the press, then I started to get my life back. If I'd have stayed in this house sober and on my own for one more night, I'd have topped myself.'

Darcy had a flashback of reaching up to take down cereal and then pouring a full pint of milk into the bowl that then flowed all over the kitchen floor. There was no mop to clean up, so she'd got the idea of inviting all the stray cats off the road into the kitchen. When her mother came down the stairs with a hangover, she'd found a dozen cats licking up all the milk. She'd screamed blue murder at Darcy and, while trying to kick the cats out, she'd slipped and crashed backwards onto the kitchen floor. Then she'd suddenly burst into laughter and Darcy had joined in until the cats had drunk all of the milk and scurried out the back door.

Darcy's heart thawed a little with the memory. 'You taking your medication?'

In reply, she held up several containers of pills and shook them like maracas.

'Do they help with the pain?'

Her mother shrugged. 'I think my body's had too many chemicals in it already for these to have much effect. I'm sure I could get something better for the pain from one of the lads down the road.'

'Please don't do that,' Darcy said.

She shook her head. 'I won't. I can't anyway. Frank warned them off me years ago. I'm in a no-buy zone here. I suppose he means well in his own way.'

Darcy scoffed at that.

'Think what you like about him, he always looked after his own. You should know that more than anyone.'

When Darcy had received anonymous deposits of money for her education, she'd always assumed it had originated from a teacher who had helped her and encouraged her and who'd promised he'd do everything within his power to help her. It was only recently that her mother had decided to share the information that all the funding for her education had come from her biological father, Frank Kavanagh. She had been supported for years and received a degree in criminology from drug money.

Darcy wanted to leave.

'I'm tired.'

'We're all tired,' her mother said.

Darcy nodded and turned to leave.

'I wanted to ask you!' her mother said.

Darcy was surprised and turned back to face her. Her mother looked away, as if embarrassed to make a confession.

'What is it?' Darcy asked.

'It's ... *em* ...' her mother said. 'It's Christmas next week. I was wondering, if you had no one ...'

Darcy stared down at her mother.

'You're inviting me to Christmas dinner?'

'No. It was just a thought if you had no one. Frank told me you weren't with that other copper anymore.'

Darcy took a step forward, flushed with anger. 'First of all, tell Frank to stay the fuck out of my business. Who I go out with or don't go out with has nothing to do with him. Or you.'

Her mother nodded.

Darcy continued, 'And I've had over twenty Christmases without you and I've managed just fine. I've had them in five different foster homes, one of which I spent in my room on my own as I was kept away from the rest of the family. I've even spent one Christmas Day homeless on the streets of Dublin. Where were you then with your invitation?'

Her mother lowered her head and Darcy heard her mumble something.

'*What did you say?*' Darcy shouted at her.

'I said that you left me. I never sent you away.'

Darcy was standing over her now.

'*I was seven years old, for fuck's sake! You never came after me. You never looked for me!*' She knew her voice was too loud as she pointed her finger accusingly at her mother, but she couldn't control herself. 'Not at any time did you request to be re-evaluated by Social Services in order to have me put back into your care. I know how the system works. You never made that phone call. So yes, I made the choice to walk out that door, that's my fault, but my mother never once asked me to come back. That's your shame and that's your negligence. My seven-year-old decision does not excuse your failure as a mother to me.'

Still standing over her mother, Darcy breathed in and out as if she had sprinted around the block. She checked herself and controlled her breathing.

'I'm sorry. I shouldn't have ...' she said. 'I have to go.'

Then she marched out, down the hall and out the front door.

As she approached her car, she saw the large letters in red spray paint written along the side of her car — PIG.

'Little bastards,' she said to no one, got in her car and drove off.

# Chapter 20

'Hello?'

'Yes.'

'Is this ...?'

'Don't say my fucking name.'

'So, what do I call you?'

'Don't call me anything on the phone. What do you want?'

'The cops were here today. At the school. They know I was there the other night.'

'How do they know that? Did you tell them?'

'Of course I didn't tell them. What do you take me for?'

'So how do they know?'

'It doesn't matter how.'

'Riding that little schoolgirl, were you? You dirty bastard. So, what's that got to do with me?'

'Nothing. I just thought you'd want to know.'

'You didn't tell them anything about me, did you?'

'Of course not. But I've been thinking.'

'What have you been thinking?'

'The fact that I am now directly involved changes things.'

'How does it change things?'

'Twenty K isn't enough.'

'Oh really?'

'No. Not when it's my neck on the line now.'

'So how much is enough?'

'Fifty.'

'Fifty grand? Are you fucking mad?'

'That's what I'm going to need to set up abroad. I'm going to Australia.'

'I couldn't give a fuck where you're going.'

'So?'

'So what?'

'So, my fifty K?'

'Here's what's going to happen, you little prick. We're going to stick with the original plan. The money's nearly in place. You're going to keep your mouth shut and then fuck off to wherever the fuck you're going. Otherwise, the school board or the cops are going to get a call from me about you and your fetish for little girls in school uniforms.'

'She's seventeen. It's not illegal.'

'Whatever you want to tell yourself, you do that, but try ever getting a job again as a schoolteacher after the cops are finished with you. Now stick with the plan, and I'll be there with your money as arranged. And don't fucking call me again.'

'Hold on a second ... Hello ... Hello? Fuck!'

# Saturday

# 21 December

# Chapter 21

Before Chief Superintendent Glenn O'Riordan's mother died many years before, and in the weeks leading up to her last breath, he had sat by her bedside every day. Most of the time, however, she had slept. Glenn believed that by sleeping for longer and longer hours, her body was preparing itself for the biggest sleep of all.

Nowadays, as Glenn sat at his desk on the fifth floor of Harcourt Street, overseeing his NBCI detectives, his mind wandered more and more to the days when he would be retired and when he and his wife could move back to Oughterard in Galway and he could fish in the lake or even walk along the shore and they could just live as many years as possible looking after each other.

One day soon, he would leave Harcourt Street, hand in his pass, and never come back. There was nothing more pathetic, in his opinion, as the old-timers who came by to relive past glories. When Glenn O'Riordan left the fifth floor for the last time, he promised himself, he would never come back, or look back.

He found it harder, much to his frustration, to focus on what he was paid to do. If he were to be honest with himself, which he tried not to be, sometimes he would struggle to remember names or passwords or acronyms and, God knows, An Garda Síochána love their bloody acronyms.

He had watched his own father suffer a long and slow death with Alzheimer's, so now whenever he looked at a face, and a name didn't immediately pop into his head, a slither of fear ran down his spine at the possibility of having inherited his father's curse. He pushed that thought, as he always did, from his mind and sat up straight in his chair.

But when Doyle and Kelly knocked on his glass door, for a moment he had forgotten on which case they were working.

'Give me your update,' he told them.

'We've just been handed Rachel Robinson's bank details, Chief,' Darcy said. 'And it makes for some interesting reading.'

'Rachel Robinson?' Glenn asked.

'The body in the Forty Foot,' Mick reminded him.

'Oh yeah.' Glenn nodded.

Darcy held up the sheets of paper. Several lines had been highlighted with a yellow marker.

'Go on,' Glenn instructed.

'Well,' Darcy continued, pointing at one of the lines, 'you see here. There are several, let's call them anomalies, in her accounts. These three in particular.'

Glenn took the pages from her, put on his glasses and looked at the numbers.

'The oldest dated line is related to Kevin Brennan's bank account,' Darcy said. 'It appears that he has been paying four hundred euro every month into her account for the past four years.'

'Why?' Glenn asked.

'We'll get to that in a minute,' Mick said.

'The second one, the one for €300 a month, is being lodged from the bank account of a local parish.'

'A parish? You mean a priest?' Glenn asked.

'We don't know yet, Chief. We're still looking into it.'

'Holy God! What has this girl got herself into? And the third line?' Glenn asked. 'The one for a thousand euro a month?'

'Barry's Beds,' Mick told them.

'Who?' Glenn asked.

'You know that guy from the ads on the telly, Chief,' Darcy said. '*A better sleep than taking sleeping pills*, some shite like that.'

'Oh, right, yer man,' he said. 'Explain to me. What does it all mean? Or at least, what do you think it means? And what has it got to do with our missing boy Alfie?'

When Mick didn't say anything, Darcy took the lead.

'Well, Chief, if you look at the dates of the lodgements, Kevin Brennan is first, two months later Barry's Beds, and then the priest's.'

'Go on ...'

'There has to be a connection between the three men,' Darcy replied. 'Kevin's reported-missing phone call correlates roughly with Alfie going missing. Then we find the dead boy, who we believe was named Luke. All three men deposited various sums into Rachel Robinson's bank account on a monthly basis.'

'Why?'

'Well, we're not 100% sure yet, but it's not a huge leap of faith that she was playing them all. Especially given that the sums have been paid into her account for as long as the two boys have been alive. We'd like to start with either the parish priest or Barry Boyle. Apply a little pressure and see what pops up.'

The Chief stared at them both, deep in thought.

'A parish priest and a well-known businessman,' he said. 'OK. But I want this treated with kid gloves. You understand me, Mick? I want you both to tiptoe around this. I don't want you going in and taking big chunks out of either of them until we're sure. So, talk to the priest and talk to Barry Boyle, and if either of them puts in a complaint about you, the Commissioner will be back to me here quicker than either of you can say "disciplinary hearing".'

# Chapter 22

The two well-groomed Oxford Hotel doormen, who Darcy thought looked more like coffin bearers, hesitated before stepping aside to allow her dishevelled, shambling superior officer to enter. For a moment she'd thought even she was going to have to produce her ID just to be allowed enter the five-star hotel.

Mick didn't help matters by careering through the rotating doors and almost tripping on the deep-pile carpet. In the middle of the foyer there was a towering Christmas tree. Its perfect pine needles and branches stretched out in welcoming arms with golden baubles and sparkling white lights. Darcy thought it exquisite and yet soulless. She stood with folded arms as she watched Mick lean towards the pines and smell them to check if they were real.

'May I help you?'

Darcy looked at the name-tag of the man who had approached her and read *Concierge*. His tone was laced with superiority, and it irritated her how much it grated on her. She wished she could banish that confused and insecure little girl inside her forever and acknowledge the woman she was today. But, like a scab on her face, sometimes it only took a little scrape to turn it back into an open wound.

Darcy decided not to rely on her charms, and shoved her ID in his face.

'We have a meeting with Barry Boyle,' she told him. She heard her working-class Dublin accent grow even stronger. 'He said he'd be having lunch here.'

The concierge paused before replying, as if disbelieving her badge. He turned his head slightly and found Mick standing uncomfortably close to him, craning over his shoulder.

The concierge took a few steps away from them.

'Mr. Boyle is lunching in the Yeats Suite,' he told them, and then walked away.

'So, where the fuck is the Yeats Suite?' Mick asked Darcy.

Darcy pointed at a floor plan on the wall and Mick walked over towards it. A woman, about her own age, brushed past Darcy who watched her as she strode through the foyer as if the expensive decor were simply a part of her. Her stride was confident, and Darcy saw men and women look as she went by.

There was an enormous mirror, almost the size of the entire wall, to Darcy's left. Darcy glanced at her reflection. She looked tired and her clothes had a marked functionality. How could she wear anything that even bordered on fashionable when at any time of the day she could be required to jump a back garden fence in pursuit of a criminal?

'Your appearance won't serve any purpose in here,' Mick said. 'And that goes for your badge too. You'll find it doesn't get the same respect in these places as it does on the street. You know what they respect?'

'Money?' Darcy suggested.

'The girl catches on fast,' Mick said. 'Come on, I found the room we're looking for.'

The Yeats Suite was as plush, ornate and, Darcy thought anyway, as pretentious as the foyer. They stepped into the room and most eyes rose from the thin China cups and little triangular sandwiches and squinted at the two new figures. They were quickly deemed to not be worth more than a cursory glance, and all eyes returned to their former positions.

But two pairs of eyes stayed focused on Mick and Darcy, and they returned the stare. They snaked their way around the lush sofas and armchairs, trays of pastries and delicacies, until they reached the table in the far corner. The table had been chosen wisely, Darcy thought, close enough to remain in a public area and yet far enough away from prying eyes or ears.

Barry Boyle stood and stretched out his hand. Joan Boyle did not. She looked at them with an expression that said they were a short step above the dirt on her shoes. That was probably as expressive a look as she could manage, Darcy reckoned, given the amount of Botox in her face. She was attractive or at least had been when she was younger. Her natural bone structure was still evident, and her impeccable hair was probably aided by daily visits to her hairdresser. She had gravity-defying breasts and was impossibly thin, and Darcy couldn't imagine her body being able to digest any of the culinary delights that were spread around the room.

'Mr. Boyle,' Mick said.

'Please, please call me Barry,' Boyle said. 'And this is my wife, Joan.'

She gave them a curt nod.

'My name is Detective Inspector Mick Kelly, and this is my colleague Detective Sergeant Darcy Doyle.'

They both reached inside their jackets for their IDs, but Boyle held up a hand. 'No, no, no,' he said. 'That won't be necessary.'

His eyes shifted to the neighbouring table to see if they had been overheard.

Darcy and Mick sank into the two empty high-backed armchairs. There were two three-tiered displays on the table between the Boyles. On one was a selection of small beautifully made sandwiches, on the other colourful cakes.

'I ordered two extra servings in case you'd like a cup of tea,' Boyle told them, indicating the dainty China cups in front of them.

'I don't think ...' Darcy began, but she was interrupted by Mick.

'Don't mind if I do,' he said and reached across for the pot of tea. 'Will I play Mother?' he asked and raised the spout above Darcy's cup.

Darcy allowed him to pour the tea and watched as he leaned across the table again and helped himself to several triangular-shaped sandwiches.

'Mr. Boyle,' she said.

'Please, call me ...'

'I'd rather keep this formal. If you don't mind.'

Boyle put on a face like a little boy who had been scolded. His wife had not failed to notice it, and she gave him a disapproving frown.

'Mr. Boyle,' Darcy began again, 'we are here to gather any information you might have that may help us with the case of Rachel Robinson's murder.'

'Yes, yes, of course,' Boyle said. 'As I said on the phone, I am only too happy to assist in any way I can with the investigation or with –'

'We are the victims here,' Mrs. Boyle interrupted him. 'We're the ones who have suffered at the hands of Ms. Robinson.'

Darcy didn't say anything, but she looked at her. She found it hard to understand how Rachel's lifeless body compared to this woman sipping tea and overlooking the park. How incomprehensible that she saw herself as the victim of the two!

She returned to Boyle. 'If you don't mind,' she said.

Throwing a quick glance at his wife, as if seeking approval, Boyle started again.

'We, I mean Rachel and me, met one night in a local club. I had been out with my employees celebrating a new store opening. I wouldn't normally be in a club on a Saturday night, I can assure you.'

He looked at his wife again, but she had turned away from them all and was looking out the window. The bright winter light accentuated her age and hardened her facial lines. Darcy had no doubt that she had already heard her husband's story, or at least the version he was about to confess.

'We're not here to judge,' Darcy told him. 'We're only interested in the facts.'

Boyle nodded and sighed heavily as if it were all too much for him. He took a sip from his tea and made a show of composing himself.

'I was on my own at the bar when she, Rachel, approached me,' he said, eyes downcast. 'I forget what we spoke about, to be honest. She was a very beautiful girl, and I had drunk too much. I should have just gone home at that stage, to be honest. Leave the late hours for the kids.'

He laughed and looked up. Not receiving an empathetic response, he carried on.

'After a while she said she was going to go home and would I show her to a taxi, which I did. When I opened the door of the taxi, she got in but then said that we could share it. So, I got in as well. She told the driver her address and after a minute or two she just jumped on me. I swear I never made a move on her. She forced herself on me. I was drunk and one thing led to another, and I woke up in her apartment the next morning.'

Boyle glanced over at his wife. She was still staring out of the window. He looked back at Darcy and Mick.

'A few months later, I started getting emails from her telling me that she needed to meet. I ignored them but then she showed up one day at one of my shops. Obviously, she had known who I was from the start. She told me she was pregnant and that I was the father. Long story short, she wanted money. She said she'd tell my wife if I didn't start paying her a grand a month.'

At this, Mick reached out and grabbed a handful of the sandwiches. He threw one into his mouth and began chewing as if he were in the cinema watching a movie. Boyle watched him for a moment and then continued.

'So, I paid her. On the dot, every month. Through the books though. I did nothing illegal. I just put her down as one of my employees so as not to raise any suspicion. Whatever can be said about the situation, I did pay my taxes.'

He let out a nervous laugh that was too inflated but none of his audience shared his amusement. Mick glared at him, his mouth chewing a cucumber sandwich like a cow chewing the cud.

Boyle swallowed hard and finished off the remains of his tea.

'Then about two weeks ago, she comes to me and says she wants to leave the country. She tells me that if I pay her a final lump sum, she'd be out of my hair, and I'd never see her again.'

'How much did she ask for?' Darcy asked.

'Fifty grand,' Boyle told her.

Mick let out a whistle.

'Sorry to interrupt you Mr. Boyle,' Darcy said. 'But when did you, Mrs. Boyle, first know about the blackmailing of your husband?'

'It was ...' Boyle began.

'I believe that question was directed at your wife,' Mick said.

Joan Boyle faced them, her face so full of resentment it looked as if it could explode at any moment.

'My husband confessed his affair to me when Ms. Robinson demanded the ridiculously large sum of money.'

'I don't have that sort of cash to throw around and certainly not to give to a blackmailer,' Mr. Boyle said.

'And you certainly wouldn't have been able to pay her off without your wife noticing, would you?' Darcy asked him.

'What do you mean by that?' Mrs. Boyle spat.

'Isn't it obvious?'

'These egg-mayo sandwiches are absolutely delicious,' Mick said to no one in particular. 'Can you tell me, though, what's that bit of green in them? Parsley, is it?'

They all looked at Mick and at the small, perfectly made sandwich in his hand.

'Cress,' Mrs. Boyle told him and, having reigned in her emotions, turned away from them again.

'I think we have everything for now, Mr. Boyle,' Darcy said. 'Can I ask you, though, just to rule you out of our enquiries, where were you on Wednesday evening?'

Boyle made a show of having to think about it. He stared up at one of the chandeliers.

'I believe I was home with my wife that evening.'

'All evening?' Darcy said.

'Yes.'

'And you, Mrs. Boyle,' Darcy asked. 'Can you corroborate that?'

'Yes,' she said, without looking at them.

Darcy looked at Mick and he stood up.

'Thank you, Mr. and Mrs. Boyle, for your time,' Darcy said and stood up.

'How's Frank these days by the way?' Mick asked.

Boyle opened his mouth to reply but then closed it again, as if trying to pull his answer back in.

'Who?' he eventually asked.

Mick smiled. 'Frank. Frank Kavanagh. '

Darcy saw Mrs. Boyle turn further away from them.

'I haven't seen Frank Kavanagh in a long time,' Boyle told him. 'He's an old school friend, but I do bump into him every now and again.'

'Tell him Mick Kelly says hello. Just in case you happen to *bump* into him anytime in the future.'

'What the fuck was that about Frank Kavanagh?' Darcy said as soon as they were outside the Yeats Suite.

'I'm not sure, to be honest. But Kavanagh's like a bad smell and everything and everyone around him stinks.'

Darcy grimaced. 'OK then. But I just know they're hiding something from us.'

'We're Guards,' Mick told her, as they reached the foyer 'Everybody is hiding something from us. Even if they've nothing to hide.'

# Chapter 23

From Trinity College, Oskar Hallik strode down Pearse Street, blending in with the other foot traffic, and then turned right onto Mark Street. It had cars parked on either side of the road, but also some pedestrians so he continued north and turned right again onto Mark Lane.

He stopped alongside a Honda Accord and allowed a screwdriver that he had hidden up his sleeve to slide down his arm and into his hand. He checked up and down the lane one more time but then spotted a large white Ford Transit further down. He pushed the screwdriver back up his sleeve and walked towards it.

Again, he checked for witnesses, but the lane was quiet. He placed the screwdriver against the small fly window of the van and tapped it with his open palm. The window smashed, glass falling both inside and onto the road. He paused, looked and listened, then pushed his arm through and unlocked the door.

In one single swift move, he opened it, hopped inside and closed the door behind him. Using the hard handle of the screwdriver, he smashed the plastic console under the steering wheel. With the console exposed, he pulled down the ignition switch and using the shaft of the screwdriver, he short-circuited the ignition points.

The van's engine turned over noisily for several moments but then the big, old 2.5 litre diesel engine jumped to life with a roar. Oskar sat up straight in the driver's seat and checked his mirrors. Then he ground the gearstick into first gear and pulled out into the lane.

The Sat Nav on the phone he had bought earlier instructed him to drive through the inner city, across the Samuel Beckett Bridge and towards the North Strand. He drove into Clonard Terrace and pulled in along a row of terraced houses that were lined up like Lego bricks. He killed the engine, and sat back, his focus now on Number 42, four doors up and to the left.

From inside his coat, he took three 5x7 photographs, and choosing one, put the other two back in his pocket. He stuck the chosen one into a corner of the plastic dash and stared at it. On it was the skinny face of a boy in his late teens who sported a scar on his right cheek and a tattoo that said ÉIRE on his neck. On the back of the photograph was written the name *Evan Meehan*, and an address*: 42 Clonard Terrace*.

Oskar paid attention to his breathing, feeling the air fill his lungs and then slowly escape through his nose. In and out. In and out. *Tick tock. Tick tock*.

He did not have to wait long. The grey door with the Numbers 42 pinned to it opened and Evan Meehan stepped outside. The sound of the door slamming shut echoed down the terrace. Evan did not even look in the direction of the white van before shoving large headphones over his ears and walking in the opposite direction.

The van started up and moved slowly along the narrow road. It followed behind the boy as he seemed to sway to the music in his ears, oblivious to everything and everyone around him. The streets were busier here but that wasn't a real worry for Oskar anymore. Evan crossed over the Royal Canal and past Ballybough Jewish Cemetery, which had stood there for over three hundred years.

On the corner of Philipsburgh Avenue was a busy junction and Evan stopped at the pedestrian lights before crossing. He took out his phone and looked down at it while he waited on the lights to turn green.

Oskar stopped the van about four metres before the crossing. A car beeped for him to move on as the lights were green for him, but Oskar ignored him. The traffic lights turned red and the car behind him beeped its horn again in frustration.

Evan looked up and seeing the green pedestrian light stepped out onto the road. Oskar slammed his foot down on the accelerator and, keeping the van in first gear, pointed its nose at Evan. Only when the van was a second or two away from him, did the roar of the diesel engine penetrate through the music in his headphones and cause Evan to look up, with enough time for his eyes to bulge wide in terror.

The front of the van struck Evan with such violent force that instead of running over him, it lifted and carried him as if he were stuck to the front. With his face pressed against the windscreen, his eyes found those of Oskar and the terror in his face increased.

A thin smile cut across Oskar's face, cruel and fleeting, like a knife wound, and he gave Evan a small wink as he steered the van over a kerb and slammed into a brick wall, crushing Evan against it.

The van bounced back slightly, and Evan's limp body slid downwards. With Oskar's foot still pressed hard on the accelerator, the van lurched forward again, ramming into Evan's chest. Blood spouted from his mouth, dark and syrupy, splashing across the van's windscreen.

Oskar kept eye contact with the boy and his foot on the accelerator until he saw the life drain out of his eyes and fade away, and his body relax into death. He reversed the van back out onto the road. Evan collapsed on the ground, his arms splayed out in front of him like a rag doll's, but Oskar didn't see him fall. He had no interest in the boy anymore.

He tapped the brake and shifted from reverse into first. The old gearbox ground its cogs as if in protest. Driving away as car horns beeped furiously in protest, he fished inside his jacket for the other two photographs and, from these, he chose another boy's face with another boy's name. He replaced Evan's photo with the new one as he continued up Philipsburgh Avenue.

He switched on the radio and turned the dial until he heard a song he recognised by the 70's singer Blondie, and hummed along to the tune, tapping the steering wheel to its beat, as out his right window the sun set over Dublin Bay and turned the sea from blue to black.

# Chapter 24

The afternoon light was fading into the dark horizon when Darcy and Mick pulled up outside the Montessori. Some of the room lights had already been switched on.

'Remind me why we're back here,' Darcy asked, looking out at the darkening windows.

Mick didn't reply at first, and for a moment she wondered if the lustre of Mick's famous hunches was beginning to fade.

'Everything comes back to here,' he said eventually. 'There's more going on than we know, and there's questions about this place that still need answers.'

'So, what *do* we know?'

'We know Rachael worked here and she was killed. We know Alfie attended here and is still missing. There's something here staring us in the face, and we can't see it.'

'That we can't see *yet*,' Darcy said, and opened the car door.

Mick followed her and stood beside her as she rang the bell.

'Hello?' a female voice answered.

'Gardaí,' Darcy said. 'Would you mind opening the door for us?'

'Oh, yes, of course. I was just about to lock up.'

'We'll only take a minute, I promise,' Darcy told her.

'One sec. I'll buzz you in.'

'*Deja vu*,' Mick said as they waited for the buzzer to unlock the door.

A woman was standing there as they entered the premises, her bulk almost touching each side of the narrow corridor. Her face was flushed, and her sleeves were rolled up.

'In this way,' she told them, sounding a little out of breath. 'Mind your step with the buckets. I've just spent the last ten minutes mopping up one that I knocked over already.'

Darcy didn't bother showing her ID as she walked into the main classroom where they had last met Rachel.

'I was hoping to get out of here by three,' the woman said. 'This mopping isn't as easy as the cleaner makes it look, the poor woman!'

'We promise to only take up a few moments of your time, eh ...' Darcy said.

'Bernie. Bernie Moloney. I'm one of the Montessori teachers. Do you need me to show you some ID or something?'

'Not at all,' Darcy said, putting the woman at ease. 'I'm Detective Sergeant Darcy Doyle and this is Detective Inspector Mick Kelly. We weren't too far from here and thought we'd just call by for a look. I know the other Missing Persons detectives were here already and took statements, but we said we'd swing by anyway.'

'Ah, the whole thing is just shocking business,' Bernie said, using the interruption as an excuse to sit down. 'It's getting so you're not safe in your own bed these days. Is there any word at all about Rachel's killer? Or poor Alfie?'

'No, I'm afraid not,' Darcy said. 'Did you know him?'

'Oh, of course I did,' Bernie said. 'A lovely little fella. I pray every night that he'll show up. The Scanlans must be going through hell.'

'It's a tough time for them alright.'

'She was a nice lady, Mrs. Scanlan,' Bernie continued. '*He* wasn't much use, in my opinion anyway. The dad, I mean. He'd barely even bother coming in to talk to the teachers to see how Alfie had got on that day. Just waited at the door, and called Alfie to him. Like a dog. He'd also park his big van right across someone's driveway, even though we'd written to all the parents asking them not to do that.'

Bernie stared down at the floor. She put her hand to her face and wiped her eyes.

'I'm sorry,' she said. 'It's been a tough week for us all. We used to spend all day worrying about where Alfie was, and now we're all so upset about Rachel as well. The poor cow.'

Darcy gave her a few moments to gather her emotions.

'Bernie,' Mick said, and Darcy noticed how soft his voice was, 'did you ever think there might be any connection between Rachel and Alfie's disappearance?'

Bernie looked up, her eyes shining. 'What do you mean?'

'I mean, Alfie disappears and then Rachel is killed. Did you or anyone else who worked here not wonder if it was connected in any way?'

'Alfie and Rachel?' she asked. 'No. It was never mentioned. I never suspected that anything was going on there at all.'

Darcy imagined that there was a lot in the universe that Bernie was unsure was going on.

Mick took a step forward. 'Did you ever see Rachel and either of the Scanlans talking privately?'

Bernie shook her head. 'Not that I remember.'

'That's OK, Bernie,' Darcy said, almost wanting to put her out of her misery.

'Rachel had time for everyone,' Bernie said. 'I don't remember her talking "privately" as you call it with anyone in particular.'

'What about a boyfriend? Did she ever mention anyone?'

'No. She was quite private about that sort of thing. But she was closer to some of the other girls. Maybe you should ask them.'

'We will,' Mick said. 'Did you notice any changes in her behaviour in recent weeks, Bernie?'

'What do you mean?'

'I mean, was she more distracted or anxious about anything at all?'

Bernie took a minute to think about this but, even as she was thinking, her head was shaking from side to side.

'No, sorry. I suppose I kind of keep to myself as well. Don't get me wrong, Rachel was a good teacher but I wasn't her boss or anything like that, and we weren't really friends as such. Sorry.'

'Thank you, Bernie,' Darcy said. 'We'll be on our way.'

'We'll see ourselves out,' Mick told her, but Bernie didn't move. She just stared down at the bucket, lost in thought.

'She's being buried on Christmas Eve,' she said. 'The poor thing. The whole world is out shopping for presents, and she's going in the ground. It's just not right. It's just not right.'

# Chapter 25

Rachel Robinson had owned an apartment in a four-storey building that had a name Darcy could never remember. Central Block or East Pointe or some anodyne name drummed up at a committee meeting at 4.55pm on a Friday evening. She knew where it was though and headed for there as soon as they left the Montessori.

'Central West,' she said when she saw the sign, then turning to Mick asked, 'How can it be central and west at the same time?'

The building complex was a carbon copy of dozens of residential apartment blocks that had been built during Ireland's boom years in the '90s and after. Darcy didn't bother finding a parking spot in the underground car park, instead parking as close to the main entrance as possible.

The apartment itself, Number 87, was under Garda protection. Though Rachel didn't die there, the apartment had been mined for any traces of DNA other than her own, or any possible piece of evidence that might link a killer to her. As always in these cases, everything was deemed of interest until it was cleared by forensics or the detectives working the case.

'What exactly should we be looking for here?' Darcy asked Mick when they were inside.

'We won't know until we find it, Detective,' Mick told her. 'This is the real work we do. It's not what the public sees, and it's definitely not the glamorous side of the job but right here is where we get our breaks.'

Darcy looked around the one-bedroom apartment as she snapped on a pair of blue latex gloves.

'Despite what the man on the street thinks when he sees us tearing through traffic with the sirens on, this is our real job, sitting in a car for hours on end, hoping for a peek at a suspect. And shit like this, going over every detail again and again until something jumps out at us that we failed to notice before. I'll take the bedroom, OK?'

Darcy stepped into the main living area. Just like the exterior of the building, the interior of Rachel's apartment was bland, as if she were trying not to offend anyone's tastes. Everything in the room was aligned sensibly, and she could easily imagine Rachel standing where she stood now, when she had first moved in, her hands on her hips, mentally arranging and re-arranging the furniture. The couch against a wall that was decorated with photographs; the coffee table placed precisely between the couch and the TV, where she would sit in the evening and eat her takeaway delivery; the neutral-coloured throw, cushions and plain floor mat from a single trip to IKEA one Saturday morning.

There was a narrow shelf beneath the coffee table. Darcy crouched down and pulled out a handful of glossy magazines. They were mostly celebrity or women-oriented glossy magazines like *VIP*, *RSVP* and *Woman's Way*. She fanned through their pages, before dropping them onto the coffee table in a loose stack. Three candles sat beside them. She picked each one up and brought it to her nose, testing their scents.

She stood up and crossed to the small shelving unit. She scanned its book titles. A lot of cookery books, a few about being the perfect weight, whatever that meant, a dozen or so titles on parenting and early childhood development and the rest were self-help books of one sort or another. Apparently fiction wasn't her thing. Darcy checked each book in case there might be a letter or notes inserted between them or inside them. Nothing. She could hear Mick in the bedroom opening drawers and cupboard doors.

She went into the small kitchen and did the same, forcing herself to focus on what she was doing, trying to see something, anything that she had failed to notice before. Nothing significant.

Walking back into the living room, she pulled up the big cushions on the couch and looked under them, but there was nothing. She lay on her stomach between the couch and the coffee table and searched under them, but there was barely even any dust. Rachel was obviously a bit of a neat freak.

Mick came out of the bedroom and went into the bathroom.

Darcy got up. Her eyes drifted above the couch to the photographs on the wall. They seemed to be arranged arbitrarily in variously shaped and coloured frames but, somehow, their arrangement made sense and added an aesthetic quality to the room.

She stood and glanced from one to the other, never focusing too long on each one. Then she looked at them again. She leaned over the couch and, now close up, her eyes flicked from one to the other, over and over.

Rachel's graduation from college, her mother standing proudly next to her; two little girls in school uniforms, one redhead, one blonde; a holiday snap with friends sitting on a yellow banana boat in the Mediterranean; outside the Montessori with the rest of the teachers and possibly a councillor wearing a thick ceremonial gold chain celebrating the school's opening; a black-and-white photo of a little girl standing next to a tall man, with hills stretching out in the background.

Each one had meant something to Rachel and, despite herself, Darcy felt a melancholy creep into her for the loss of a person's life. She must have worked in the Montessori from the day it opened. She knew from the files that was four years before.

Darcy looked back at the photo of the Montessori. She had been so young. She was still so young. She looked along the line of faces of the other staff members. Bernie stood in the middle. She wondered if anyone ever called her 'Big Bernie' behind her back. Rachel had her arm around a woman at the end. The woman was heavily pregnant. Who was she?

Darcy checked her watch. The Montessori would be closed by now, so she made a mental note to call them first thing on Monday morning to identify the woman.

Darcy took the photo down from the wall. She looked closer at Rachel's face. She had been a very attractive girl. It must certainly have been easy for her to entrap Barry Boyle and even possibly a priest and lure them into bed with her. Had there been others? Others who had paid a once-off lump sum to make her go away? Others who had just paid cash?

Then there was the junkie, Kevin Brennan. He must have been the first. Another dead body. Mick was right that there was a malevolent force at play connecting them all.

It was a swanky apartment and Darcy imagined it had a rent to match. Too nice for the single salary of an assistant in a Montessori. No doubt some of Rachel's blackmail money had been used to pay for it.

She looked at her watch. 'I have an appointment with Seán's doctor in an hour,' she called in to Mick.

Mick came out of the bedroom. 'I can drop you there and take the car. That OK?'

Darcy nodded and gave the room one final look but her mind had drifted to the Rehabilitation Hospital and to Seán, who at that moment would be on his way to meet her there.

Mick hauled himself out of the passenger's seat, walked around the car and got into the driver's seat. He lowered the window.

'You sure you don't want me to come with you?' he said to Darcy.

The last silver strips of light were disappearing into the horizon as the cold blackness of a winter night spread across the sky, enclosing them below. Darcy looked up at the grey, immutable and somewhat intimidating building of the National Rehabilitation Hospital. It appeared to be looking down at her like a sleeping and unyielding elephant with one half-closed eye observing her.

'No, I'm OK,' she said. 'Thanks though.'

'Tell Seán I said hello.'

'Will do,' she said and walked towards the entrance.

It was brighter and more cheerful inside than she imagined it would be. The building was probably older than Ireland itself. A conscious effort had been made to decorate over the horror stories and sights that the now colourfully painted walls must have witnessed through the years.

At the reception was a nurse in a pristine blue uniform, so young she looked like a schoolgirl dressed up for Halloween. Darcy asked her for directions to the room where her meeting with Seán and his consultant was scheduled.

As she scurried through the corridors, she avoided looking at her phone, knowing she was already running late.

She knocked and entered the room and saw Seán seated in his wheelchair, and the consultant sitting behind a desk. When they both stared at her silently, she wanted to leave.

'Hi, Seán!' she said, but it came out with more forced enthusiasm than she'd intended.

If Darcy had imagined the consultant's office before stepping inside, she would not have been too wrong. A large dark wooden desk took up most of the room, with a bookcase and filing cabinets running along one side. There were enough medical charts and diagrams to hide most of the institutional grey paint on the walls.

'Please have a seat, Ms. Doyle,' the consultant said.

He hadn't bothered to stand, and he didn't offer his hand. His voice was smooth, and his accent had a moneyed south-Dublin lilt. He was broad, and his frame impeded most of the light outside attempting to sneak its way in through the small window. She could imagine him as one of those overzealous rugby fans in a pub, standing in front of the large TV screen and blocking everyone else's view, just as he did the light from outside now.

'Please, call me Darcy.' She took off her coat and hung it on the back of her chair.

'Very well,' he said. 'My name is Dr. Dermot Cullen. These meetings are extremely important for Seán's rehabilitation, and your punctuality would be appreciated, especially during these critical early-intervention consultancies.'

'I know, and I'm sorry,' she told him, meaning it. 'I promise to make more of an effort to be on time.'

'Early immobilisation and treatment are important factors in –'

'I said I'm sorry,' Darcy interrupted him. 'I'm here now, so let's move on.'

After a pause acknowledging his victory, he joined his hands together as if in prayer and placed them on the desk.

'What I was saying, before you arrived, Ms. Doyle,' dismissing any first-name informality, 'is that we would like to start Seán's further rehabilitation as soon as possible. It is important to realise, though, that this will be a long process. We are not miracle workers, but I can guarantee Seán that his results will be based on the effort he is prepared to put in. From his charts, I can see that he has already exceeded the expectations of his initial team at the Mater Private. '

Darcy looked at Seán. His face was impassive, but he didn't return her gaze, keeping his eyes fixed on the doctor.

'It's important to be aware that most of the recovery occurs within the first six to twelve months,' he continued. 'Any remaining loss of function present after twelve months is likely to become permanent. Physiotherapy has gone well — core-strengthening, as well as occupational therapy.'

Darcy stirred in her chair. She gave Seán a sideways glance and saw that his jaw was clenched.

Dr. Cullen picked up on the change of energy in the room. He looked at Seán.

'Look, I know this is hard to hear, but I don't want to make promises that are impossible to keep. As you know, there is no cure for spinal-cord injury. Having said that, there have been many promising advancements in recent times, and these advancements may lead to a cure one day in the future but, for now, we need to deal with what we have. It's a lot to get your head around, but maintaining a positive outlook is extremely important, especially in these early stages, and I know that's going to be harder than it sounds. I'm aware of that, but your mental state, Seán, will have as much to do with your progress as your physical rehabilitation.'

A silence settled in the room as the doctor allowed Seán to absorb his words.

'I know all that, Doctor. But sometimes it's a struggle,' Seán said without raising his head. His voice was low and almost childlike.

Darcy looked at him. She reached out and placed her hand on his knee. He didn't respond to her touch.

'Seán,' the consultant said. 'Seán, look at me.'

Seán raised his head slowly.

'I may not be able to promise you miracles, but I *can* promise that you can have your life back if you choose. You can return to work, but not in the same capacity as you had before. You can go out with friends. Family, relationships with women, even sport — all of these can be yours again. It will be the same, but different. Thankfully, you don't have to rely on me or your family or your partner. It's all up to you. And I know that that's both liberating and terrifying at the same time.'

Seán's head dropped slowly, like the air being let out of a tyre.

'Seán,' Dr. Cullen said, 'you can do this. I know you can. It'll be the biggest battle you've ever fought, but you can win it. And the next stage of your rehabilitation can start this evening, if you like?'

'Now?'

'Why not? We have everything you need here.'

Darcy squeezed his knee. She knew it would sound trite and cliché before she even said it, but she felt she had to at least say something.

'I'm here too, Seán,' she muttered.

When Seán looked up at her, she could see the struggle in his eyes. Seán Murphy, the man who ran towards danger his whole life, the man who put others' safety before his own, now having to learn the skill of reaching for a kettle without tripping up. This institute and this doctor could provide him with all the therapies under the sun, but Darcy wanted to play a role in his acceptance of this great burden and to help shoulder some of his grief and loss of identity.

'Our pool is open till ten every evening,' Dr. Cullen said. 'We could try some hydrotherapy before you go home?'

'I could stay too,' Darcy offered.

'That's up to Seán,' Dr Cullen said. 'We can organise transport for him once his session is over.'

'Seán?' Darcy said.

He looked up at her, but she was unable to read his expression.

'If it's OK,' he said. 'I'd like to do this alone.'

'Are you sure? I could wait for you, if you like?'

'I'm OK. But thanks. I'll see you at home.'

He turned away from her and there was silence in the small office. The doctor made no effort to ease the atmosphere in the room, so Darcy stood, took her coat and left.

The corridor was quiet. She wanted somewhere to hide. Somewhere to run. Without knowing where she was going, she marched down the corridor, the click of her shoes echoing off the gloomy grey walls, all the brightness and cheerfulness she had thought was there now gone.

The receptionist didn't even look up as the automatic door swished open and Darcy walked out into the bitterly cold air.

From the back of the taxi, Darcy looked out at the city streets, its buildings and shopfronts decked out in a mismatch of Christmas decorations. Revellers with glasses and bottles in their hands spilled out from the pubs and onto the streets, like rats from burst sewer pipes. Darcy had forgotten it was Saturday night. She didn't miss those nights walking the beat in uniform, mingling among the drunks, with sobriety as her only weapon of defence.

The taxi cut through the city and out towards the Liberties and home. She peered up at Christchurch, its silvery concrete lit up against the black sky like a child's pop-up book, and an idea popped into her head. Suddenly she didn't want to go home.

As they drove down the hill of Clanbrassil Street, she leaned forward. 'Stop here, please,' she told the driver.

He looked around, confused.

'Here, here,' she told him, and he glanced in his mirror and pulled in. She checked the taxi meter and handed him a twenty. 'Thanks,' she told him and, before he could say anything, she was gone.

She pulled her coat tighter as she strolled by the redbrick blocks of flats and crossed the street to St Patrick's Cathedral. She took a sharp left and disappeared down an alley before stopping in front of a metal door that, unless you were actually looking for it, you wouldn't notice.

Without thinking too much, she banged on the door. In less than a minute, she heard the bolts being pulled back on the other side. It edged open, the light momentarily blinding her, but as her eyes adjusted she saw the big frame of the security man — Pat.

He looked at her and then up and down the alley.

'You look like shit,' he told her and then nodded for her to follow him inside.

He opened the door a little further to allow her to come in and, when she had, he slammed the bolts closed behind her.

'I was just about to put the kettle on. Fancy a cuppa?'

She nodded and offered him a weak smile.

'Of course you do. Come on then,' he said and walked on ahead of her.

On either side of them were the tall bookcases of Marsh's Library, the oldest library in Ireland. For over three hundred years, the library had been used by the British to meet with clandestine undercover agents. After Ireland's independence a hundred years ago, its use had remained the same. It shared its back door with the wall of Kevin Street Garda Station, an ex-British army barracks, and in more modern times Gardaí working undercover could meet here with superior officers away from the prying eyes of the public.

Unknown to most was the fact that the security men were always ex-Gardaí who had served more than thirty years' service. The library never had to pay for security and never asked any questions.

'Where's the other fella?' Pat asked when they were in the small canteen waiting on the kettle to boil.

'You mean Mick?' she said.

Pat nodded and poured the boiling water into a teapot. He only ever made tea with tea leaves, the old-fashioned way, and compared the taste of tea made with tea bags as tasting like the devil's balls had been dipped in the cup.

'I'm not sure. Home, I think. He doesn't tell me a lot about his private life.'

'I wouldn't take it personally if I were you. He's not used to sharing information. Comes from his years spent undercover. I think if you spend too much time being afraid to say too much, you learn that it's sometimes best to say nothing at all. No milk, right?'

Darcy nodded her thanks and took the cup from him.

'Speaking of undercover,' Pat said. 'How's Seán doing these days?'

'Angry,' she told him.

'I don't blame him. What about you?'

'Me?'

'Aren't you angry?'

'Why should I be angry?'

'You had this good-looking bloke who worked in the job. Always hard for a cop's partner to understand or appreciate the job unless they're a part of it. Especially the dedicated ones, and Seán was most certainly one of the dedicated. The job was his life. One of our best undercovers, I'm told. Maybe better than Mick was in his day, although I wouldn't say that to Mick.'

'No, I never got angry,' Darcy said. 'My anger's not going to help him.'

'So, what will? Love?'

'Maybe. If that's all I can give him. Besides, you're wrong. He's still very good-looking.'

'I never said "very".' Pat stirred two sugars into his milky tea. 'Come on through here.' He picked up his cup and strolled back into the library.

At the end of the shelving was an open space with large windows that looked out onto St Patrick's Cathedral. It looked magnificent, lit up on all sides in white light. Darcy sat at the large study desk that dominated the room and looked out at it.

Pat allowed her to take in the reverence of the room and absorb some of the serenity that it exuded. Then, as if suddenly remembering that he was there, she focused back on him.

'What happened to Captain America?' Pat asked.

Darcy laughed. 'Jamie, you mean? I see him every now and again. Another angry man. I seem to be leaving a trail of them around the place.'

He sipped his tea and peered at her over the rim of his mug.

'What?' she asked him. 'Why are you looking at me like that?'

He put his cup down. 'You know, Darcy, I never made detective grade. I never wanted to, and I was never good at the politics and whose arse I was supposed to lick that year to get a promotion — but, after forty years in a blue uniform, I know people.'

'And pray tell me, oh wise one,' Darcy teased him, 'what do you see in me?'

'You don't have to admit or deny it, it's none of my business but I reckon, since you asked, that you joined because someone in the force once did something for you that had a profound effect on you or perhaps even saved your life.'

The smile fell away from Darcy's face and Pat didn't fail to notice it. She looked out at St Patrick's Cathedral.

'It's OK,' Pat said, noticing how uncomfortable she had become. 'You don't have to share any information with me.'

'It's not that I don't want to share, it's just that ...'

Pat raised his hand and cut her off. 'Darcy, it's OK. My point is that one day, someone saved you. You and I know from our job that the abused often become the abusers, whether that's violence or sexual. The same can be said for the saved. They often become the savers. Unfortunately, the irony is that those who join the force to help others also end up needing the most help of all, because no one can really be saved except those that want to be.'

Darcy stared at him for a long time, his words running around in her head. When she turned away, she felt tired. Tired enough to lie across the table and sleep.

'I should go. Try and get some sleep,' she said. 'Thanks for the tea.'

Pat stood up and looked down at her. The lights from St Patrick's Cathedral cast his face in shadow and the golden buttons on his uniform shone like distant stars, and for a moment Darcy was taken back to when she was a little girl and a Garda had hovered over her and put out her arms and saved her.

'I'm only telling you this because I know you can take it,' Pat said. 'You're a rescuer, Darcy. It's in your DNA. Just a word of warning as I've seen many a rescuer in this job come to no good. They spend all their time rescuing everybody else that they forget to save the most important person of all. Themselves.'

Pat moved back into the light and walked towards the metal door. After a few moments she got up and made her way back down the aisle of books after him. He unbolted the door. It was like opening a fridge, the cold air rushing inside. Without thinking about it, and without even knowing why, she turned around and gave him a hug. He felt like a hundred-year-old oak tree — an immutable, calm giant. He stood there, stoically, for a few moments, before he put his arms around her. After a while, she let him go and stepped outside.

She turned back. 'So why did *you* join?' she asked him.

Pat looked down at his security jacket. 'I love dressing up in blue uniforms,' he told her and smiled.

'Would you change anything if you could go back?'

He nodded. 'Yep. I would've been a postman.'

She smiled as she walked back down the alley out onto St Patrick's Street and headed for home.

# Chapter 26

Mick stood on the steps of the house staring at the red door he had walked through innumerable times. A door he used to close behind him from the inside, like a barrier where he could leave all the troubles of the day outside. A door he would open and hear happy children inform the house and the whole wide world that 'Daddy's home'.

He rang the bell. And waited.

Inside, he could hear the crisp clicking of his ex-wife's heels as they clip-clopped across the Italian marble hall. The sound stopped, and there was a pause. He was expected, and Mick imagined his ex-wife taking a moment to check herself in the hall-table mirror beside the door, and he smiled at how well he knew her. The door eventually opened with all the enthusiasm of a discarded teabag in a sink.

'Michael,' Marion Quigley said. It was a statement not a greeting.

Marion Quigley came from money, old money. Eyebrows had been raised when she began dating a mere Garda, which was nothing compared to when she had the audacity to actually marry the man. But she had loved him. He was kind and loving and a part of her had enjoyed the excitement of his job.

Of course, she couldn't live on his salary or accept the burdens of a working-class lifestyle, like a three-bedroom house, or a two-week holiday in a Spanish resort or even a ten-year-old car. She would always accept a family invitation for a quick getaway to her father's villa in Saint Lucia, or the Mercedes cabriolet for her thirtieth birthday or a nanny to help mind the children.

Mick had little say in any financial decisions in the home as his salary was used merely as petty cash. He was in work all the time anyway, and as more and more demands were made on him and bigger cases were given to him, any real connections with his family became tenuous. Apart from those with Michael.

Michael had been born with Down syndrome and it had broken Marion's heart. His birth had also filled her appointment books, and Michael's life, with every medical professional, therapist and expert that money could buy. Mick had never dared say it to Marion, but it had not taken him long to see that that little extra chromosome shone a light in his son that he wouldn't remove for all the money in the world, including the Quigleys'. Of course, there were tough times, and everything took longer for Michael, and the world around him moved at a slower pace. But what was so terribly wrong with that? And, besides, whose child didn't have their own special set of problems?

Mick's other child, Lucy, was testament to that. After the divorce, Lucy took out her dissatisfaction with her life on everyone around her. She was blamed for a fight in her school that resulted in another girl sustaining a black eye. Meetings with the school board resulted in Lucy being shipped off to an all-girls boarding school in England. Somehow, Mick got the blame for that one, and his daughter was only too happy to lay the blame on him too. Marion turning the screw against him whenever she got a chance didn't help.

Standing in the door frame, someone who didn't know Marion might well have asked her if she was on her way out to dinner or the theatre.

'You're looking very nice, Marion,' Mick said with a smile.

Marion winced at his insincerity.

He walked inside and closed the door behind him.

'I have some friends coming to the house, so you have exactly one hour with him,' she said.

The door to the kitchen at the rear of the house opened and a woman walked out. She was wearing a light-blue uniform and was sliding her arms into a long, padded winter coat, a woollen scarf already wrapped around her neck.

'I'm finished now, ma'am,' the woman said, crossing the marble floor. 'I'll be back on Monday. Enjoy your night.'

'Oh, Amelia!' Marion called to her as she reached the front door. 'In future, I'd prefer if you used the back entrance to come and go.'

Amelia stopped, her hand reaching out to open the door. She was obviously unsure whether she should continue out the front or withdraw her hand and walk out the back. She looked from Mick to Marion and then back to Mick.

He stepped forward and opened the front door for her. He gave her the biggest and most apologetic smile he could muster.

'Thank you,' she said, lowering her head as she scurried outside.

Mick watched her go and then closed the door behind him.

'Our regular cleaner is sick. But they're all the same,' Marion said in such an accusatory tone that Mick thought she might very well be referring to him.

She turned and walked back in the direction of the kitchen.

Her father had given them the money for the house when they'd moved back to Dublin. It cost more than Mick could earn in his entire career as a Garda.

Mick heard a baritone voice in the kitchen and then the clattering of someone rummaging through a cutlery drawer. Marion's new man, he figured. Mick had too much pride to go in and say hello, and the other man had too much arrogance to come out.

There was a Christmas tree in the hall that Mick reckoned was even bigger, but just as fake, as the one he had seen in the Oxford Hotel. He climbed the stairs two at a go to his son's bedroom.

After exactly one hour that went too fast, Mick heard Marion calling up. '*Michael! Time for bed!*' A euphemism, Mick knew all too well, for '*Mick, get out!*'.

Mick had to check his watch that it really had been an hour. 'Sorry, kid. I got to go.'

'Ah, Dad, can you stay for just a bit more?'

They had been playing Michael's latest game on his PS5.

'You're coming over to me on Christmas Day,' Mick reassured him.

'And can I have a sleepover?' he asked.

'I'll have to ask your mum, but since it's Christmas, I don't see why not.'

'Really?'

'Sure.'

'*Wow*, that'd be great! I prefer your house to this one.'

Mick looked around his son's bedroom and imagined it was quite possibly the same size as his whole apartment. There were very few people in Dublin that would have agreed with his son. No, there was probably none, but that didn't matter as the most important person to him did think it.

Michael pursed his lips and closed his eyes and Mick kissed him. On the landing he walked a little further than he had to and peered into his old bedroom. It was more girlie now, decorated in purples, pastels and pinks. It was like, and probably was, something from a glossy magazine page. Every morning, he had woken up in that bedroom, so refined and clean, a sterilised version of the reality he dealt with outside this house. He felt out of place now and disconnected from the room, like a coffee stain on the magazine's page.

He went downstairs to where Marion was waiting. She looked at her watch as if to emphasise a point, but Mick ignored it. He didn't want the good time he'd had with Michael to be spoilt.

'Where's Lucy tonight?' he asked.

'In her friend's house.'

'Will she be home tonight?'

Marion didn't reply. Obviously she felt she had given him enough information regarding his daughter and didn't have to, nor feel like, sharing anything further with him.

But, again, Mick ignored her hostility.

'I'll be over for himself on Christmas Day,' he informed her as he opened the front door.

'Not too early,' she warned him.

'No, not too early. 7 a.m.,' he told her and closed the door before she could protest.

Mick drove out along the coast, taking the long way back to the city. The surface of the sea was calm, and it looked black and thick like oil, as if it were waiting to rise and loom over the land and swallow up the pretty little houses vying for space on the hills.

He passed empty residential streets, out along Bullock Harbour and into Sandycove. A pub called The Sand Dunes, with a large car park out front, had a group of five or six girls standing in a circle, smoking and chatting, their drinks in their hands. A lock of blond hair glimmered under the streetlight and caught Mick's eye. He pressed the brakes and slowed down. He checked his mirror and swung the car around, stopping the car on the opposite side of the road from the girls.

A voice in his head told him to drive off, but he pushed it away, got out and crossed the road.

'Lucy,' he said as he approached the group.

The girls turned and stared at this overweight, grey-bearded, ancient man approaching them. Then they turned to Lucy, as if for an explanation. Mick was too close to her not to have spotted his daughter's cigarette as it sparked when it hit the ground. Too close also not to see her mouth form the words '*For fuck's sake*' as she lowered her head.

'Lucy,' Mick said again, giving her another chance.

The girls moved back and opened the group, exposing Lucy to this *stranger*, perhaps in hope of adding some excitement to the evening.

Some friends you lot are, Mick thought to himself.

'What do you want?' Lucy asked him.

'Merry Christmas to you too.' Mick smiled at her.

'Lucy, are you alright?' one of the girls asked her. 'Do you want me to call the Guards?'

'I *am* the Guards,' Mick told her. 'And if you lot don't go back inside then I'm going to start asking for some ID. I'm sure though none of you are underage drinkers, are you?'

They all stood and looked at one another.

'Alright then if that's what you want,' Mick said. 'Show me your IDs.'

'We're going,' one of the girls said. 'Lucy, we'll see you inside.'

They all shuffled away, mumbling under their breaths, some of them even daring to make eye contact with Mick.

Lucy watched them go and then turned back to her father.

'Thanks for embarrassing me,' she said.

'That wasn't my intention.'

'What was your intention then? To warn me about the dangers of drink and drugs and then drive me home?'

The children of Dalkey and the surrounding neighbourhoods all the way up to Killiney had a different accent to the rest of the city. The vowels were stretched and each word was sounded out. Even given that, Mick noticed Lucy's accent was more enunciated and clipped from her time spent in private English boarding schools. He wondered if it was a fascination to her friends, or an isolation for her.

'Something like that,' he admitted.

'Well, consider me warned then,' she told him and went to walk away.

'Lucy, wait,' he said, softer this time. 'I don't want to fight with you.'

'Then don't. Just leave me alone.'

Mick felt his heart cave in a little. She must have seen it on his face, because she sighed.

'I'm not a kid anymore,' she told him.

'I know that. I'm sorry. I just sometimes wish you still were.'

'Well, wishing gets you nothing,' she said, and he heard the anger in her voice, and saw it in her eyes.

'I know it hasn't been easy for you,' Mick told her. 'I know it's been rough.'

'Do you? Do you really?'

He shook his head. 'Probably not.'

She didn't reply.

'I've been so focused on myself the last couple of years,' he said, but she was shaking her head.

'You haven't been focused on yourself. In all fairness, look at the state of you.'

Mick looked down at his protruding belly.

'You've been focused on your job,' she told him. 'And Michael.'

'Well, I have to look after him,' he told her with new conviction. 'I had to reassure him. Comfort him. Help him understand what was happening between your mother and me.'

'That's exactly the problem,' she told him. A single tear fell from her eye, and she swatted it away. 'And what about me?'

He stared at her, unsure what to say.

'Where was *my* reassurance?' she asked him, her voice angrier than before. 'Where was *my* comfort? Who was going to explain things to me?'

'But you ... you understood,' he said. 'I had to protect Michael. I had to look after him.'

'No, Dad,' she said calmly, the anger gone. 'You were supposed to look after *both of us*. Michael is great because of you. I know that. And he needs extra help. I get that too. But ever since he was born, you only ever seem to have eyes for him. He shines so brightly and casts such a shadow over me, that you just stopped seeing me.'

He tried to keep eye contact with her but he couldn't, so he turned away. The realisation dawned on him, and he nodded. He dared to look at her again.

'And then the divorce just made everything ten times worse,' she said, as if resigned to her fate.

'I'm sorry,' he said.

She shrugged. 'Doesn't matter.'

He walked over to her and put his hand on her shoulder. 'No, it does matter. It matters a lot. I didn't ...'

'Miss, are you OK?'

A bouncer, with an eastern European accent, was standing beside them. Mick hadn't noticed him walking over to them.

'What?' Mick asked him.

'I'm not talking to you. I'm talking to the lady.'

Mick faced him. He was taller than Mick. His winter coat hung loosely on him, but Mick could tell he was a bodybuilder by his neck and broad shoulders.

'Tell him you know who I am,' Mick said.

Lucy looked him up and down.

'No. I don't know who you are. And you don't know me either.'

Mick stared at her.

'You are on private property, sir,' the bouncer said, blocking Lucy from his view. 'Please leave the area or I will be forced to –'

'Or you'll be forced to do what?' Mick said and took a step closer to him.

Instinctively, the bouncer put his hand on Mick's chest. Mick grabbed his hand and in one motion twisted it hard so that the whole of the bouncer's body was forced to follow it around. He fell to his knees and Mick held his arm up in the air. The bouncer's face convulsed in pain.

Before Mick could do anything else, Lucy had marched away and back to the pub. He watched her walk away, and it wasn't until several moments had passed that he heard the bouncer grunt in pain, and he remembered he was there. Mick let go of his hand, and the bouncer pulled it in to his chest and rubbed it.

The front door of the pub slammed shut. Mick looked down at the man on his knees in front of him. He held out his hand.

'I'm sorry,' he told him.

The man didn't accept his offer of help, but instead stood up himself, and still holding one hand in the other, backed away. He kept his eyes on Mick until he reached the door and went inside.

'Sorry,' Mick said out loud, but even he was unsure, now, who he was apologising to or why.

# Sunday

# 22 December

# Chapter 27

Every time Darcy hit the punching bag, the thud bounced off the low ceilings and the brick walls and echoed around the empty gym. She did her best thinking whenever she ran, but she always felt better after a workout on the punching bag and when her arms felt as heavy and hard as the leather bag she was punching.

Once, when she was in uniform, she had pulled over a car that had broken a red light right in front of her. The driver had no licence, and the car wasn't insured or taxed. She informed the driver that she was going to have the car impounded, and he spat straight into her face. Before a thought had even passed through her mind, she had given him a hard enough punch to break his nose with a crack.

After claims of police brutality from the driver, who had a litany of previous convictions, and Darcy filing a mountain of paperwork, she narrowly missed being suspended. As part of her 'sentence', she was ordered to seek counselling from a psychotherapist about her 'anger management' issues. Although initially she attended the hour-long sessions half-heartedly, she soon found herself looking forward to her weekly chats.

It was the psychotherapist who recommended that whenever she felt like things were getting on top of her, she should 'hit the shit' out of a punching bag for as long as her arms could take it. When she had woken this morning, Darcy's only thought was that things were most certainly getting on top of her, and so, while Seán was still asleep, she had made her way to where a set of gloves and a punching bag waited patiently for her.

She thought about Seán and when he'd come back from the hospital. Sitting opposite each other, eating a vegetarian pizza that tasted bitter in her mouth. Awkward silences and awkward conversations. Seán had given up after the first slice. She should have got a regular pizza with meat on it and claimed she wasn't hungry. It was stupid of her. Every time she tried to do something nice for him it seemed to backfire. Like trying to run fast on a lake of ice. Always falling on her arse whenever she made an effort.

Five minutes into her workout, Amos, the Israeli owner of the gym, appeared wearing a Batman dressing gown and sipping from a mug that said *World's Best Mum*.

'I've only a few regrets in life,' he told her. 'Getting married was one. Not buying stock in Amazon twenty years ago was another, but giving you the code to the front door tops the list.'

She ignored him and continued her attack on the bag. He watched her for a while.

'You want some coffee?' he asked her.

*BANG — BANG — BANG.*

She stopped and tried to catch her breath.

'No,' she told him, untying the laces of the gloves with her teeth. 'I'm sorry I'm here so early. I didn't know you slept here.'

'I don't,' he said, taking a mouthful of coffee. 'Well, what I mean is, I don't normally. My girlfriend kicked me out, so I've been here for a couple of nights. It's harder to find a room to rent in this city than it is to get a good Guinness in Tel Aviv.'

'I didn't know you had a girlfriend.'

'Well, I can't wait around for you forever, you know.'

Darcy looked away, a little embarrassed. 'I better go. Thanks though. And I'm sorry if I interrupted your morning coffee.'

'That's OK,' Amos told her. 'I do have a life outside this gym, though.'

'Do you?'

'No. Not really.'

They stared at each other for a few moments. Amos looked away first.

'Did I ever tell you the story about the Great Pagliacci?' he asked her, as she removed her gloves.

'No,' she said, smiling. 'But I've a feeling you're about to.'

'This man goes to the doctor and tells him he's depressed. Says life is hard and painful. He says he feels all alone in the world. Doctor says, "Your treatment is simple. The Great Pagliacci is in town tonight. Go see him. That will pick you up." The man starts crying, and says, "But, Doctor, I *am* the Great Pagliacci".'

Darcy surprised herself by laughing loudly, and Amos smiled in satisfaction at having made her laugh.

'I'm going to go shower,' he said. 'I'll probably get a few diehards coming in later. I haven't had anyone in this early on a Sunday since Jimmy McGrath.'

'Jimmy McGrath, the boxer?'

'Yep,' Amos said.

'I didn't know he came here to train.'

'He didn't. He came here for the same reason you do.'

He turned and walked away.

Darcy watched his back. She didn't want to ask, but she had to. 'And what was that?'

He stopped and turned. 'To avoid being somewhere else,' he told her. 'Or *with* someone else.'

Darcy stood watching where Amos had been but left when she heard the shower turn on.

Seán wheeled himself out of the bedroom into the kitchen and saw Darcy standing at the cooker, the frying pan sizzling loudly in front of her.

'That smells good.'

She turned around and smiled at him. 'It's been a while since I cooked these,' she told him, 'but I thought I'd give you a treat. I noticed the supermarket open, so I popped in and got some sausages.'

'You're cooking sausages?' he said, the excitement palpable in his voice.

Two pieces of bread popped out of the toaster. She put them on a plate, brought it over to him and went back to the kettle.

'I know I messed up with the pizza,' she said as she poured the hot water into the teapot. 'And I was hoping we could have a little chat.'

'OK,' he said. 'Go ahead.'

She brought over the teapot, placed it on the table and then sat down.

'So, I was thinking ...'

'Your sausages,' Seán said and nodded his head towards the kitchen.

Darcy turned around and saw smoke rising off the pan. '*Oh shit!*' she said.

She ran back to the cooker, lifted the pan off and transferred the sausages to a bowl. She placed the bowl in the centre of the table beside the toast and then poured tea into both the cups. She lowered the pot heavily onto the table.

She sat down opposite him. 'I've been having a think about you and me and this ...' she struggled to find the word but avoided looking directly at his wheelchair '... situation.'

'OK.'

She spooned a couple of the half-burnt sausages onto Seán's plate, and he looked down at them. She noticed his mouth tighten.

'Is there any butter?' he asked. 'For the toast?'

'What? Oh, sorry, yeah.'

Darcy got back up. She returned with a tub of unopened spreadable butter and put it in front of Seán. She watched him open the tub and dip his knife into it, then spread some of it onto the toast.

'Why not come with me to the shops next time,' she told him. 'We'll need a lot of stuff if we're to cook Christmas dinner together.'

He lowered his eyes to the table. 'You know I can't.'

'Yes, you can. You just don't want to. We can go and you can choose all the regular brands that you love. We could make the place really homely.'

'Is this what you wanted to talk about?'

'No, of course not.'

''Cause I'm just not in the mood for any motivational advice. I'm sorry.'

She nodded. 'What I was going to say was that I apologise for not being around more often the last few days and giving you a proper welcome, but that I promise to make up for it. I promise. A new start. What do you say?'

He looked at her.

'You don't believe me, do you?' she said.

'It's not that I don't believe you, it's just that I don't think it's possible. I know, more than anyone, Darcy, what your job involves. And the demands they put on you. I'm really not upset with you for not being around more often.'

'You sure?'

'I'm sure,' he said.

Seán stuck his fork into one of the sausages and took a bite. 'It tastes just like the hospital food.'

Darcy opened her mouth in shock and then smiled. 'I think that's a compliment in there somewhere hidden in that insult.'

Seán chewed on the sausage and then swallowed. 'Today I'm going to work on some of my rehabilitation exercises. Gabriela will be here soon. And you go do what you have to do. I'll be fine. When do you have to leave?'

Darcy looked at her watch. 'Mick said he'd collect me in five minutes.'

'Please don't let him come in. Can you do me that favour?'

She nodded. 'OK. Sure.'

'Thanks. But, listen, I want to apologise too.'

'Apologise to me? For what?'

'There are lots of things I don't have any more, Darcy. Use of my legs for one. A career. A future to look forward to.'

'That's not true, Seán. The doctor said –'

He held up a hand and she stopped.

'There's one thing I do have a lot of now, and that's time. I have time to sit around here and to think about things, and I realise that I've expected too much of you. And maybe too much of myself also. I think about when we first met and the nervous flirting and the foolish games and how much I wanted to spend every minute I possibly could with you but was afraid to tell you. I think about how attracted I was to you, and still am by the way. And I spend way too much time thinking about how it could have been for us.'

'You mustn't think like that.'

'No, wait, let me finish. Please, Darcy. I also realise, and I want you to know that it hasn't been an easy decision, but I think it would be best, for me as much as for you, if I leave here and work hard at my rehabilitation, like you suggested, but just not here.'

She managed a small nod, but she suddenly felt off balance. She placed her arm across the table as if to steady herself, as if a rug had been pulled out from under her.

'Not here? You mean, not with me?'

Seán nodded and reached for her hand. 'My parents have offered to help me out. In their place.'

'Wait,' she said, her voice low. 'Do you mean that you're leaving for proper treatment, or you're leaving me?'

'I don't know. I'm sorry.'

'But I wanted us to make a start again. Please, Seán.'

'I know, and I'm so grateful for that. I really am, but this is not how you imagined your life with me when we first met. You have to admit that.'

'What difference does that make?'

'It makes all the difference.'

The noise of a car coming into the little square made them turn towards the window.

'That's not your parents, is it?' Darcy said and jumped out of her seat.

When she saw Mick driving in, she let out a sigh of relief. 'It's Mick,' she said.

'Please, Darcy, don't let him come in.'

Darcy's phone beeped and she looked at the message.

**I'm outside. Bring the interviews from the Montessori with you.**

She opened the curtains and held up a finger to Mick — one minute. He nodded. She took out the folder of witness statements from under the coffee table.

'I'm sorry,' she said, but she was unsure exactly what she was sorry for. Sorry they had come to this. Sorry for what had happened to him. Sorry she had to go. Sorry for everything.

She took her coat off the hook and put it on. She opened the front door slightly but then stopped and turned to face Seán.

'Can we talk about it some more before you make any big decisions? At least think about it some more. A lot more.'

'It's all I do all day, think about things.'

'Please?'

He let out a deep sigh and smiled at her. 'OK,' he said. 'I promise. Now go. Go save the world, Darcy Doyle.'

She was about to leave, but turned around quickly and walked back to him. She bent down and kissed him on the lips.

'I'm sorry I lied to you,' Seán said.

'Lied? Lied about what?'

'The sausages. They're worse than the hospital. Much worse!'

She laughed and kissed him again. Longer this time.

Then, without saying anything else, she left, the sound of the door banging shut echoing around the small square.

# Chapter 28

Like most churches nowadays, even when Sunday Mass was in full swing, St. Augustine's car park was only half full. Darcy parked the car outside the church's sacristy and switched off the engine.

'I don't understand what you're looking for. What did your wife say exactly?' she said to Mick, who was riffling through the stack of witness statements on his lap.

'Ex-wife,' he corrected her, without looking up. 'It hit me as soon as I woke this morning. She was giving out about the regular cleaner.'

'And?'

'Every time we've gone to that Montessori, what have they been doing? First Rachel. Then Bernie.'

Darcy thought for a moment. 'Cleaning.'

'Exactly,' Mick said, holding up each page, one at a time and looking at them. 'Where's that list of staff?'

He found it and handed it to Darcy. 'Count the names of the employees.'

She counted them silently as Mick counted the statements.

'Thirteen,' she told him.

'So why do I only have twelve statements?'

Darcy shrugged.

'Because one of them never gave one,' he told her.

'Who?'

He placed his finger under a name on the employee sheet.

Darcy looked at it.

'Ciara Ward,' she read aloud and then looked up at Mick.

'The cleaner,' he said.

'Oh, yes ... off for a couple of weeks. Isn't that what Rachel told us? But didn't say why.'

'Exactly. Why? Why is she never there? And why hasn't she come forward? The records here show she's been working there since it opened.'

Darcy leaned her head back on the headrest. 'The woman in the photo,' she said, almost to herself.

'What?'

Darcy already had her phone open and was calling Eoin.

'The pregnant woman in the photo in Rachel's apartment. The one Rachel was cosying up to.'

Eoin answered on the second ring. She skipped any greetings.

'I need you to get me the home address for Ciara Ward. She's an employee at the Montessori. Call me when you have it, please. It's urgent.'

She took the phone away from her ear, but then paused.

'Eoin. You still there?'

'Yes.'

'Also get me all her medical records. Specifically, I need to know if she had a baby. And its gender. Got it?'

'Got it.'

They slid along the pew at the back of the church just as the priest was saying the final prayer. From his elevated view on the altar, they saw him raise his head and fix his gaze on them for a brief moment before bowing it again in prayer.

'*The Lord be with you*,' he said, his arms held up in the air on either side as if surrendering.

'*And also with you*,' the congregation murmured.

'*Now go in peace to love and serve the Lord*.'

'*Thanks be to God*,' they replied, and began to stand up.

'*Thanks be to God is right*,' Mick said, and they also stood up, their eyes never leaving the priest as he made his way into the small antechamber on the far side of the altar.

Darcy nudged Mick with her elbow and, as everyone made their way down the church aisles and outside, they jostled their way in the opposite direction and towards the altar.

'The important thing to realise here, Father,' Mick told him, 'is that we're not here to arrest or even charge you. You've done nothing illegal. We don't work for the Vatican, and we're not the moral police.'

Mick forced a smile but neither Darcy nor Father Aidan made an attempt to copy it. Darcy had already decided she was going to be the bad cop in this good cop/bad cop routine. She tried to keep her expression as emotionless as possible as she stared at the priest.

Father Aidan Brady, Darcy had to admit, was an attractive man. Or rather, he had an attractive face. His unkempt grey hair seemed more styled than carefree, and his light-blue, soothing eyes would not have gone amiss in a Hollywood gossip magazine.

'In fact,' Mick continued to the priest, 'it is you who have been done wrong by. You are the victim here — you are the one who was blackmailed.'

'On the other hand,' Darcy told him and couldn't help offering him an insincere smile, 'I doubt your superiors, or your parishioners, would see it like that.'

Mick cut in. 'We are here today to gather as much information as possible about your blackmailer, Rachel Robinson.'

'The *murdered* Rachel Robinson,' Darcy added.

'There's no need to be so base and gruesome, Detective,' Father Aidan told her. 'I am aware of the situation and, as I've already stated, I promise to do everything in my power to cooperate and assist you in your enquiries.'

'And we are very grateful for that, Father,' Mick told him.

Darcy was about to tell him that he had little choice in cooperating with them unless he wanted to be brought down to the station and his lawyer called, but Mick gave her a look that told her to ease up. Instead, she took a moment to imagine herself walking up the aisle of the church and arresting him on the altar in front of his Sunday Mass worshippers.

'What we're trying to establish here ...' Mick continued, but there was a gentle knock on the door of the sacristy, and a middle-aged woman came in carrying a tray.

'Ah, Sadie, thank you,' Father Aidan said, and moved back to allow her to place the tray on the coffee table between them. 'We'll pour ourselves.'

'Yes, Father,' the woman said.

Darcy's gaze rose from the assortment of biscuits on the plate and was shocked by the vicious look that was directed at her. Sadie's cold grey eyes stayed focused on Darcy as she left the room and gently closed the door behind her. Darcy looked at Mick to see if he'd noticed, but he was already chewing a digestive biscuit, its crumbs resting on the lapel of his jacket.

'Who knew about your financial arrangement with Rachel?' Darcy asked him, as the priest poured his tea.

Father Aidan put down the pot. 'Only myself and Mrs. Griffin.'

'Mrs. Griffin?' Mick asked.

'The church secretary.'

'The woman who just brought us tea?' Darcy guessed.

'Yes. Sadie Griffin.'

'I don't suppose,' Mick said, 'that she's any relation to Mark Griffin? He used to live around here, didn't he?'

Father Aidan made an attempt at a questioning stare but gave up halfway through. 'Yes. She's his mother,' he admitted.

Mick sat back in his chair. 'You weren't the parish priest here at that time, were you?'

'No,' Father Aidan said.

Mick turned to Darcy. 'I wasn't involved in the case myself,' he told her, 'but this whole area was like a war-zone for several weeks while Mark Griffin was on the run. Apparently, the kidnappings he'd done hadn't been sanctioned by his buddies in the IRA, and they were pretty pissed, to put it mildly. Luckily for Griffin, we found him first.'

'He's still locked up, isn't he?' Darcy asked.

'Oh, yeah. And most likely will be for another twenty years.' Mick turned back to Father Aidan again. 'Did you know that Griffin cut off that man's ear and sent it to his wife in the post?'

Father Aidan nodded. 'I'm aware of the details of the case.'

'And that's the psychopath's mother?' Darcy asked.

'Sadie had nothing to do with her son's actions,' Father Aidan said, raising his voice. 'She was as much a victim of her son's behaviour as were the victims of his crimes.'

'Somehow,' Darcy said, 'I find that hard to believe.'

'Believe what you like,' Father Aidan told her. 'It's the truth.'

A silence settled in the room before Mick spoke again.

'Speaking of the truth,' he said, 'how about we get back to the circumstances that led to your depositing €300 into Rachel Robinson's account each month.'

Father Aidan sat up in his chair. 'It's a little uncomfortable for me to talk about.'

'Well, then, perhaps you'd be more *comfortable* answering our questions down at the station?' Darcy asked.

Mick raised his hand to her. 'I'm sure there'll be no need for that, will there, Father?'

Father Aidan grimaced at the thought of it. 'No, Detectives. There'll be no need for that. It was at a wedding actually. A girl from this parish decided to have her wedding ceremony in her future husband's local church. A beautiful spot outside Glenbeigh, along the Ring of Kerry. Her mother had asked me to officiate, a request I was only too happy to grant, but it did mean a night away from my own parish. Rachel was one of the bridesmaids. We spoke a couple of times, before and after the ceremony, and she made some inappropriate comments to me.'

'Such as?' Darcy asked.

'You know, things like, "You're the best-looking priest I've ever seen", and "Have you ever kissed a girl?". There were other things, more lascivious, but I laughed them off. I was a little embarrassed, of course.'

'And a little flattered perhaps?' Darcy said. 'Rachel was a good-looking girl.'

Father Aidan scowled at her. 'Yes, I suppose I was. Humility is a virtue I have struggled with in the past.'

'Go on,' Mick told him.

'Anyway, as I was staying the night, I had a glass of wine with my meal. It was a wedding in the country and, as I'm a priest, quite possibly everyone at the wedding bought me a drink. I didn't consume them all of course, but I was courteous and took a few sips from each when it was put in front of me.'

'How magnanimous of you,' Darcy said and gave him a smile.

Father Aidan ignored her. 'I went to bed. Early. They had provided a room for me in the hotel. Despite my rationing of the alcohol, my head was spinning. I undressed and fell asleep to the muffled sound of the music below in the hall. It must have been several hours later when I woke up, as the music had stopped, and the room seemed darker. I think I'd woken because I thought I'd heard my room door being closed. I wasn't sure whether I'd locked it or not.'

Father Aidan reached down, picked up his teacup and took a large mouthful.

'Excuse me,' he said. 'This is not easy for me.'

'You're doing just fine,' Mick told him.

He put the cup back down. 'At first I thought I was still asleep and dreaming, because I saw a woman's figure at the end of my bed. She was dressed in a white robe and, to be honest, when I realised I was awake I thought I was experiencing an apparition of the Blessed Virgin Mary. But then she ... she ... unrobed and stood completely naked in front of me.'

'That certainly doesn't sound like the Blessed Virgin Mary to me,' Mick said, in such a deadpan manner that Darcy had to bite hard on her lip to suppress a laugh.

'I'm only trying to tell you the truth,' Father Aidan said, getting upset. 'This is very difficult for me.'

'I apologise, Father,' Mick said. 'Go ahead.'

'Well, I'm sure I don't have to narrate every sordid detail of what happened next. My only excuse or defence is that I was still half-drunk and half-asleep. It was over before I knew it. She put her robe back on and was out of the room. On awaking the next morning, I thought it had all been a dream. It was only when I saw her at breakfast that I knew it had really happened. I knew by the way she looked at me. I have been living with the shame every moment since.'

Father Aidan placed both of his hands over his face and held them there long enough for Mick to look at Darcy, and for Darcy to shrug.

Eventually the priest removed his hands and appeared to have composed himself.

'When did she start blackmailing you, Father?' Darcy asked.

'She contacted me a few months later. Maybe four months after that night. Came to Mass one Sunday. She already had a small bump and she said she wanted to talk. I brought her in here, into this room and we made the deal.'

He lifted the cup of tea to his mouth, his hand noticeably shaking, and drank some. He swallowed loudly and let out a sigh again.

'Oh God. I'm sorry. It's been a very difficult few years. In a way, I'm glad that it's out in the open now. Oscar Wilde once said that it's the confession, and not the priest, that gives us absolution. I hate to admit that he was right.'

'As I said to you, Father,' Mick said, 'this is not a confession box. We're not here to admonish you for anything you think or may think you have done. If the press ever gets hold of your little secret, it won't have come from us. Isn't that right, Detective?'

Darcy didn't reply.

'*Detective Doyle?*' Mick said in a more commanding tone.

She nodded.

Mick turned his attention back to Father Aidan. 'Did Rachel come to you in the last week or two and offer you a once-off payment that would put an end to the monthly ones?'

Startled, the priest looked at Mick and nodded.

'And what did you tell her?' Mick asked.

'I told her the truth. That I didn't have ten thousand euros to hand over. I wanted an end to the whole rotten business, but I couldn't explain ten thousand missing from the books.'

'And what did Rachel say about that?'

'She said she'd put my story all over social media if I didn't pay her. She said I'd be the laughingstock of the whole country, and that every newspaper would have my face on the front page, and that she'd make me more famous than Bishop Casey. I can tell you in all honesty, Detectives, that I haven't had a good night's sleep since then.'

'I understand,' Mick said. 'And did you take any action? Try to get a bank loan? Or borrow the money?'

The priest hesitated. 'No.'

'You did nothing?'

'Well ... I spoke to Mrs. Griffin.'

'You told her about the situation?'

'I did.'

'And what did she say?'

The priest paused before answering. 'She said that she would look over the books and that I could leave it with her for now.'

'Leave it with her?' Darcy said. 'What do you think she meant by that?'

'I assume she meant that she would go over the church's finances and try to come up with the money.'

A silence fell in the room, Darcy and Mick pondering on that unpalatable information.

'I have one more question, Father,' Darcy said then.

'Yes.'

'Did you ever meet the little boy? Rachel's child?'

'No,' he said.

'Why? Were you not curious about him?'

'*Curious* isn't the correct word. I made a decision early on to never meet the child. With cameras everywhere nowadays, all they needed was a photo of me pushing the little boy on a swing. It would be the end of me.'

'And I guess Rachel was more than happy with that arrangement?'

'Yes, she was, actually,' he replied curtly.

Darcy looked at Mick, ready to leave.

'May *I* ask one question?' Father Aidan said.

Darcy shrugged.

'Now that Rachel is ... now that Rachel is no longer with us, what will happen to the little boy?'

'Do you know his name?' Darcy asked him.

'Yes, I saw photos of him. He seems quite the little chap. A lovely little boy. His name's Luke.'

'Luke's dead, Father,' Darcy told him. 'He was found on the side of a mountain. He'd been lying there for days. You probably read about it in the news recently.'

'Sweet Jesus in heaven!' the priest said and blessed himself. 'I did see it on the news. That little boy was ...'

Darcy became conscious of Mick staring at her. She looked at him, and he nodded.

'If it helps,' she said to the priest, 'at this stage of the investigation we don't believe that you were his biological father. In fact, we don't believe Rachel was ever even pregnant.'

He looked up at her, his eyes wide in disbelief.

This was something that he would have to deal with in his own time, come to terms with it, and make peace with his God. There was nothing either Mick or Darcy could say to him now.

Mick stood up and walked to the door.

Darcy followed him, placing her hand on the priest's shoulder for a moment as she walked by him.

'If we need anything else from you, we'll be in touch.'

On the way out, they found Mrs. Griffin sitting at a desk with a large calendar in front of her.

'How's Mark these days?' Mick asked her.

'*None of your business!*' she spat at him.

'Ah, now. That's not very Christian of you.'

'Is it true what they say, that the apple doesn't fall far from the tree, Mrs Griffin?' Darcy asked.

'What's that supposed to mean?' She scowled at them both.

'It means we believe you're quite the fixer,' Mick said.

'I don't know what you're talking about,' she said.

'That you help Father Aidan out whenever you can.'

'I serve the Church in any way I can.'

'I'm sure you do.'

'You might want to take himself in a cup of tea,' Darcy told her. 'He's had a bit of shock.'

Mrs. Griffin left them and went straight into the sacristy, closing the door behind her.

Mick looked at Darcy. 'I thought for a moment there, you were going to leave him hanging,' he said.

'*Let he who is without sin …*' Darcy said as they walked back out into the cold air.

# Chapter 29

'Not great weather for fishing,' Jack Leonard of Leonard's Fishing Supplies told his customer, but Oskar didn't reply.

Instead, he watched Jack roll the long filleting knife in bubble wrap and then place it carefully into a plastic bag.

Oskar handed Jack a twenty-euro note, the price written on the little sticker, reached across the counter and took the knife from him.

On the way out, he spotted a dark-green waterproof poncho with a hood and took it off the shelf. This price-tag said twenty euros. Oskar took out his old black leather wallet and removed another twenty-euro note. He placed the money on the counter, not even looking at Jack this time.

A mechanical bell chimed on the door as he left the quiet of the shop and stepped out into the busy pedestrianised streets of Temple Bar.

Next to a public bin, Oskar unfolded the knife from its wrapping and slid the long blade down the side of his trousers with only the wooden handle visible. He shoved all the superfluous packaging deep inside the bin and walked away, throwing the heavy poncho on, the hood over his head, as he manoeuvred across the ancient cobblestoned streets of the city.

Earlier, he had followed Ryan Durkin to Temple's Arcade and had watched him go inside with two other boys. He had stood outside and watched them start to play a Zombie-shooting simulator game. He now looked through the window and saw them still playing the same game. Two of them, one fat with scraggly wisps of a black beard and the other tall and scrawny with ginger hair, were firing plastic guns at the screen, while the third boy, Durkin, who was wearing an open Canadian Goose black puffy jacket, stood to the side smiling.

Oskar reached into his inside jacket pocket and took out the three photographs. He found the one with the third boy's face and looked down at it. On the back was written *Ryan Durkin, 17 Chester Avenue*. He put the photographs back into his jacket.

At the entrance to the arcade there was a bin, and from it Oskar pulled out a cardboard takeaway coffee cup. Close to the entrance, he put his back to the wall and crouched down, pulling the poncho's hood over his face. The cup he placed in front of his legs.

Some people threw coins into the cup as Oskar crouched there, his head bent low. Thirty minutes went by. Eventually, he heard them, their bravado artificially fired up from violent video games. He watched their footwear pass in front of him, their bright trainers contrasting with the centuries-old cobblestones.

'A few euro,' he begged.

'*Fuck off!*' one of them spat at him and the other two laughed.

'*Asshole,*' Oskar said loudly.

He still hadn't lifted his head, but he heard their steps halt.

'What did he say?' one of them asked.

'I think he called you an asshole,' another said, laughing.

Their footsteps came back in his direction. Two shoes stood in front of him now.

'Hey,' the voice belonging to the shoes said. 'What the fuck did you call me?'

Oskar said it more quietly this time, but loud enough for them to hear.

'I say, you an asshole.'

The other two sniggered, and Oskar saw the foot rise as it aimed at his head. As it swung towards his face, Oskar caught it mid-air and held the ankle tight, and the boy struggled to stay upright.

Only now did Oskar look up and make eye contact with the boy. The boy recognised something in Oskar's eyes and all aggression fell from his face and was replaced by fear. His sudden realisation of the gravity of the situation caused Oskar to smile, before he used the wall to launch himself upwards, his fist rising with him until it connected under the chin of the ginger-haired boy. His mouth slammed shut and he was lifted off the ground and backwards.

Before the other two could even register what had just happened, Oskar drove his open palm into the fat boy's bearded face. He knew speed mattered more than force, and the second boy shot backwards in agony, blood gushing from his nostrils.

Ryan Durkin was about to run when Oskar grabbed the lapels of his padded coat and pulled him inwards. Ryan didn't even see from where the long fillet knife had appeared, but he certainly felt it as it went up and into the top of his leg, the sharp blade cutting easily through the muscle until it found the femoral artery.

Oskar twisted the handle of the knife, and the artery sliced open. Ryan's eyes almost popped out of his head and his hand automatically shot down to grab at the source of the pain, but Oskar held his wrist and would not allow him to touch it.

The thick, dark blood flowed out of him and so too did life itself. It spread down and outwards and stained Ryan's jeans as if he had wet himself. If the cut was not attended to within moments it would be too late to do anything. When Oskar felt the fight go out of the boy, he knew it was already too late. He let his wrist go, turned him around and leaned him against the wall. Ryan, still conscious, slid down onto the path, and by the time the first pedestrian decided to show any real interest in him, and saw his blood, Oskar was so far away from the scene that he barely even registered the scream.

# Chapter 30

Ciara Ward's home was a two-storey terraced house a few minutes' walk from the Montessori where she worked part-time as a cleaner. It wasn't in one of the most desirable neighbourhoods in Dublin, but the front gardens were tidy, and all the cars on the street, although more than ten years old, were roadworthy, taxed and insured.

The house itself had a lived-in and somewhat tired look about it. The curtains were dark in colour, old-fashioned and drawn shut. No light could be seen emitting from anywhere inside.

'What do we know about her?' Mick asked, as he looked up at the house.

'Nothing much so far. Eoin is chasing her medical records from Galway, but it's hard to pin anyone down at this time of year. She also seems to have escaped any attention from the Missing Persons detectives who were first assigned Alfie's case.'

'OK then. Let's see if she's up for a chat, shall we?'

They both walked up the driveway. In the front window of the next-door neighbour's house the curtains twitched. It caught Mick's attention and when he looked over, a woman was standing there watching him.

Mick waved at her and she pulled the curtains closed and disappeared.

'That's a bit weird,' Mick said.

'Yeah, it'd be weird if it happened to someone else, alright. Be honest, Mick. That's not the first time someone's legged it after you've waved at them.'

Mick shrugged and stepped onto the porch. He couldn't see a bell, so he banged his fist on the door.

'Jesus, Mick. Is that what they taught you in Templemore a century ago? We've learned to knock these days.'

As if to demonstrate, Darcy knocked gently on the front door. 'We're not trying to wake the dead.'

After a few moments, Mick said, 'Looks like there's no one home.'

Darcy cocked her head. 'Wait, did you hear that?'

Mick went to speak, but Darcy shushed him. She brought her head closer to the wooden door and placed her ear against it but then shook her head.

Mick took a step back from the porch and looked up at the bedrooms above.

'No one's home,' he said.

'Or they don't want to open the door for us.'

'Maybe they think we're Jehovah Witnesses.'

'No, those are usually young, groomed and well dressed.'

'What's your point?' he asked as he followed her back down the driveway. He couldn't help but look back at the window where the woman had stood staring at him. The curtains were still closed.

Back in the car, Mick turned the heating up full blast.

Darcy's phone rang. She showed Mick the screen.

**Chief Inspector Glenn O'Riordan**

'I'm putting you on speaker, Chief. I'm in the car with Detective Kelly.'

'I'm looking for a progress report.'

'Well, sir ...'

'But not right now,' O'Riordan interrupted her. 'Make sure you come see me the next time you're in Harcourt Street.'

'Yes, Chief.'

There was silence for a moment. Darcy glanced at Mick.

'There's been two more murders,' O'Riordan said. 'Teenagers. Looks like separate incidents at this stage, but also coincidental. And what do we not like at the NBCI?'

'Coincidences,' Darcy answered. 'Do you think they're connected to our case, Chief?'

'I'm not sure yet but either way that's your job to find out. I've sent Detectives Finnegan and Rossiter to the scenes, but I want you to do a little digging to see if anything's connected.'

'Yes, sir. Why do you think there is? A connection, I mean.'

'Both kids go to St. Michael's school in Dundrum, and they're – I mean they *were* best mates with Sam Gallagher who happens to be Jimmy Gallagher's grandson. I'd like to rule out any gangland connection to Rachel Robinson and our missing boy.'

'And why do you think it has anything to do with the gangsters?' Darcy asked.

'Because we don't live in Juarez, Mexico, Doyle. Three murders in three days is still unusual for Dublin — for now anyway. I just want that angle ruled out. Keep your investigation on the straight and narrow and don't muddy your waters. Or whatever metaphor you want to use.'

'Yes, sir,' Darcy said. 'We'll get on it pronto.'

'Jaysus,' O'Riordan said, 'she's already speaking Spanish.'

Darcy was about to reply, but he'd already hung up.

She looked at Mick. He seemed lost in thought, as if he hadn't even been listening to the conversation.

'What're your thoughts?' she asked him.

'I'm thinking that if the Chief's right, then there's one person who could be at the centre of all this, and I'd love to have another little chat with him.'

'Who?' she asked, but she already knew what he was going to say.

'Frank Kavanagh.'

The mention of his name made Darcy's stomach twist.

'Missing kids? You really think that's his style?' Darcy asked him.

'No, but he always seems to know more than us. Mind you, sometimes even the dogs on the street know more than us.'

'Of course he does, Mick. That's why he's not in jail.'

Mick turned and looked up at Ciara Ward's house.

'There's a connection there with Barry Boyle,' he said, as if speaking to the closed windows and the closed door. 'I think Frank doesn't want to have anything to do with that kid, or with any dead kids, and that gives us an advantage.'

'So what? You're going to just call him and say you want a chat?'

'No, of course I'm not,' he said. 'You are.'

The smile fell off Darcy's face, but she knew she couldn't refuse him. She let out a deep sigh and took out her phone.

Halfway up Fishamble Street, Darcy parked near the entrance of Darkey Kelly's pub. One of the oldest if not the oldest streets in Dublin, it wound down to the quays and was used for hundreds of years to carry fish up from the River Liffey into the heart of the city. It was an open-air slaughterhouse, and they said the blood would run as fast and as deep as a small stream out into Dublin Bay and that it was strong enough to carry away a small dog or a crawling baby.

They got out and walked up to the entrance.

'Ah look,' Mick said when he spotted one of Frank Kavanagh's men, Tony, standing in the porch. 'We should call Dublin Zoo and let them know we've found that missing gorilla.'

'Better to be a gorilla than a pig,' Tony told him.

'And it's learnt how to talk,' Mick said. He stopped and sniffed the air. 'It still smells of shite though.'

Tony pushed the door open and walked in ahead of them. He walked towards the back of the pub as Mick stood for a moment breathing in the warmth and smells of an Irish pub.

He followed Tony, with Darcy a few paces behind him.

They passed a group of young men who were sitting around two circular tables that had been pushed together, and on which were resting pint glasses filled and half-filled with black stout and piss-coloured lager.

One of them clapped his hands together loudly and called out, '*Great, lads! Looks like the stripper's arrived!*'

Darcy was so focused on her meeting with Frank that the remark caught her off-guard and when she turned her head in their direction, her expression caused raucous laughter to spread throughout the group.

When they entered the snug, she was even more surprised to see a young girl sitting by Frank's side. They were laughing as if sharing a private joke and, for a moment, they even looked disturbed by the intrusion into their space. In front of them was a whiskey and a tall glass of Coke.

'Frank,' Mick said, looking around the small snug. 'This is cosy.'

'Hopefully you won't be here long enough to get too cosy,' Frank said. 'You want a drink?'

'I'm driving. It's illegal, in case you forgot,' Mick said and looked at the girl. 'So is underage drinking.'

Frank smiled and ignored him. 'And how's Detective Darcy Doyle?' he asked. 'Columbo Kelly still showing you the ropes?'

Darcy shrugged but didn't say anything. She didn't trust herself to say anything.

'Can I introduce you both to Chloe,' Frank said, but kept his gaze at Darcy. 'She's my daughter.'

There were a few moments of silence as Darcy and Frank held each other's stare.

Darcy watched Chloe bury her face into Frank's jacket sleeve and felt an ache in her heart looking at her, this girl feeling the protection of her father against the cruel world. This beautiful girl who was her half-sister, and Darcy was unsure whether she felt a sense of loss for the love of a sister or the protection of a father, or merely the hollow longing for something she never even had.

Then another thought popped into her head.

'Chloe, is it?' she asked.

'Yes.'

'My name's Darcy. How old are you, Chloe?'

'I'm sixteen.'

'You're very grown up for sixteen. And what school do you go to, Chloe?'

'St Michael's.'

'The one in Dundrum?'

'Questioning kids now, are you, Doyle?' Frank interrupted but not before Darcy saw Chloe nod.

'She's only making conversation, Frank,' Mick said, a smile on his face. 'Just trying to be nice.'

Frank gave Mick a malevolent scowl, but then he turned to Chloe and his face relaxed.

'The thing about the cops, Chloe, is that they never do *nice*. It's not in their nature. They just want to arrest and hang someone, and often it doesn't even matter to them if it's even the right person or not.'

Mick said, 'Perhaps the young girl would be more comfortable waiting outside while we asked you a few questions, Frank?'

'Maybe *you* would feel more comfortable if Chloe waited outside?' Frank replied.

There was a pause before Chloe said, 'I don't mind waiting outside.'

Darcy detected a French accent, and she also noticed something else that both surprised and angered her: a streak of jealousy in herself towards Chloe.

Frank stood and they all watched Chloe squeeze around the table.

'Stay with her,' Frank told Tony who followed her outside.

Mick and Darcy were about to sit down when someone from the group of lads out in the bar called out, 'Look at this little beauty! Fancy a ride, darlin'?'

There was the sound of a chair falling over and then a loud crack, which could only have been a well-connected fist to the side of someone's head.

*'Jesus!'* someone called out, but then the room went silent.

Darcy looked in the direction of the fracas, but then she and Mick sat down and turned their attention back to Frank.

Frank shrugged. 'So,' he said. 'To what do I owe the pleasure?'

'It's not much of a pleasure, to be honest with you,' Mick told him. 'So, we'll cut the small talk if you don't mind.'

'No problem at all. Are you sure you wouldn't like a drink though? A thick creamy cold pint of the black stuff, Mick?'

Mick raised a hand to hide the involuntary lick of his lips, but he was too slow, and Frank saw him. He let out a huge laugh that even made Darcy feel sorry for Mick.

'What are your connections with Barry Boyle?' Darcy asked.

'Who?'

'Fine,' Darcy said, standing up. 'We'll come back with a warrant. Let's go, Mick.'

Frank put both of his arms in the air, as if surrendering. 'Hold on, hold on! There's no need to be like that.'

'There's still a little boy missing, Frank,' Darcy told him. 'So we're not here to play games.'

Frank waved his hand for them to sit down. Darcy looked at Mick before sitting down again.

'I know Barry Boyle,' Frank said. 'He's an old schoolmate.'

'Did you know about his connections with Rachel Robinson?'

'Rachel who?'

Darcy raised her eyebrows at him.

'Oh, you mean the murdered girl,' Frank said, but then said nothing else.

Darcy could tell he was trying to figure out how much he could get away with telling them, or more importantly, not telling them.

'A girl who was blackmailing Mr. Boyle is murdered,' Darcy continued. 'Mr. Boyle is an acquaintance of yours. So, I'll ask again, did you know about his connections with Rachel Robinson?'

'No,' Frank said. 'I never heard the name Rachel Robinson until after she ... met her tragic end.'

Darcy looked at Mick and could see in his face that he believed Frank was telling the truth. So did she.

'Will that be all?' Frank asked.

'Doyle,' Mick said. 'Let's go.'

'Just because Barry and me used to be old mates doesn't mean we still have a connection. I appreciate that you're desperate for answers and that you're clutching at straws but you really shouldn't go around making assumptions. It's sloppy police work.'

Mick scoffed and they both stood up.

'Take, for example, this pub,' Frank continued. 'Do you know why it's called Darkey Kelly's?'

'Some old racist slur, I assume,' Darcy said.

'Then you'd assume incorrectly,' Frank told her, a sparkle in his eye. 'You see, the thing is, Darkey Kelly was a woman. Dorcas was her real name, and she ran a brothel on these very premises. Two hundred and fifty years ago, Detectives, so no use looking her up on your PULSE system.' He let out a loud chuckle. 'One day, the body of a local shoemaker was found here and poor old Dorcas was accused of witchcraft and of killing him. So, they hung her up by the neck, as was the custom of the time, until she was only partially dead. Up there on Baggot Street, it was. And then they burnt her alive. Round the corner here, on Copper Alley, the prostitutes caused a riot. Said it was a travesty of justice and that Dorcas was as innocent as pure driven snow. But, then again, I've never known a hooker who didn't have something to complain about.'

He paused and drained his glass.

'Here's the thing though,' he continued. 'It was only after her execution that the investigators found five more bodies buried in the basement.'

Frank banged his shoe off the wooden floorboards.

'Right under our feet, here,' he said. 'Turns out that old Dorcas was not so wide-eyed and pure as the hookers wanted to believe. She might well have been Ireland's first ever serial killer. Apparently, bartenders through the years have claimed to see the ghosts of those very men when they go down to the cellars to change the kegs of beer.'

Darcy kept her focus on Frank as he kept eye contact with her too.

'You see,' Frank said, holding her gaze. 'No matter how hard you try to bury them, sometimes you just can't escape the ghosts from your past.'

# Chapter 31

'Why do I always feel like I've gone ten rounds in a ring after I've finished talking to that man?' Mick said as they walked back down Fishamble Street towards Darcy's car.

'If *you* feel drained,' Darcy told him, 'imagine how I feel.'

'You're right. I can't imagine. How *do* you feel?'

She didn't answer.

They reached the car, stopped and looked at each other for a few moments, neither of them wanting to be the one to break eye contact.

'You know, you were wrong about what you said to the priest,' Mick said eventually. 'Sometimes, the apple *does* fall far from the tree.'

She looked away.

He glanced at his watch and then up and down the street.

'What is it?' Darcy asked him. 'You got ants in your pants all of a sudden.'

'Can you take the car?' Mick asked. 'I've got to go.'

'Sure. Got a date?'

'Yeah, something like that.'

Darcy didn't say anything.

Mick looked at her.

'OK,' he said. 'It's Irena.'

'Well, this is news!' Darcy said and clapped her hands in delight. 'Why didn't you tell me?'

'Because I knew that's exactly how you'd react.'

'I'm happy for you, that's all.'

'Well, I don't want you to be happy for me, OK?'

'OK, OK,' she said, and put her hands up in surrender. 'No need to be so sensitive about it.'

'I'm not sensitive. I'm just ... I don't know. It's been a while, that's all. OK?'

'That's fine, Mick. It's understandable.'

They stood in awkward silence under the glow of streetlamps, Christ Church Cathedral looming behind them.

'So do you want any tips?' Darcy asked him.

'No, I don't want any fucking tips. I'm late already. I'll call you tomorrow.'

'Do you have enough condoms?'

'Go fuck yourself, Doyle,' Mick told her and walked down Essex Street.

He could feel Darcy still standing there and watching him. For the first time in a long time, he had the urge to run, but he kept his pace steady on the cobblestones and checked his watch again.

When Mick entered Toscana's Italian restaurant on Dame Street, he saw Irena sitting at a table by the window. He watched her for a moment as she studied the menu, holding her reading glasses in her right hand, and moving them in and out like a magnifying glass. She bit down on her lower lip as she focused, and Mick saw an innocence in her he hadn't noticed before, an innocence that drew him to her and that he wanted to protect.

Her face was lit by the glow of a flickering candle, and he noticed that her hair looked different and that she was wearing makeup. He thought her dress had a sheen to it that only a new dress could have. He combed his scraggly beard with his fingers and then pressed down on the front of his jacket, but the action only made him feel even more abashed and unkempt.

'You know what they say about people sitting at the windows in restaurants?' Mick said as he slid into the seat opposite her.

She gave him a smile that was the most genuine thing he'd seen all week, and it made him smile too.

'No. What do *they* say?'

'They say that the waiters always put the pretty ones at the window to make the restaurant look good.'

'Maybe that is true in Ireland. But in Croatia they put the fat ones in the window to make it look like the food is good!'

Mick laughed. 'Then let's say that you are proof of the Irish rule, and I am proof of the Croatian one.'

'You're not fat,' she said.

'I must be the pretty one so.'

Irena gasped in mock horror, and then smiled.

Mick leaned towards her.

'I'm sorry I'm late,' he said, picking up the menu.

'That's OK, Mick. I know you have busy detective work. I'm jealous that you have such a skill to use.'

Mick opened the menu and glanced at it up and down. 'I wouldn't call it a skill,' he said without looking at her.

'What would you call it then?'

He looked up at her and thought about it for a moment before answering.

'It's more common sense than anything. Anyone could do it, if they put a bit of effort into it.'

'So, give me an example.'

Mick looked around the restaurant.

'No,' Irena said. 'Use me as your example. As if I was a stranger and you were meeting me for the first time.'

'I'm not so sure –'

'It's your penalty for being late and keeping a lady waiting.'

The waiter appeared at their table. 'Are you folks ready to order?'

Mick kept his gaze on Irena for a moment and then looked up at the waiter. 'Would you mind giving us another minute or two?'

'No problem, guys,' he said. 'Take your time.'

Mick nodded and the waiter left. He put the menu down on the table and continued to look at Irena. She smiled self-consciously and lowered her head.

'Are you trying to use your skills as a detective on me or your skills as a hypnotist?' she asked.

'OK,' he said. 'Sorry. Here's what I can see.'

She sat up straight in her chair as if she were waiting to hear test results.

'You're an honest and genuine person, and you're patient,' he told her. 'And you're also kind.'

'So, I'm not a secret dark criminal?'

'No,' he told her. 'Although you are a little vain.'

Her eyes widened. 'Really? And how do you deduce all of that, Mr. Holmes?'

'It's no Sherlock Holmes stuff. You're honest because you didn't try to hide your relief when I arrived. You obviously thought that I might not show up.'

'The thought had crossed my mind.'

'You're patient,' he continued, 'as you've been here for at least fifteen minutes and yet you didn't call me, even though your phone is on the table.'

'And how do you know I've been here that long?'

Mick nodded at her drink. 'The ice in your Coke has melted and a third of it is gone already.'

'Maybe there wasn't any ice in it when I got it, and I just took a big gulp from the glass.'

'You're not the gulping type, Irena, and there are two tables beside us with ice cubes in their soft drinks. So why would yours not have them too?'

She looked at her glass of Coke and then back at him. 'And kind?'

'You ordered a Coke and not a glass of wine, even though you do drink alcohol, and a glass of wine would be the obvious thing for you to order with your meal in a restaurant.'

'I didn't want to make you feel uncomfortable.'

'I know. And I appreciate it, but you can have a glass of wine if you like.'

'I'm fine,' she told him. 'And what about my vanity?'

'You told me you bought new reading glasses last week because you think your old ones make you look like a granny. But you couldn't find your new reading glasses when you left home, so you took your old spare pair with you.'

She looked down at her old reading glasses folded next to her phone.

'I could have just forgotten the new ones.'

'Why would you forget your new ones and remember your old ones?'

'Fair enough,' she said.

'You need them to read the menu, but you won't put them on your face because you don't like how they make you look.'

Irena laughed, and Mick enjoyed the feeling of making her laugh.

'You're right,' she told him. 'You really are a genuine Sherlock Holmes.'

'I've read one or two of the books,' he told her. 'I'm not a big fan of fiction, to be honest. I see enough crazy stuff in my job and in the papers to keep me entertained.'

'I love my books. Maybe because I lead a quieter life than you, although I have heard the expression "truth is stranger than fiction".'

'Unfortunately, that's very true,' Mick said, and he picked up the water jug and poured them both a glass.

'Thank you,' she said.

Mick drank some water. 'Last week,' he said, putting the glass down, 'I read about a man who received a heart transplant from a suicide victim. He survived the operation and was so thankful that he wrote to the widow of the guy who had taken his own life. They met up, fell in love and got married. A few years later the guy with the new heart committed suicide as well. He put a shotgun in his mouth and pulled the trigger, the exact same way and in the exact same place as her first husband had. Now you tell me, who could come up with a story like that? And if they did, we'd say it was unbelievable.'

The waiter appeared again and this time they ordered. With the whole choice of the menu in front of him, Mick suddenly felt ravenous, and he ordered the steak. Irena ordered pasta and they both had two more Cokes. With ice.

'My books give me something your newspapers and even your career often fails to give you,' Irena told him.

'Which is?'

'Justice.'

Mick nodded slowly. 'You're right about that. Often, I'm left wondering what the point of it all is. We investigate. We arrest. And then we see the same guy a few weeks later doing it all over again. We have a revolving-door justice system that is unfair to the victims and unfair to the guards who put themselves in harm's way. To be honest, I don't remember morale ever being this low among the rank and file.'

The waiter placed two glasses of Coke in front of them without saying a word.

'You don't ever think of retirement?' she asked when the waiter was gone.

'Sometimes,' he said. 'But it's a bit of an out-of-the-pot-into-the-fire situation.'

'I don't know that expression but I can guess what it means.'

'Yes, it means you might land in an even worse situation if you try to escape from a bad one. I'm not sure I could handle it, you know. I'm afraid ... well, I'm afraid I'd have a bit too much time on my hands to do other stuff. Maybe I could start my own private detective agency. I wouldn't mind being my own boss for a change. And it'd be something to keep me busy.'

'So, you are more like Sherlock Holmes than you think?' she said.

'Why's that?'

'Because whenever he didn't have a case for his brain to mull over, he would turn to opium for his amusement.'

'Sherlock Holmes was a cokehead? I don't remember ever reading that.'

'It's true. You just have to read between the lines, as you call it.'

'Somehow, I don't think I'll be going down that road,' Mick said and took a sip from his glass. 'Anyway, you learn something new every day.'

'Next you'll be telling me that you weren't aware that Holmes and Watson were having a sexual relationship.'

Mick held his glass mid-air, his mouth partially open.

Irena burst into laughter. 'I'm kidding, but you should see your face! It seems there are things that can still shock Detective Inspector Mick Kelly after all.'

The restaurant was almost empty by the time Mick and Irena left. The cold air hit their faces, and they pulled their coats tighter around themselves. Irena slid her scarf higher up onto her face, linked her hand around Mick's arm and leaned into him as if it were the most natural thing in the world. He looked down at the top of her head, but she was tucked into him, so she didn't see the surprise and then the smile on his face.

They walked down Dame Street, around Trinity College, which had stood there for over four hundred years, and then crossed the River Liffey. The city was in full swing with most people enjoying Christmas drinks, having already finished work for the year. The festive lights reflected off the wet streets, lighting their path in a multi-coloured display as they made their way down the quays. It became quieter the further out of the city they walked, the landscape changing from business to residential buildings.

A block from his apartment, Mick spotted a fish and chip shop on the corner of Mayor Street.

'OK if I get some cigarettes?' he asked her.

Irena shrugged and they crossed the road. Even though Mick had only finished his meal in the restaurant, the smell of the fried food enveloped him and, if he were alone, he would have ordered chips. He decided to stick with the cigarettes, but Irena saw his face light up with the greasy smell.

'You can't still be hungry?' she teased him.

He shook his head. 'Twenty Player Blue, please!' he called out.

The chipper had a long counter running the length of the shop and had only a handful of people inside waiting for their orders. So, when the insult was shouted across the floor at him by a group of young men, it caught Mick by surprise.

'*Lads*,' the voice called out, '*does anyone else get the sudden smell of pork in here?*'

The rest of the group laughed. Mick looked over at them. It wasn't the first time someone had called him a 'pig'. It wasn't even the first time that day. Taking verbal abuse as a Garda was unfortunately part and parcel of the job. Mick knew that the same idiots who insulted him one day were quick enough to ask for his help the next. He felt Irena's body stiffen beside him as she turned to face them.

One of the young female employees handed him a packet of cigarettes, and Mick gave her a twenty-euro note.

'*Oink, oink, oink!*' the same guy said, and the rest of his crew laughed louder.

Mick looked over at them and made eye contact with their ringleader. He was tall for his age, which Mick guessed at about twenty-two, but Mick had seen his type a thousand times, a bully who'd been getting away with it his whole life because of his size. One day he would pick on the wrong guy and, if he was lucky, he'd live to tell the tale. Mick didn't feel like doing him a favour and being that wrong guy today and embarrassing him in front of his mates. Not with Irena beside him anyway. He could catch up with him another time.

'Please, let's go, Mick,' Irena said.

They began to walk away.

'*Please let's go, Mick*,' the guy said, imitating Irena. 'Don't worry, love. I'll sort you out with a ride if Mick isn't up to the challenge,'

The other boys burst out laughing, and Mick stopped walking.

'*No, Mick*,' Irena said.

Mick relaxed the muscles in his face and took a deep breath and let it out.

Irena grabbed his arm and pulled him tighter to her.

'*Mick the prick!*' a different boy called out.

Irena pulled at Mick's arm as if she were trying to drag him outside. Mick allowed her to lead him out.

'*You'd better hurry up, Mick the prick!*' the first boy shouted. '*Since you're paying that hooker by the hour!*'

Mick stopped again. He looked down at Irena.

'*Don't*,' she said.

'*Ohhhhh!*' the boys mocked, as the ringleader took a step forward from the group.

'Something you want to say, old man?' the guy said, puffing up his chest at Mick. 'Want to fucking start, do you? You fucking prick! We'll beat the shit out of you.'

It was all bravado and Mick knew it, a bullfrog trying to intimidate his opponent. Mick had met plenty of proper hard bastards, and they were rarely big mouths who needed to whip themselves up into a frenzy. They were violent men, but men of action, not talk.

Mick took Irena's hand and walked for the door. The guy was stupid enough to interpret this as cowardice and began to walk after him.

Mick was genuinely surprised when a hand grabbed his shoulder from behind and spun him around, forcing Irena to be pushed away to the side. Instinctively, and without even a thought, Mick grabbed the guy's hand and twisted his fingers so far back that he cried out in pain. Mick's right hand had already formed into a fist and flew upwards and hit the guy under the chin so hard that a crunching sound echoed throughout the little shop and froze everyone to the spot.

Mick was surprised that the guy was still standing. He remained standing for a few seconds until one of his friends said, 'Liamo?'

It was only then that his eyes seemed to roll into the back of his head, and he dropped to the floor like a sack of frozen chips.

Mick prepared himself for a possible attack from one of the other goons, but they all stood in silence looking down at their leader. When he was sure that none of the others fancied stepping up, he turned around, but he stopped when he saw Irena's face. She looked from the man on the ground back to Mick's face, and then she turned around and left.

When Mick had caught up with her, he took her by the arm. He stood in front of her and saw the tears in her face.

'I'm sorry,' Mick said. 'I tried to walk away.'

'But you didn't, Mick.'

'What was I supposed to do? Just ignore what he said?'

'Yes,' she said. 'That's exactly what you were supposed to do.'

She removed her arm from his grip. Mick watched her go, but she stopped and came back to him.

'My first husband was a proud man. A tough man. A man of principle, as you call it,' she said and took a deep breath. 'He died in Croatia for those principles when he could have ... when he *should* have walked away.'

'Let me walk you to your room, Irena,' he said. 'I'll make you some tea.'

She gave him a half-smile and shook her head.

'I'm sorry, but no,' she said and rested her hand on his chest. Then she turned and walked away.

Mick watched her leave, her footsteps echoing off the buildings.

# Chapter 32

Darcy was just about to get out of her car and go into the gym when her phone buzzed. She looked at the screen and knew it could only be bad news.

'It's Garda Eoin,' the voice said.

He sounded too enthusiastic for this hour of the night.

'We just got a call from Tallaght Hospital. They said there's a woman asking for you.'

'What woman?' Darcy asked, but she already guessed.

'A woman who claims to be ...'

'For fuck's sake, Eoin. Who is it?'

'She says she's your mother.'

Darcy's head flopped back onto the headrest, and she let out a deep sigh that seemed to go on forever. Her mind began to wander until she heard the tinny sound of Eoin's voice.

'You still there?'

'Yeah, I'm still here. Call them back and tell them I'm on my way.'

'Really?' Eoin said, not hiding the surprise in his tone.

'Yes, really. What's so strange about that?'

'I just never thought you had a mother.'

'What the hell's that supposed to mean?'

'Nothing, sorry. I don't know. Sorry. You just don't strike me as someone who needs a mother. You don't strike me as someone who needs anything.'

Darcy looked at the phone in her hand and pressed the button to end the call.

'Cheeky little prick,' she said, and started the car.

Darcy's shoes squeaked along the dimly lit corridor of St Cillian's Ward on the third floor of Tallaght Hospital. The Nurses' Station had told her in which room she could find her mother. She opened the door of Room 326 without knocking.

On her drive over, she had been expecting to find her mother either being hand-fed grapes by a Brazilian male nurse or blowing smoke from a cigarette out of a crack in her room's window. Instead, the room was dark, its only light source coming from the orange glow of the streetlamps and the screens of the medical equipment that surrounded her.

Her mother lay in a single bed, her chest rising and falling to the rhythmic clinical beeps of the machines which were attached to her by clear tubes and coloured leads.

Darcy walked quietly into the room and then stood looking down at her. She was under the covers with only her bandaged wrist resting over the thin blue sheets.

How could this frail old woman have ever been the vibrant young woman whom she had looked up to so much? A woman she had remembered as being the life of every party. A woman whom she had cried for during hundreds of sleepless nights alone in a strange bed with yet another foster family.

One of her mother's eyes popped open and gave Darcy such a fright that she took two steps back. The bulbous single eye scanned around the room and then the second eye opened.

'Thank God it's you,' her mother said, straightening herself up in the bed. 'I thought it was that tea lady again. Never shuts up, that one. Spent half an hour in here last night going on about her poxy grandkids. As if I give a shit that one of them is making its Holy Communion.' She looked at Darcy. 'What's wrong with you? You look like you've seen a ghost.'

'I thought you were ...'

'Dying?' her mother interrupted her. 'We're all dying, darling. The only difference is the amount of time each of us has left.'

'Why are you here?' Darcy demanded. 'You don't look that sick to me.'

'You're a doctor now, are you?' she said and then raised her bandaged arm. 'Fell over, didn't I? Got up out of my chair to use the bathroom, and I fell.'

'Just fell?'

'Well, not exactly. TIA they told me.'

'A mini-stroke?'

'Oh, so you *are* a doctor then.'

Darcy let out a long and tired sigh. 'A mini-stroke is serious. What else did they tell you?'

'Too much. I came in here with a broken wrist and now they tell me I'm diabetic and have high blood pressure. Want me to quit the cigs as well. Fat chance of that. I was perfectly fine till I came in here.'

Darcy took a second to process that information, and then asked, 'What do you want from me?'

'Open that wardrobe, will you?'

There was a small wardrobe standing in the corner. Darcy opened it.

'Grab those clothes hanging up,' her mother instructed her. 'Give them here. I won't be a minute.'

'A minute for what?'

'I need to get dressed.'

'You're leaving?'

'Of course I'm leaving. That's why I called you. I need a lift home.'

'A lift? You called me for a lift?'

'Well, it was either you or Frank. And sometimes Frank's guys can be a little rough around the edges, if you know what I mean.'

Darcy threw the clothes onto the bed. 'What exactly do you want from me?'

'A lift, I told you.'

'You don't need me for a lift. You don't need me for anything. I can drop you off at home, no bother. Pop the kettle on and tuck you into bed if you want. But what do you really want from me?'

Her mother shifted in the bed. 'Have you ever spent a few days in a hospital?'

'No.'

'You get a lot of time to think, you know.'

'And what? You realised that maybe abandoning me when I was a little girl wasn't perhaps the greatest idea in the world?'

'I didn't abandon ...' but then she stopped herself. 'We've been over this already.'

'So what is it then?'

A silence between them grew that was amplified by the beeping of the machines and the darkness of the room.

'Fine. I'll ask the nurse to order you a taxi,' Darcy said as she walked back around the bed.

'No wait, Darcy!' her mother called out.

An innate childhood memory of her mother's voice calling her stopped Darcy from walking out, but she didn't turn around.

After she had stood for a few moments there in the dark room, her mother asked, 'Was it true what you said? About being homeless?'

Darcy didn't reply or turn around.

'I'm sorry,' her mother said. 'I didn't know.'

Darcy shrugged. 'Doesn't matter now anyway.'

'I know you were angry with Frank for having you followed and for all those photos, but it was me who asked him to do it. I know I shouldn't take credit for how you turned out, but I couldn't help feeling proud of you anyway.'

Darcy turned and faced her mother.

'You're right,' she told her. 'You shouldn't take credit for it. You shouldn't take credit for anything I've done.'

Her mother nodded in agreement, and Darcy felt angry at her mother's understanding.

'I don't,' her mother said. 'For what it's worth, I went to see a psychotherapist years ago. It was part of a suspended sentence that a judge gave me for possession. At first, I hated it but the lady was really nice and she was probably the first person I ever met that didn't judge me for who I was or what I looked like or where I came from.'

Darcy glanced at the door. Only three steps, and she'd be back in the corridor, but her mother continued to talk.

'I know it was hard for you, but at the time I felt that I was doing the right thing in not looking for you or asking for you to come back to me. I was a user, an addict, and you couldn't be with me, and that lady explained to me that the guilt of you not being with me was keeping me a user. I know it doesn't make up for the years, but I thought that if I could just at least explain.'

'*It doesn't explain anything!*' Darcy said, turning to face her and raising her voice above the beeps. '*It would have been better to have a junkie for a mother than no mother at all!*'

'But you had all those other mothers. The foster mothers.'

'*But I wanted my real mother!*' Darcy shouted at her. '*I wanted you! I missed you! I asked them if I could go back, and they said no and that you had to come get me, but you never came, did you?*'

All thoughts of caring for her mother abated and a mountain of rage erupted inside her. Darcy could feel the pain and sorrow of that little girl, and she felt angry at herself and her mother for bringing those feelings back to the surface.

'I didn't ...' her mother said, but Darcy cut her off.

'No, you didn't. You didn't do anything. And that's something I have to live with. Something we both have to live with.'

Darcy kept her mother's eye contact for several moments but then couldn't look at her anymore.

'It's too late now anyway,' Darcy told her and turned around.

'Is it?' her mother asked as Darcy opened the door, the light from the corridor coming into the room.

She stopped in the doorway for a moment, but then stepped outside and closed the door behind her, returning her mother to the darkness of the room.

# Monday

# 23 December

# Chapter 33

Brian Meany wasn't a fan of early mornings. Each weekday he woke with the dread thoughts of having to face that god-awful school again, so when the first Monday morning of the Christmas holidays came around, he'd much rather have kept his head on the pillow and the alarm clock switched off. But he had to give in a little to her demands, and for twenty grand in cold hard cash, he was prepared to miss an hour or two of shut-eye.

She was a fool, though, if she thought he would meet her at some lonely harbour at night, or on a deserted forest trek in the mountains. Eight in the morning in a Costa Coffee, in the public eye, seemed as safe a place as any for their little meet-up, but at the same time quiet enough not to attract too much attention. Just another normal couple having an early-morning cappuccino.

He looked at the clock on his car's dash as he pulled in and then saw her already seated at an outdoor table. She was early. He slowed as he passed her and scanned the area for anybody whom he might see as a potential threat. He wasn't out of the woods yet and wouldn't feel safe until he was driving back out of the car park with an envelope stuffed with euro bills in his jacket pocket.

She was wearing a hoodie top, the hood pulled up over her head. Her face was hidden as she sipped on her takeaway coffee. The car park had only one other car in it, and there was no one inside. He got out, walked over to the other car and peered inside, just to be sure it was empty.

If at any point he felt he was being over-cautious or even paranoid, he reminded himself that he had seen this very woman he was about to meet shoot someone in the chest at close range. And then push her off a pier into the sea.

He went inside the coffee shop, while keeping her in his peripheral vision. She didn't look up, just kept her head down, sipping on her coffee. The man ahead of him, wearing a high-viz jacket, stepped aside and Brian ordered a cappuccino from the barista. He was feeling peckish, perhaps from nerves, so he ordered himself a cheese toastie. He glanced up at the CCTV cameras and counted three of them.

'Do they work?' he asked the barista as she placed his coffee on the counter.

'Excuse me, mate,' the man in the high-viz said, leaning across Brian to snatch a handful of napkins, blocking him from the barista.

'Do what work?' the barista asked vaguely when the man had moved out of the way.

'The bloody cameras. Do they work?' Brian repeated.

She nodded, her eyes glancing from side to side as if she were about to get robbed, and then pointed at the office door behind them. It was partially open, and he could see two monitors with live video footage of the café both indoors and outside.

'I'll bring your toastie over to you when it's ready,' she told him.

'I'll be outside,' he said and took his cup and saucer from the counter.

As he approached the table, where she sat with her back to him, he scanned the area again before he sat down opposite her, trying to spot something or someone out of place.

'Good morning,' he said.

Anita Cooney raised her eyes from her takeaway coffee and looked at him.

'What's the matter? You don't like heat?' he said. 'It's fucking freezing out here.'

He ripped the top off two white sugar sachets and poured them into his coffee. They looked at each other as he stirred with the wooden spoon. He put the spoon down and then picked up his cup. He blew on the foam and took a sip, all the time looking into her eyes.

'I assume you have the money on you, and we're not going to play some silly game about not having enough time.'

Anita said nothing.

'So, how about you give me the cash, and you can fuck off, and we can just go about our business.'

'Take it easy, Mr. Meany,' Anita said. 'I don't want us attracting any undue attention.'

Anita unzipped the top of her hoodie and put her hand inside.

Brian's eyes widened, and he sat up straight.

'Relax,' she told him. She pulled out a thick padded envelope and slid it across the table. Looking around only once, Brian picked it up and shoved it inside his jacket pocket.

'You know if it's not the right amount, even by one euro, then all bets are off. You do understand that, don't you?'

She nodded.

Brian looked back inside the café.

'Did you forget something in there?' Anita asked him.

'I didn't forget anything. That stupid bitch forgot my cheese toastie,' Brian said, stood up and went back inside.

It was waiting on the counter.

'*You said you'd bring it out to me!*' he called over to the girl.

'Oh sorry, sir,' she said.

'It's probably gone cold by now,' he muttered.

'I can heat it up for you, if you like,' she said, but Brian walked off with the plate.

When he placed it down hard on the outdoor table, he thought that he'd actually broken the plate. He sat, lifted the toastie and took a large bite out of it.

'I'm starving,' he told Anita, his mouth full of the lukewarm sandwich. 'You want some?'

She shook her head.

'I can't wait to get out of this fucking country,' Brian said, and took a large mouthful of his coffee to wash the food down. He laughed.

'What's so funny?' Anita asked him.

'Nothing really. I just don't understand how that Montessori teacher met you all alone in the middle of the night with no one around. How she could be so stupid? Was she that stupid?'

Anita stared at him, not returning his laugh.

'You know who my father is, don't you?' she asked him. 'I mean, you know who my whole family is?'

'Of course I do,' he said. 'How else do you think I recognised you on the pier? And why the fuck do you think you passed all your exams in school? Let's just say your talents didn't involve any academic strengths.'

Anita smiled at him. A cold hard smile. 'You know, there are many different types of smart. And while you may be what they call *book smart*, when it comes to real life and the street, I'm the smartest person in the room.'

Brian shrugged, ate the rest of his toastie and drank the last of his coffee in silence. He tapped his jacket where the money was.

'Well, I think our business is concluded here, Miss Cooney. I wish I could say it's been nice chatting to you, but you're still the same braindead cunt you've always been, and I hope I never see your ugly face again.'

Anita failed to hide the shock on her face.

Brian stood up, and she looked up at him.

'Wait a second,' she said. 'Sit down, and I'll give you some advice.'

Brian looked over at his car as if it were the finishing line in a race. He touched the money again in his jacket.

'OK,' he said. 'I suppose twenty grand gets to buy you a few more minutes.'

When he was sitting down, Anita leaned across the table at him. 'I probably shouldn't tell you this, as it'll ruin the surprise, but since you're being such a prick about it, then I feel I've no choice.'

'What the fuck are you talking about?'

'You're right that I'll never get a great job by passing exams, and you're right that I'm not the smartest when it comes to studying and shit like that, but I'm smart in other ways. I know, for example, that there are lots of ways of killing someone other than shooting them or sticking a knife in their belly.'

Brian said nothing, but he was listening.

'My grandad did fifteen years for murder. Most of my family, in fact, were locked up for one reason or another when they were even younger than that little schoolgirl you're riding. Crime has always been in our family. You could say it's in our blood.'

Brian looked around the car park and out onto the road. A woman went by pushing a pram. On the far side of the road there was a man walking his dog.

'You wouldn't try anything here,' Brian told her. 'It's too public and you're on CCTV cameras. I've checked.'

'What cameras? I don't see any out here.'

'There are three in the shop and one behind you. If something happens to me, you'll be picked up in a few hours. You want to spend the next fifteen years in jail like your grandad?'

'Jail for me doesn't hold the same threat as jail for you. I probably already know half the people in there.' Anita laughed. 'But don't worry, I'm not going to jail. None of the cameras have seen me. I have my back to that one behind me, and I've had my hoodie up all the time. That wouldn't stand up in court.'

'OK,' he said. 'But when you went inside, the cameras saw you there.'

'Who said I went inside?'

'When you bought your coffee.'

Anita shrugged. 'I didn't buy any coffee.'

Brian reached over and lifted her takeaway coffee cup. It was empty and cold.

'Maybe I picked that out of a bin just to give you the impression that I'd been inside in order to relax you a little. Maybe the gloves I'm wearing aren't just because of the cold weather either.'

Brian felt a lump in his throat.

'You know who Elaine Baker is?' she asked him.

Brian shook his head.

'Of course you don't. She's the receptionist for your doctor. She's a struggling single mother with three kids who you walk by every three months when you go see the good doctor for your check-up. And for a small fee of five hundred euro, Elaine was kind enough to share your medical history with us.'

Brian put his hand up to his chest. Anita didn't fail to notice.

'Everyone at school knew you had a dicky ticker. We used to call you Breathless Brian. But now I read the exact information about your heart's aneurysm, and other Latin names that I skipped over. So, what could I do with that? It wasn't something I could just Google as there'd be a record of it, so I went onto the dark web and found that a certain drug taken for chemotherapy, I've forgotten the name to be honest with you, but mixed with a little cocaine can cause so much pressure in your aorta that it'll just pop like a burst water pipe.'

Anita made a popping sound with her mouth.

Brian could feel his heart quickening.

'Your coffee,' she said as if answering a question. 'That tingling feeling you're getting now all over your body isn't the caffeine. It's the coke.'

'What? But, how did you ...'

'I didn't. The man at the counter poured it in. My cousin, Rob. Sleight of hand. He's gifted like that. He'd have let me know if he hadn't pulled it off.'

Anita stood up.

'I imagine when they find your body it won't even be treated as suspicious,' she said. 'Your medical records will confirm a dodgy ticker and the autopsy will suggest you were fond of the white stuff. I've also had one of the school kids plant a small bag of cocaine in your office. To be honest, I probably went to too much trouble with the hoodie and the gloves and the fake coffee, but you were right about one thing — you can never be too careful.'

Brian stood up clutching his chest. He was barely even listening to her now. He needed to get to a hospital.

'The only question they'll even ask at your funeral is why were you carrying an envelope packed with a neatly cut stack of old newspapers. That'll be the real mystery.'

Brian lurched towards his car, staggering across the car park. He fumbled for the keys in his pockets and unlocked the car. He got in, started it and screeched out onto the road. A car blared its horns at him.

Anita Cooney stood on the path and watched his car charging into the distance. She was about to walk away when she saw his brake lights come on and the car veer to the other side of the road, narrowly missing a bus, and then smashing into the wall of a school.

She stood and watched it for a few moments, but nobody got out of the car. Then she turned and walked away in the opposite direction and did something she couldn't remember doing for years. She whistled.

# Chapter 34

When the lift doors pinged open for Darcy on the fifth floor of the NBCI in Harcourt Street, she could already see Mick at his desk. With only two days until Christmas, most of the detectives had found a reason to be anywhere but here. Not one coloured string of tinsel brightened the grey walls or covered the grime and dust on the windows.

'Morning, Casanova!' Darcy smiled at him, but as soon as she saw his face she knew things had not gone well for him and Irena. 'Jesus, that bad, was it?'

He didn't reply.

'Any idea what the Chief wants?' she asked him.

'The Chief wants what he always wants,' he told her. 'Results.'

In unison, they both turned to face the Chief's office. From behind his desk, Chief O'Riordan was staring out at them like a cat eyeing two cowering mice. He pointed a long thin forefinger at them and then curled it, beckoning them to him. Mick rose, his chair scraping the floor and echoing through the office.

'I'm sorry — I forget,' the Chief said when they were seated. 'Which one of you is Cagney and which is Lacey? I'm always getting you mixed up.'

'I'm Cagney,' Mick told him. 'That's the pretty lesbian one.'

Darcy looked at him. 'She wasn't a lesbian.'

'Was she not?'

'Just because she was an assertive attractive female, you assume she was a lesbian. That's a typical misogynistic view that I'd expect from Kane and Burns, not you.'

'Well, then, maybe she was a lesbian in real life. I read it somewhere.'

'There was never anything about her being a lesbian. She was a –'

'*Would you two shut the fuck up!*' the Chief yelled at them. '*I'm getting a headache just listening to the pair of you!*'

'Sorry, Chief,' Darcy said.

'Should we leave?' Mick asked, getting out of his chair.

'Don't fucking start with me, Kelly!'

Mick lowered himself back into the chair.

They all looked at each other for a few moments as O'Riordan allowed the energy in the room to settle before stating, 'You're both off the murdered boy and the missing boy's case.'

Darcy exploded out of the chair. '*No way, Chief!*' she shouted. '*That's not fair!*'

'Fair?' O'Riordan laughed. 'What has fair got to do with it?'

'But we're making progress,' she said.

'Are you? Where is it? You're no closer than you were last week. Tomorrow's Christmas Eve, for Christ's sake!'

Mick, who was still leaning back in his chair said, 'What's the real reason, Glenn? Where's this coming from?'

O'Riordan let out a deep sigh. He raised his hand and motioned for Darcy to sit back down, which she obeyed.

'The media's all over this one, and we haven't given them anything concrete yet. The Super spends more time reading what the press have to say about a case than what his detectives' opinions are. He's on to me every few hours wanting an update.'

'So this is his decision?' Mick asked.

O'Riordan nodded. 'You've to hand over all your intel to Kane and Burns –'

'*Ah, for fuck's sake!*' Darcy erupted.

'Watch your tongue,' O'Riordan told her.

'Sorry, sir.'

'This is more about politics than your ability,' O'Riordan told them. 'Sometimes, you just have to suck it up.'

'Can you buy us some time?' Mick asked.

O'Riordan shrugged. 'Normally, no. But given the time of year, I could stall him until the day after Christmas Day.'

Darcy's phone rang in her pocket. It continued to ring, filling the room with its chime.

'Well, answer it then,' O'Riordan told her.

'Sorry, sir,' she said.

Mick looked at her as she listened.

'OK, Eoin. We're on our way now.' She ended the call and put it back in her pocket.

'Well?' Mick asked.

'It's the teacher. Meany. He's dead.'

The traffic was busy as Darcy made her way to Whitehall and to the morgue. Beside her, Mick was on the phone to Chief O'Riordan.

'I know what day it is, Glenn,' he was saying. 'But I wouldn't be requesting a warrant unless I felt it was urgent.'

Darcy could hear the Chief's voice on the other end of the line.

'Well, then, get a judge at home,' Mick said. 'You must have a home phone number for at least one of them. Christmas doesn't mean all the rank and file get to take two weeks off, so why should the courts and judges get to shut down?'

Darcy glanced over at him as she pulled into a space near the front door of the morgue. It looked like most of the staff had finished up earlier here too.

'OK, just do your best and get back to me,' Mick said and hung up the phone.

'Well?' Darcy asked.

Mick shrugged. 'I say whether we get a warrant or not, we find a reason to get into the cleaner Ciara Ward's house as soon as we're finished here.'

'OK, good,' Darcy said and got out of the car.

When they were both dressed in their white overalls and face masks, they joined Dr. Catherine Daly who was hovering over the naked body of Brian Meany.

Darcy glanced up and down the teacher's body. He was in good shape, even if he'd received several cuts from a smashed-up car only a few hours before.

'He really died from a car crash?' Darcy asked.

'He died in a car crash,' Dr. Daly told her. 'But did he die *of* a car crash?'

'What do you mean?' Mick asked.

Dr. Daly bit her lip and leaned in closer to the body.

'Before I open him up, I'm already suspicious of the exact circumstances of the man's death.'

'Go on,' Darcy said.

'Obviously, I'll need to get in there and have a good root around and then wait for some toxicology results but look at his face.'

They all leaned closer towards him.

'Did you know the man before the accident?' she asked.

'Yes, we'd both met him,' Darcy said.

'And do you notice anything different in his face now?'

'Well, now that you mention it, I do,' Mick said. 'I'd say compared to when we met him last Friday, he's more dead now.'

Dr. Daly and Darcy both raised their heads to look at him.

'Look along the left-hand side of his face,' Dr. Daly continued and, without touching him with it, she ran a scalpel along the contour of his jaw.

Brian Meany's jaw had a slackness about it as if it were trying to fall away from the rest of his face.

'Heart attack?' Mick suggested.

'Yes. Sudden cardiac arrest, I'd guess,' Dr. Daly said.

'So, he had a heart attack and then crashed his car?' Darcy asked. 'Is that what you're saying?'

Dr. Daly nodded. 'The signs are there, but like I said I'd need to examine his heart to be one-hundred-percent sure.'

Mick straightened up.

'Too coincidental?' Darcy asked him.

'I think we need to retrace Mr. Meany's steps this morning,' Mick told her. 'Check if there's any CCTV footage in the area. What the hell was he doing on the road at that hour of the morning anyway?'

'Thank you, Catherine,' Darcy said. 'We appreciate the early heads-up.'

'Hope I didn't ruin your Christmas,' she said.

'No, Doc,' Mick said. 'Christmas was ruined for us a long time before today.'

# Chapter 35

On a cold December day, the city morgue in Whitehall was the only place you could walk out of and feel warmer.

At first Darcy and Mick didn't recognise the girl standing by the side of their car. Even with her coat pulled tight around her, she was still visibly shivering and rocking from one foot to the other.

'Sophie?' Darcy said when she approached.

When the girl turned to face them, they could see the redness of her face and the tears she had wiped away that were quickly replaced by yet more tears. Darcy felt the instinct to hold out her arms and hug her but held back.

'You shouldn't be here,' Mick told her.

Sophie straightened herself up in front of the two detectives. Her eyes narrowed and her expression switched from one of grief to anger. She raised her arm and showed them a white envelope she had clutched in her closed hand.

'*That bitch!*' she cried. '*That fucking bitch! It was her!*'

'Who?' Darcy asked, taking a step closer.

'The one we saw on the pier. The one we saw shooting the other woman. It's all here in Brian's own handwriting. She's the one who killed him.'

'You know who that was?' Mick asked.

'*Here!*' Sophie said, thrusting the envelope into his face. '*Here she is!*'

Darcy took the envelope from her hand. She looked up at Mick before opening it. Inside was a single page and a USB memory stick. She read the letter quickly and then handed it to Mick to read.

'Anita Cooney,' he said.

'Anita Cooney,' she responded. 'He was trying to blackmail her.'

Darcy turned Sophie who was staring off into the distance.

'Sophie ...'

'He told me that if anything happened to him, I was to give that to the police. It's Brian and the woman talking about the murder. We were going to run away together. We were going to run away to Australia. Make a new start, he said. Just him and me.'

Darcy could feel only pity for the girl. Pity for her age and her innocence. She had no doubt that Brian Meany had plans to move to Australia as soon as he had the money in his hands, but doubted he had any real intention of taking Sophie with him.

Out of the corner of her eye Darcy saw Mick move to the side and take out his phone.

She took a step forward and put her arms around the girl. Sophie responded to her and hugged her tightly and cried harder. How many times, Darcy thought, had she herself wanted someone to put their arms out to her when she was Sophie's age and younger? Darcy had learned quickly not to expect anyone to do that and that even wanting it was a show of weakness. But that didn't mean that others needed to suffer as she had done. That didn't mean that the world had to be a cruel cold place for everyone.

Mick tapped her on the shoulder, and she let Sophie go.

'Sophie, we should have enough with this letter and Anita Cooney's voice on the USB stick to put her away for years.'

Sophie nodded.

'Do you have somewhere to go?' Darcy asked her.

'I'm going home,' she said.

'A Garda car's going to be here in a couple of minutes,' Mick told her. 'They'll take you home, OK?'

Sophie just nodded, grief taking over her world again.

Mick put his hand on Darcy. 'Let's go pay a visit to Anita Cooney. This time, let's invite the ERU to come along.'

Two Audi Q7 SUVs with their windows blacked out were already waiting for Darcy and Mick about half a mile from Barry's Beds. Jamie got out of the passenger seat of the lead vehicle as Darcy parked her car in front of them.

She lowered her window as he walked slowly to them, his black military uniform ironed and crisp, a semi-automatic pointed at the ground.

'Are we really here to help you arrest just one woman from a bed shop?'

'No,' Darcy told him. 'You're really here because we think you should be, and because you were told to be here.'

Jamie had his mouth open to reply but Mick cut him off. 'That woman happens to be Anita Cooney, the daughter of the crime boss Charlie Cooney, and who also happens to be the main suspect in two recent murders.'

Jamie was still trying to stare Darcy down, but then he looked back at his men as if someone had called him.

'Anyway, the lads are always happy to get out and stretch their legs,' he said, forcing himself to smile. 'Wait outside until we have the premises secured.'

They both watched him walk back to the SUV.

'I never noticed before,' Mick said quietly, 'how much he walks like John Wayne.'

Darcy couldn't help but smile, but she lowered her head in case Jamie turned around and saw her. She didn't need him rattling his cage at her again. The sooner he found himself a new girlfriend and moved on the better.

Darcy's phone pinged. She read the message and then showed it to Mick. It was from Garda Eoin.

**Been on the phone all morning to University Hospital Galway. Better late than never! Ciara Ward admitted on numerous occasions for various illnesses. Too many to text. She gave birth to a baby boy over four years ago, but no records since that date. Do you want me to check Dublin hospitals?**

The car rocked from side to side as the two jeeps tore past her like two shots fired from a gun, and roared up the road in the direction of Barry's Beds.

'I'll call O'Riordan. They have to give us that warrant now,' Mick said, and Darcy pulled out onto the road and followed them.

By the time they got to Barry's Beds a couple of minutes later, the two black SUVs were outside, their doors left open. A small crowd of onlookers had their faces pressed up to the glass of the shop, one girl had her phone out and was recording Jamie's team at work inside.

Darcy and Mick strolled into the store, neither one of them even mentioning Jamie's request for them to wait outside. All the staff and customers were looking in the same direction, towards the back of the shop where Barry's own office was.

An ERU officer walked out of the office. Jamie followed close behind him with Anita in handcuffs in front, his assault rifle in one hand pointed downwards at a 45-degree angle, and his other hand gripping Anita's cuffs.

'*Fucking pigs!*' she spat at Darcy as she walked by.

'Did your mammy teach you to talk like that?' Mick said, and headed straight towards Barry Boyle's office.

There was an ERU officer standing outside Barry's office door, staring at it. Inside, shouting, screaming and the odd object being thrown and then smashing could be heard.

'A domestic argument?' Mick asked him.

'Yes, sir,' the officer replied.

They didn't bother knocking as they entered. Joan Boyle was standing at one end of the room with a glass dish held high above her head.

'*I've turned a blind eye to your blatant cheating before but this time, you horrible little shit, this time I want you gone! You hear me?*'

To make her point, she hurled the glass dish straight at her husband. It smashed against the wall just above his head, and judging by the glass debris around the room, her aim was getting better.

'Please, Joan,' Barry pleaded. 'Stop breaking my awards.'

Joan picked up another one. She looked at it and read the inscription aloud: '*Barry's Beds — Retailer of the Year 2014. Retailer of the year? Shit-bag of the year!*'

'*OK, that's enough!*' Mick called out. '*Put the vase down please, Mrs. Boyle!*'

'Don't call me Mrs. Boyle,' she said. 'I'm finished being Mrs. Boyle — the good wife waiting at home while her husband bangs anything that'll come near him!'

Darcy stuck her head back into the hall. 'In here, please,' she told the ERU officer. 'Please escort Mrs ... this lady to her car.'

The officer walked towards her and the fight seemed to go out of Joan Boyle. She looked down at the vase in her hand as if she'd forgotten why she was holding it.

'This way please, ma'am,' the officer told her.

She stopped looking at the vase and allowed it to fall as if she had no further use for it. It smashed against the floor. She was escorted out of the room.

Darcy looked at Barry Boyle. He was slumped into his chair. She walked slowly towards him, glass crunching under her feet, and stood above him, looking down at a man who looked like he had lost everything of value in his life.

Mick joined her.

'Looks like you'll be sleeping in the doghouse tonight, Barry.' Mick smiled at him.

Boyle's head slumped further down.

When Darcy had first attended the interview of a suspect, she had found the behaviour of the detectives towards him to be very cruel. Now, she knew that was simply a part of the interview technique. There was a logic to their cruelty, unlike the interviewees who had shown cruelty to their victims for sometimes no reason at all.

When suspects were at their low point, you put further pressure on them. That is how you get the answers out of them. If you show them any kindness, they see that as a weakness, and you'll lose.

'I trusted her,' Boyle said.

'Who?' Mick asked. 'Cooney or your wife?'

Boyle lifted his head up. 'My wife?' He laughed. 'I haven't trusted her since the day I married her.'

'Did you order Anita Cooney to murder Rachel Robinson?' Darcy asked him.

'Order Anita Cooney?' Boyle scoffed. 'Have you met her? No one has ever ordered her to do anything in her life that she didn't want to do. Anita does whatever Anita wants.'

'Did you casually mention it to her?' Mick said. 'Did you say something like "Wouldn't it be great if Rachel Robinson suddenly disappeared?"'

'No,' Boyle said. 'And you have no evidence otherwise. And it's the truth.'

'The truth?' Mick laughed. 'What would you and your lot know about the truth?'

'About the same as you and your lot,' Boyle told him.

Mick looked at Darcy, deciding what his next move would be.

'*Where's Alfie Scanlan?*' Mick shouted at Boyle.

'*I don't fucking know!* What have I to do with missing kids? I sell beds, for fuck's sake!'

'If I find out you're lying to us, Boyle ...'

'You won't. But come to think of it, you'd probably be doing me a favour by locking me up for a few days. I'd rather face Mountjoy than my wife right now.'

Mick looked at Darcy again. She shrugged.

'Don't leave the country,' Mick told him.

They left Boyle alone with his mess of a life to sort out, which was as broken now as his glass awards scattered on the floor.

Mick had felt his phone buzzing in his pocket while he was interviewing Boyle but, only now when they were sitting in the car, did he take it out and look at it.

'The Chief has come through for us on the warrant,' he said.

Darcy started the engine and drove in the direction of Ciara Ward's house.

# Chapter 36

Mick banged hard on the front door of Ciara's house twice before taking a step back, aiming the flat of his foot at the area just beside the lock, and kicking it. The door stayed closed. He repeated the action, and this time it flew open on its hinges.

Darcy walked ahead of him, stepping into the hall. It was dark. All the curtains were drawn shut and none of the lights were on. She reached behind her and switched on the hall light but it didn't come on.

'*Ciara!*' she called out.

She waited. Silence.

Mick stood beside her. 'Upstairs or downstairs?' he asked.

Darcy answered him by taking the first step of the stairs. It creaked loudly.

Mick reached inside his jacket and drew his sidearm. Darcy did the same, pressing her back against the wall as she slowly climbed the stairs.

The evening light from the front door illuminated the hall a little but upstairs it was darker. When she got to the top, she saw four doors. The door to her right was half opened and she could see a bathroom inside. She pushed it open. Empty.

She took another step forward and turned the handle of the first door. It creaked open and although she was sure it wouldn't work, she flicked down the light switch. Nothing.

'Ciara,' she whispered, but didn't know why she was whispering. She cleared her throat and tried again. '*Ciara!*'

The room had a double bed in it with clothes and bags on top. Black bin liners and storage boxes filled the rest of the room. Old and broken toys, a plastic fire station, robots and soldiers, were littered on the floor. She was tempted to open the curtains but didn't want to disturb anything.

Back on the landing, she yelled down '*There's a room full of boys' toys up here!*'

There was no reply from Mick.

'*Mick!*' she called out, but again he didn't reply.

She leaned over and looked down the stairs. No Mick. The front door was still open.

She turned and moved on to the next door. She took two steps towards it and pushed down on the handle. This room was neater. It had an unmade double bed in it but very few personal decorations or ornaments.

Darcy walked to the locker beside the bed. There was a cup on it, and she placed the back of her hand against it. It was cold. The tea inside didn't have any fungus on top, which Darcy knew would occur after three or four days.

So whoever had slept in this bed, had been here less than two days ago, possibly this morning. Or even yesterday when they'd knocked.

She went back onto the landing and to the final door but as soon as she touched the handle a hand was placed firmly on her shoulder.

Darcy leapt. She swung around, raising her gun.

'*Jesus!*' Mick said and shied away.

'*Mick, what the fuck? Why did you do that?*'

'Why did *you?* You frightened the life out of me.'

'*I* frightened *you*?' she said, trying to catch her breath.

'There's nothing downstairs.'

'Why didn't you answer me when I called you?' she asked him.

'I didn't hear you. I went out to the back garden to look in the shed. OK, open the door.'

Darcy took a deep breath and put her hand back on the door's handle. She pressed down on it, but the door didn't open.

She tried again, but it didn't budge.

'It's locked,' Mick told her.

'No shit, Sherlock.'

'Stand back,' he told her.

He kicked the door and it opened in one go.

Darcy went in first. The room had a mouldy smell. There was a small single bed pushed up against the wall that had a duvet cover with a montage of superheroes. Mick pulled back the curtains and saw that the window was completely blacked out with a black bin liner and grey masking tape along its edges. There was a small chest of drawers and Darcy opened the top one. It was filled with empty Calpol and Nurofen bottles.

She turned around and looked at the bed. She lowered her face to the pillow, studying its surface and then, reaching inside her jacket, she pulled out a pen. She used it to touch something on the pillow.

'What is it?' Mick asked.

Darcy moved the pen to the darker duvet cover and Mick bent down to look closer.

'*Fuck,*' he said as he stared at a single long blond hair.

'We need to get forensics in here now,' Darcy said.

'OK,' Mick said. 'Let's get out of here before we touch anything else.'

Outside, Darcy inhaled the fresh air as if she'd been stuck in a cave.

Mick hung up his phone having called the Chief with an update.

Soon, forensics, in the form of Dr. Phoebe Pepple, were *en route*.

'She's not in there,' a woman said. 'She's gone away.'

Darcy turned. The woman was wearing an overcoat but beneath the hem Darcy could see bright pink pyjamas and matching fluffy slippers.

The woman eyed Darcy up and down as well, her cigarette held close to her lips.

'Do you know when she left?' Darcy asked her.

'Yesterday,' the woman said and took a drag from her cigarette. She blew out the smoke. 'A taxi pulled up outside, and I saw them get into it.'

Mick and Darcy walked over to her.

'Them?' Mick asked.

'Yeah. Her and her little lad.'

'Her son?' Darcy asked.

'Yeah,' the woman said. 'Luke. God love him. With his mother. That poor woman.'

'Do you know where they were going?' Darcy asked.

'No. I try to stay out of other people's business. I like to keep myself to myself if you know what I mean.'

'Did Luke look any different?' Darcy asked.

'Different? Different how?'

'I don't know ... his hair, his posture or maybe his facial expression. Anything.'

'His facial expression?' the woman said, sucking hard on her cigarette. 'Who do you think I am? Miss Maple?'

Darcy sighed. 'It doesn't matter. Would you mind giving a formal statement to one of my colleagues later?'

'If you like,' she said. 'But like I said ...'

'Yeah, we know,' Mick interrupted her. 'You like to keep yourself to yourself.'

'That's right,' she said, and she dropped her cigarette onto the grass and stamped it out with her slipper.

They both watched her pink fluffy slippers hike through the tall grass of her front garden, then she went inside and closed the door without turning around.

'Why does everyone keep calling Ciara Ward that?' Mick asked, his focus still on the closed front door.

'Calling her what?' Darcy asked.

'*Poor*. That *poor* woman. That's another person who's called her that, with such sympathy. Why the fuck is she a poor woman? And "God love him". What's that about?'

Darcy shrugged but then felt something click in her thoughts, like a lock's combination aligning with all the right numbers. She walked out of the garden.

'Where are you going?' Mick called out.

'Can you wait here for Fifi? I want to check something.'

Mick shrugged. 'Speaking of crazy old bats,' he mumbled.

Darcy turned before getting in the car. '*I heard that!*' she called back to him.

# Chapter 37

Jimmy Gallagher was too long in the game to believe in coincidences. The two other boys involved in the case against that French slut were dead. After the hit and run, and an apparent random attack by a street beggar with a knife, he'd felt the need to step in.

Who really was this little bitch, he had asked his grandson Sam. As he was unable to answer the question to his grandfather's satisfaction, Jimmy had ordered some of his men to find out. In the meantime, he would close ranks until a suitable plan of action was orchestrated.

A heavy-set man in his seventies, Jimmy had a face that made new-born babies cry and grown men step onto the road when he walked down the street. He had an immense presence whenever he walked into a room and liked to see himself as a Godfather figure like in the Marlon Brando movies. He was of the gangster generation that robbed banks and wealthy households. A career criminal who saw jail time as part and parcel of life. Nowadays it was all about flashy cars and expensive holidays to places he'd never even heard of.

Not that he blamed this generation for dealing in drugs as the rewards were astronomical compared to his day of four men dividing up the proceeds of a safe. Nowadays, clever accountants kept your money safe and out of the hands of the tax man, and well-paid lawyers kept you away from the courts and out of goal. He wouldn't say things were better in his day, they were just different.

But he knew an angle when he saw one, and the deaths of those two boys was about as coincidental as night following day.

He had told his son to bring Sam over to his place for the Christmas as a precaution. His older and wiser eyes would be more able to spot someone coming and deal with them in a way that would put an end to this little vengeance spree, as he saw it.

So, on Christmas Eve, Jimmy invited his grandson with several other members of his family to Capelli's on Francis Street. The group sat at a large table at the back of the restaurant, the table laden with pasta and pizza and opened bottles of wine and beer. The mood was jovial and festive, and Sam was even looking forward to spending some time with his grandad. Everyone knew who Jimmy Gallagher was, and Sam enjoyed basking in the limelight of his notoriety.

As an extra safety precaution, Jimmy had ordered two Eastern European henchmen to watch over them for a week or two. They had not been hired for their subtlety and they cast an intimidating shadow over the staff and the rest of the restaurant diners.

Although the funerals of his two mates were postponed until after Christmas Day, and he put on an appropriate mournful expression for their families, Sam Gallagher felt relaxed with his own, and laughed and joked with them over the food and alcohol. He was naturally gregarious and liked being the centre of attention. Many had even mentioned his name as a possible successor to his grandfather's crime interests. He was the youngest of the sons but had the traits of a bully mixed with a ruthlessness that his brothers lacked.

'Where are you going?' Jimmy asked his grandson when he stood up.

'Grandad, I appreciate your protection but when I need to piss, I gotta piss.'

One of his cousins laughed, but when Jimmy cast him a cold look he fell silent.

'OK,' Jimmy said and then turned to one of the two goons. 'Go with him.'

'Yeah,' Sam said. 'I'll get him to hold it for me.'

This time no one laughed as they walked off in the direction of the toilets.

'Wait,' the goon said when they reached the toilets and walked in before Sam. He had a quick look around — four sinks, six urinals and three cubicles. Only one of the doors of the cubicles was closed. The goon crouched down, looked under it and saw two feet. He got back up and knocked on the cubicle door.

'Yes?' a voice inside said.

'*Open the door*,' the goon said, his Eastern European accent strong and loud.

'I'm busy,' the voice said. 'Go away.'

The goon shook the door. '*Out now*.'

'*What the hell?*' the voice said, but the rattling of a belt could be heard and the toilet flushed. The door opened.

A man in a white cleaner's coat, carrying some cleaning products and a spray came out. The goon was about to search him, but he saw that the man was missing an arm. The right sleeve to his coat was folded up and held in place by a safety pin.

'What's going on?' the cleaner said in a foreign accent. 'All day I clean and now I cannot even take shit in peace.'

Despite his size, the goon looked a little embarrassed and took a step back. The door to the toilet opened and Sam came in. He looked at the one-armed man and at his goon.

'Wait outside,' Sam told him.

'I will wait here,' the goon replied.

'Why? Are you going to wipe my arse? Get the fuck outside, you moron!'

The goon went to say something, but then kept his mouth shut. He walked back outside, and Sam went and stood in front of a urinal. He unzipped himself and urinated into the bowl.

The cleaner began to whistle, and Sam looked over his shoulder at him. When he was finished at the urinal, Sam went to the sinks. The cleaner sprayed and wiped the white ceramic tiles and taps. Sam gave him a sideways glance. He began to spray and clean the sink beside Sam. Some of the spray went onto his clothes.

'What the fuck?' Sam said, holding up his sleeve. 'You know how much this shirt cost? More than you earn in a week, you prick!'

'Sorry,' the cleaner said.

Sam placed his hands under the running water, and the cleaner sprayed again. This time some of the spray hit his hands and Sam felt a slight sting from it.

'Are you for fucking real, pal?' Sam said and pushed the cleaner's shoulder.

The cleaner held up his one arm in apology, the spray bottle in his hand.

'I'm sorry,' he said.

'Are you looking for a ...' Sam said, but the spray hit him directly in his face and went into his open mouth, eyes and nostrils and cut him off. '*Ah, Jesus!*' His hands went shooting up to his face.

'I'm so sorry,' the cleaner said. 'Here, clean it with water.'

Sam allowed the cleaner to remove his hands from his face but, as soon as he did, a second spray of liquid hit him full in the face. This time, the liquid cut the breath from his throat, and he felt as if there were hot metal burning into his eyes. His whole head felt as if it were about to explode and his hands stretched out in front of him.

He tried to call out for help but only a croaking sound came out. He fell to his knees and one hand went to his throat. With his other hand on the floor, he crawled to the door and hammered on it with his fist.

The goon outside open the door.

'*What the fuck?*'

He pulled Sam to his feet but, once the boy was standing, he pushed the goon away and stumbled back into the restaurant. He could feel his throat closing in and squeezing his airways shut and his heart was beating so fast it felt as if it would bounce out of his chest.

He wanted to reach the table. He wanted to tell his grandfather something, although he had no idea what he wanted to say. With immense pain, he opened his eyes long enough to see the big table in the back, and he staggered towards it.

Sam heard a woman scream and chairs being pulled back as he approached. A sound came out of him as he reached the table. The sound of pure agony. The sound of death.

Sam fell forwards, his whole body slamming onto the table as glasses and plates smashed.

The second goon ran towards the toilet and burst inside, but the cleaner was already gone.

# Chapter 38

Mick's heavy steps echoed off the stairwell of his apartment building. Halfway up the final flight, he placed his hand against the wall to catch his breath.

He had stayed at Ciara Ward's house even after Phoebe had taken away every piece of evidence available. It would be at least a couple of weeks before he would hear of any DNA confirmation from her. It being less than two days to Christmas didn't help matters.

When the Scanlans had shown up, the media had followed, and the police had used the media to their advantage. Every news channel tonight and every newspaper in the morning would have Ciara Ward's picture on them. One of the Gardaí had told Mick that her name and picture had gone viral on social media already. He wasn't particularly sure what that meant exactly but the officer made it sound like a good thing.

It wasn't until the Chief himself had shown up and told him to go home that he finally left. He knew in his heart there was nothing he could do at this stage anyway. All air and seaports had been notified. It was a waiting game now. Someone would see her and they would find her. His only thoughts were for the little boy.

He continued up the final steps. He had stopped at a late-night convenience store on the way home and everything he had bought was in a plastic bag, which he placed at Irena's apartment door. He pushed the key into his own door's lock but, before he had turned it, Irena's door opened.

She lifted the bag up and opened it without saying anything. She took out the flowers and sniffed them. Mick spotted the price tag still attached to the side with a big red sticker and cursed himself.

Irena took out the chocolates and placed them under her arm and then opened the white envelope and read the card. He watched her lips move as she read it slowly. Only then did she look up at him.

'You didn't embarrass me,' she told him.

Mick didn't know what to say.

'I may have overreacted a little,' she admitted.

'I suppose I did too,' Mick said.

'No, you *definitely* overreacted.'

'I'm sorry,' he said.

'I know you are. Thanks for these.'

Mick nodded and after a moment of silence opened his door.

'You know, I haven't been in a relationship since my husband,' Irena told him. 'I don't need to give you the details now, but it did not end well.'

She looked down at the card and read it again.

'Everyone has their own sad story to tell, I suppose,' she said without looking at him. 'Mine is just one more on the pile.'

'Everyone has one, yes. But they're all different. And they're all important to somebody.'

'Maybe.'

'I just wanted to let you know that you weren't someone I took lightly. If you know what I mean.'

Irena nodded. 'You're a good man, Mick Kelly. That I do know.'

'Goodnight,' he said and pushed his door open but, before he went inside, he took a step back. 'I've invited my son, Michael, for Christmas dinner, if you'd like to join us?'

Irena walked out from the doorway of her apartment and came up to him. She reached up and when he lowered his head she kissed him on the cheek. Then she walked back to her own apartment.

'As long as I can cook the food,' she told him, and then went back inside.

Mick stood for a moment staring at the closed door. A lot of the tiredness had left him and for a brief moment he considered knocking on her door. Instead, he stepped inside his own place and closed the door behind him.

The clouds opened on an already dark sky as Darcy pulled into the little square of houses in the Liberties. Normally someone could always be seen coming or going, but the heavy rain had forced everyone indoors. She pulled up outside her own home. It was in darkness. She wondered if Seán was still inside. Perhaps he had left. Gone to his parents.

It was up to the boots on the ground to find Alfie now. He was alive, that was the main thing. They all hoped so anyway. All they had to do now was to get him home safe. That was all.

But all Darcy wanted was to cook Seán a proper dinner to make up for being away all day, shower and then read a book until she fell asleep. She looked at her darkened living room window again and hoped she would find him relaxing in her bed with his iPad watching some old Western film that he loved. So many people had given up on her in the past, she would never give up on Seán as long as he wanted her.

She got her key ready, opened her car door and ran the few paces to her front door. She shoved the key in the lock, opened the door and stepped inside. She shook the rain off and removed her coat. The house was freezing. She switched on the overhead light.

'*Turn off the light!*' a voice called out.

She jumped but then saw Seán curled up on the sofa, a cushion covering his eyes to block out the light.

'*Turn off the light!*' he yelled again.

She did as he asked, but then switched on the small lamp on the hall table.

'I need to see where I'm going,' she told him.

Seán groaned in response.

'It's freezing in here,' she said. 'Did you not turn on the heating all day?'

She took up the breakfast dishes from the table and put them in the sink.

Seán coughed and for a moment it seemed as if he was unable to stop.

'Are you OK?' she asked him.

'*Am I OK? Am I OK, she wants to know? Of course I'm not OK. I can't fucking walk for one thing. Is that enough for you?*'

She spotted the empty whiskey bottle lying on its side at the edge of the sofa. She walked over to him and picked it up.

'Is this the full bottle of Jameson I had?' she demanded.

His hand came up and snatched the bottle from her.

'It's not empty yet,' he told her. 'There's still a few drops in it.'

'You're drunk,' she said.

'Well, aren't you the smartest detective in Ireland!'

'Oh, I see,' she said. 'So, this is the new plan, is it? Get drunk and angry at the world and be a victim?'

'You know what?' he mumbled from beneath the cushion. 'That sounds like a great fucking plan to me. I'm going to stay drunk for the rest of my poxy crippled life.'

'Not on my couch, you're not. If you want to drink and feel sorry for yourself, you can go find yourself a pub. It's full of men who think the world is against them. Clichés, the lot of them!'

He removed the cushion from his face. Darcy failed to hide her shock at the sight of his tired and tormented face.

'At least in a pub they don't have to listen to their nagging girlfriends or partners or whatever you are!'

'Whatever I am? You know who I am! I'm the one here trying to help you.'

'Help me?' He laughed.

'I'm doing my best, Seán.'

Darcy felt as if her head was going to explode. There was no point in talking to him like this.

'If you want to do anything of use, go get me another bottle of whiskey.'

'You must be joking.'

'Then I'll go myself.'

'It's raining.'

She had her back to him and when she heard the thud she turned around. He was sprawled out on the floor. She ran to him and grabbed him.

'*Get away from me!*' he yelled.

She recoiled from the anger in his voice. His arms stretched out, and he dragged himself along the floor.

Darcy put her hands to her face, unable to watch him as the pain tore at her heart.

'OK, OK,' she said. 'I'll get you another bottle.'

He stopped crawling and she had to step over his body to get to the front door. She took down her coat and put it on. She looked at him again and he wasn't moving, his arms still stretched out along the floor.

She walked over to him and bent down. 'Seán?'

He was snoring.

She stood up again, unsure what to do. She had her coat on and the keys in her hand. She looked at her front door and then again at Seán on the floor.

She bent down and placed the cushion under his head. Then she went to the bedroom, pulled the duvet cover off the bed and brought it back to the living room. She put it over him and then watched him snoring softly for a few moments.

She opened the front door, turned off the lamp and walked back into the rain.

In the car, she slumped into the seat. The rain pounded onto the roof of the car. She stared out at her lovely little house in the darkness. It was more than just her house though. It was her sanctuary. The first place she could lock the door and not allow anyone inside if she so chose. She couldn't help shaking the feeling that she'd been barred from her own haven. She shivered from the cold and felt the rain soaking into her bones.

Then a sudden volcanic anger erupted from inside and she screamed and roared and banged her fists off the steering wheel.

'*Fuck!*' she yelled over and over. '*Fuck, fuck, fuck!*'

She stopped. Her chest rose and fell quickly as she tried to catch her breath. She closed her eyes, forcing herself to breathe, in and out, slower each time, until calm finally returned. Then she opened her eyes and started the car.

She sat motionless and waited but couldn't think of anywhere to go, so she turned the engine off and took comfort in the patter of the rain and the solace that it brought, cocooned under the orange glow from the street lights that lit up and folded around her and her car and the little square outside.

# Chapter 39

Frank Kavanagh threw back the black silk sheets of his super king-sized bed and went into the ensuite. He switched on the light and blinked. He looked at himself completely naked in the full-length mirror as he pissed into the toilet. He always needed to urinate after sex these days, and he wondered if it was an age thing.

Perhaps, he thought, he should get the finger up the arse test, but he quickly dismissed it. He wanted to be that guy who one day walked into a hospital to check out some belly pains and be told that he was riddled with cancer, had two weeks to live and it was a miracle that he had been able to walk in by himself.

He would never be one of those men who lay in a hospital bed for years enduring dull family visits and vile-tasting grub. He'd suffered enough of both in prison over the years. At least in prison there was always the possibility of parole. There was little chance of any pardon for those men in their hospital beds looking out at the world like live lobsters trapped in a restaurant's glass tank, their fate already determined.

When that day came, he would have no hesitation in coming back home and lying down in this room and blowing his brains out with the Glock he had hidden in the floorboards.

With his left hand, he grabbed his gut and straightened himself up. He needed to cut back on the whiskeys and the late-night snacking.

Other than that, he wasn't in such bad shape for an old geezer. There were still a few years of frolicking and fornication left in him yet.

He flushed the toilet and then ran the tap, cupping the water and splashing it onto his face. He dried his hands with a large white bath towel and then styled his hair with his fingers.

'Turn off that light, will you, darling?' Joan Boyle asked him when he came back into the bedroom.

He switched it off and she removed her hand from her eyes as he climbed back into bed. She cuddled up beside him and kissed him on the chest.

'Ten out of ten as usual, Frank,' she told him. 'You have no idea what sort of a day I've had.'

'Actually, I know exactly what sort of a day you've had,' Frank said. 'I've had both you and your husband in my ear all evening.'

She let go of him and sat up in bed, the blankets cupped above her breasts.

'I hate when you mention him when we're in bed. You have no idea how he gets under my skin of late. I'm finding it hard to even be in the same room as him and now all this. It's such a mess.'

'He's not that bad. He's loyal and that means a lot these days. It means a lot any day.'

'Loyal?' she laughed. 'He fucks anything that he can get his hands on. I've put up with it for years, his floundering and adultery, but this last one, Anita Cooney, is a step too far.'

Frank turned and looked at her. 'Don't you think that's a little bit of the kettle calling the pot black?'

'You mean us?' she said. 'Frank, what we have isn't the same as him attempting to mount everything with a pair of tits. I don't sleep with anyone except you, darling. I certainly wouldn't let him put his hands on me. How is that cheating?'

She moved back over in the bed and cuddled him. Frank looked down at her.

'Maybe I'll tell him to go away for a while,' he told her. 'Go to Spain until things cool down a bit.'

'It's all such a mess,' she repeated.

'It is that,' he agreed.

'Maybe,' she said and bent her neck up to look at him, 'maybe he should go away for a long time.'

'No. I need him here to run those shops. There's too much legal cash coming in from them. No one knows their operation better than him.'

'Well,' she said and kissed him on the neck, 'there is someone who could do a pretty good job.'

Her hands caressed his torso and slid up to his head.

'You?' he asked.

'Why not?' she said, her voice becoming a whisper as she kissed his chin and jaw. 'Things would be so great then. I'd have full control of the shops, and you'd still get everything that was owed to you, I'd make sure of that. I've been wanting to spruce things up in that business for a while. I have so many great ideas, but he's so old school about everything.'

Her hand moved back down his chest, and she slid it under the sheets.

'And also,' she said, 'we'd be free to meet up for our little catch-ups whenever we wanted. You could even pop by my office and surprise me.'

Frank reached down and took her hand and pulled it back up.

'You know, Joan,' he said, 'you're probably the only person who could take over my whole operation.'

'How right you are,' she told him. 'If anything were to happen to you, God forbid, I could make sure things continued as smoothly as if you were still around.'

Frank leaned over the bed and picked up his phone. He pressed a few numbers.

'Lurch,' he said. 'Tell the Estonian not to leave the country just yet. I have one more job for him.'

Frank switched off his phone and slid back into the bed.

'You're such a real man,' Joan hummed in his ear. 'Always ready to do whatever needs to be done.'

She slid her hand back down the sheets, and this time he allowed her to have her way with him as he lay back on the pillow and stared up at his reflection in the mirrors on the ceiling.

# Christmas Eve

# Chapter 40

Darcy woke at the sound of a van door slamming shut. She knocked her head off the glass of the driver's window and groaned. Her mouth felt sticky and numb and when she put her hand to it, she felt drool at the side of her mouth.

It was still dark but at least the rain had stopped. In the side mirror, she saw a milkman's van leaving the square. She searched for her phone.

**06:30**

She moved her head from side to side. Every part of her body ached and was cold. She opened the car door and dragged herself outside. She stood and stretched, and then took the keys out of the ignition and opened her front door.

Seán was still on the floor and snoring loudly. She went into the bedroom. Her bed looked tempting, but she still had a sense of awkwardness being in her own home. A sense that her home was no longer hers.

She took out the gym bag that she always had ready to go. It had a complete change of clothes folded inside. She carried the bag, stepped quietly around Seán again and went back outside. She closed the door gently, got back in her car and headed for the gym.

Amos was in the reception of the gym drinking coffee and reading an early edition of the *Independent*. There were large photos of Ciara and Alfie on the front page. He peered over the top of his newspaper as Darcy walked in.

'Jesus,' he said. 'You look like you slept in your car.'

Darcy took the half-empty cup of black coffee from his hand and swallowed it back in one go. She pushed open the double doors into the gym area as Amos reached back and switched on the kettle.

An hour later, Darcy had run five miles on the treadmill, showered and changed into her work clothes. Amos was still in the reception when she came in. He slid his coffee cup out of her reach.

She walked past him without saying a word.

'Have a great day!' he called to her in as cheerful a voice as he could manage.

Without turning around, she stuck out her arm and gave him a thumbs-up. The most sarcastic thumbs-up she could manage.

Apart from the desk sergeant and two cleaning ladies, Darcy didn't meet another soul until she reached the fifth floor of Harcourt Street HQ. There were two detectives at their desks whom she didn't know that well, chatting to each other in the far corner. They turned as she came out of the lift and nodded a greeting to her.

Six months ago, they would have turned away as if she were a bad smell on the NBCI floor, so she took that as some sort of a victory.

She couldn't see Mick at his desk, so she strolled down to the coffee machine in the hall and rooted in her pockets for a two-euro coin. Not finding one, she banged the side of the machine with her fist.

'Take it easy,' Mick said as he approached her. 'They'd be quicker to charge you for assault on that machine than on some of the staff in here.'

He plonked a coin into the machine and pressed the button for black coffee — no milk, no sugar.

'Thanks,' Darcy said. 'You got my text?'

'I'm here, aren't I?'

They stood there in silence as the machine whirled and gargled until eventually a plastic cup of tepid black coffee popped out.

Darcy took it and went over to her desk and Mick followed.

'Lads!' the Chief called from his office door. 'Come in!'

They looked at each other and slowly made their way inside

'Good work on the Alfie Scanlan case,' he told them when they were all seated.

'Thank you, sir,' Darcy said.

'Although it isn't over yet. We still need the kid back home.'

Darcy and Mick knew that this was about the best they could hope for with regard to any sort of praise from their boss.

'Any updates overnight, Chief?' Darcy asked.

'The switchboard tells me that every four-year-old blond-haired boy in Ireland has been spotted and reported. Everyone, of course, except *our* four-year-old blond-haired boy. We've got every available Garda searching.'

'We'll be joining them too after we're finished here,' Darcy said.

'Well, you requested this meeting, Doyle. What have you got?' O'Riordan asked.

'MBP, sir,' she said.

'Go on,' he told her.

'It stands for Munchausen By Proxy,' Darcy explained. 'I believe Ciara Ward was suffering from it. I also believe that Rachel Robinson thought the same thing about her close friend. Or at least suspected it. We'll never know. I'm sure you've heard of Munchausen Syndrome, Chief. It's when someone pretends to be ill or makes themselves ill for the sympathy and the attention they receive from everyone. Munchausen by Proxy is when they make someone who is in their care ill or exaggerate their sickness to garnish sympathy for themselves. It's usually a child. Parents have been known to induce symptoms in their own kids by poisoning, starving or even suffocating them. Before Ciara moved to Dublin she lived in Galway. I had Garda Eoin dig up her medical records, and she has a litany of various conditions and attendances in hospitals.'

She switched her gaze to Mick and he was smiling at her, but then his expression changed quickly back to a more attentive one. She went on.

'That stopped as soon as her son, Luke, was born. Since then Luke has gone from one doctor to the next with both imagined and very real symptoms. Unfortunately for him, the poor little guy, we suspect she took it a step too far and he died. Dr. Daly is still waiting on toxicology reports, but she said at the post mortem that Luke died as a result of too much sodium or, rather, as a result of someone then trying to correct that by administering too much water too quickly. That can be fatal. I don't remember the exact term, but I looked it up and one of the things a MBP parent does is to give their child too much sodium. Or basically table salt. This is usually to make their child sick enough to get the attention they crave.'

'So she didn't mean to kill her son?' O'Riordan asked.

'No,' Darcy said.

'And she kidnapped Alfie because?'

'Because he reminded her of her own son,' Darcy told him. 'The similarity was, of course, no coincidence. Without her son, or someone to care for, she was nothing. Worthless. We found empty bottles of Calpol in her home that she must have been forcing Alfie to drink in order to subdue him and prevent him from calling out after she took him. It was easy for her to take him from the sports ground last week. She didn't look out of place, maybe John Scanlan even spotted her that morning, and Alfie was happy to go with her as he knew her from the Montessori, since she was the cleaner.'

O'Riordan leaned back in his chair and tapped his fingers on the table. He stared at Darcy.

'Go on.'

'Rachel got pregnant five years ago,' Darcy continued. 'Her boyfriend at the time was Kevin Brennan, who we found OD'd in his flat. She demanded money from him, and he paid her but then she had a miscarriage. I have the medical records for that too. She knew the payments from Kevin would stop but her close friend Ciara just happened to have moved to Dublin from Galway after she got pregnant. They'd been school friends and Rachel got her the cleaning job in the Montessori. There was a photo of the two of them in school uniforms on Rachel's living-room wall. When baby Luke was born, Rachel pretended he was hers and continued demanding payments from Kevin. We know that Ciara and Rachel were as thick as thieves so anything Luke mentioned to anyone, including Kevin, about his staying at one house or another, or even that he had two mummies, wouldn't have attracted too much attention from a four-year-old. After all, he even drew himself with two mothers on that stick-figure drawing we found in Kevin's apartment. It's possible the women even schooled him to think of Rachel as a second mother. Ciara clearly cooperated with the whole scheme and allowed Rachel to let Luke spend time with Kevin in order to keep the payments coming in.'

'The priest and Barry Boyle, you mean?' O'Riordan said.

'Exactly,' Darcy said. 'But that all went tits-up, if you pardon my language, when Ciara killed Luke. Albeit accidentally. I think Rachel had already decided to cut her losses. So, she demanded lump sums from Father Aidan and Barry Boyle. There may have been others we're not aware of who paid her cash or a once-off lump sum.'

'But she got unlucky,' O'Riordan said, 'when she came across the likes of Anita Cooney.'

'Yes, Chief,' Darcy said. 'We don't know if Barry Boyle put it in Anita's head, or if he simply paid her or whether she even acted on her own volition through some sort of perverted loyalty to Boyle. We've already established a connection between Boyle and Frank Kavanagh, so we can't rule out his involvement in tidying up Boyle's mess. But either way Anita did away with Rachel and although we can't see any self-motivation on her part, I'm not sure we'll be able to touch Boyle for it either. Perhaps a plea bargain from the DPP might get her to talk, but I doubt it. The code of silence, or *omertà*, is a part of her DNA.'

O'Riordan nodded. 'All we can do now is hope Ciara shows up or is spotted, and we get Alfie back before any further harm comes to him.'

Darcy felt suddenly overcome with tiredness. She wanted to go home. She looked at O'Riordan across the table as he tried to take it all in. Then she followed his gaze to the brown folder on his table.

'We've enough people looking for the little boy right now,' he said, and pushed a folder across the table. 'I want you to take a look at this,'

Mick put his hand out to take it but then allowed Darcy to pick it up.

'Three boys have died in the last couple of days,' O'Riordan told them. 'They all knew each other and more importantly they were all once charged with the rape of a young girl. They were found not guilty, but one of the boys is Jimmy Gallagher's grandson, Sam Gallagher.'

'Jesus!' Mick said. 'Looks like some sort of payback.'

'Yes, but it'll be hard to prove,' O'Riordan said. 'They all died violently within a short period of time but at different locations and by different means.'

Darcy flicked through the folder and then stopped. She looked up at Mick.

'What is it?' he asked.

Darcy held up a photo to him. 'Is this the rape victim?' she asked O'Riordan.

'Yes. Chloe Brunelle. She's a French citizen. Why? You know her?'

'We know her,' Mick confirmed, looking at the photo. 'And we've a good idea where to find her.'

Mick stood up, but Darcy remained seated. She stared at the table where the folder had been.

'You OK, Doyle?' O'Riordan asked her.

She heard his words but felt numb and unable to stand.

Mick took a step closer to her and placed one hand gently on her shoulder.

'Let's go, Detective.'

She raised her head to him, stood up and followed him out the glass door of O'Riordan's office.

# Chapter 41

Joan Boyle wanted to look her very best before the Gardaí and the media arrived following the imminent death of her husband, who at that very moment was sprawled across the chaise longue downstairs reading the morning papers.

She was seated at the makeup table in her bedroom, applying the final touches to her face. With her forefinger, she stretched the folds of skin at the corner of her eyes and made a mental note to book herself in for a Botox session after Christmas. But it would have to do for now.

She allowed her mind to wander and to daydream about her life as a new widow. Of course, she would be a very wealthy woman. That was part of the allure. Not that she ever wanted for anything now but everything her husband owned would soon be entrusted to her sole control.

She knew Frank Kavanagh would never take her as his only lover and, to an extent, that suited her. She had her own societal plans of attending book launches and new restaurant openings and the odd play at the theatre. She had visions of seeing her photo in glossy magazines in the 'Out and About' sections, appearing alongside celebrities and politicians. They would write that she was a wealthy widow and would wonder how she managed to maintain her youthful looks and figure.

She would take a lover, no doubt. Someone in his thirties. A personal trainer or someone like that. Someone foreign. Spanish perhaps. A little cliché, but she could live with that. She would take him away on holidays to expensive hotels in the sun and have her way with him for hours on end, swaggering at his side by the pool, and the bar and the bedroom. Turning heads with jealous eyes and gossiping lips wherever she went.

A quick rehearsal might be called for. She cleared her throat.

'*Please, you need to come! It's my husband!*'

Too high a pitch. It would probably be recorded so she needed to get it right.

'*Officer, please ...*'

Officer? It wasn't America.

'*Oh my God! It's my husband! He's been shot! Please come now!*'

It would have to do.

The sound of gravel crunching on the driveway made her lean to the side of the mirror and look out her bedroom window. At first, the sight of the Estonian frightened her. He looked like a man who had seen more horrors than he would ever get to speak of. For a moment, she almost felt sorry for her husband — a man she had once loved and with whom she had shared much of her life. She pushed the thought from her mind, took a deep breath in and let it out slowly. I hope at least it's quick, she thought.

She had been instructed to leave the front door unlocked to allow access, and a map of the house had been provided. She'd been unable to give an exact location for her husband but when she saw him slumped in front of the TV, she had brought him a beer to try to keep him downstairs while she was in the main bedroom, so that the man would not have to go traipsing around the house.

She strained her ears to listen and heard the front door open and then quietly click shut. A thought came to her that perhaps she should go downstairs and be there while it happened. Would that make her innocence more apparent? No. She should stay in the main bedroom where she was, as she'd been told to do. Stick with the plan. They said that it'd be best not to see anything at all so there would be nothing to tell the Gardaí when they arrived.

Without turning around, she tried to listen, but she could hear nothing. Surely he had found him by now? Would the man use a silencer? What does that sound like anyway? Was it a TUT-TUT sound like in the movies?

She closed her eyes and forced herself to remain calm.

A creak in the floorboards behind her made her open her eyes. In the mirror she saw the Estonian standing in her bedroom doorway. Her initial thought was that he looked even scarier this close.

She turned around to tell him to get out, that this was not part of her plan. She was even about to scold him like a petulant child but when she saw the gun in his hand she froze.

Had he already finished with her husband? Did he want payment from her for the job?

He raised the gun and pointed it at her, and she stared at it, more out of curiosity than fear.

Then, like an avalanche, all her thoughts came crashing down, and she knew. She knew everything and saw everything. This was indeed not part of her plan, but it was part of someone else's plan. *Frank Kavanagh. Frank and her husband.*

She heard a car start up in her driveway. She raised herself up off the pouffe and turned to see the silhouette of her husband driving away in his Mercedes.

She turned back to the Estonian and looked into his soulless eyes.

'*Men*,' she said, the taste of bile in her throat. '*Fucking men.*'

And then he fired.

# Chapter 42

It was Lurch who opened the door for Darcy and Mick. He stepped aside, his nonverbal way of inviting them to enter. For the first time, Darcy wondered if he was actually nonverbal. She imagined he'd had his tongue removed by some previous gangster boss, then shoved the gruesome image from her head. Lurch peered down at them as they walked into the hall.

Tony was sprawled out on one of the more comfortable sofas. Frank was pouring a drink behind the bar.

'If I said it once, I'll say it again,' Mick said, surveying the expansive open-plan room. 'Who says crime doesn't pay?'

'Perhaps I'll have to repeat myself as well, Columbo,' Frank said, spreading his hands out in front of him. 'All of this was bought from the proceeds of legitimate businesses.'

'Really?' Mick said. 'Then perhaps next time you're down at the law library in the Four Courts you could point out that section to me where the sale and distribution of narcotics is now legal in this great state of ours.'

'Drugs?' Frank said, breaking into laughter. 'You're living in a dream world, mate. Sure, what would I know about drugs? I will admit to having skirted along the edge of the law as a youngster, but all of this has been bought by honest, hard work.'

'Honest work? Now who's living in a dream world?'

Darcy put her hand on Mick's arm, and he looked at her. She shook her head.

Frank laughed out loud. 'Oh, now I see who the real boss is. Columbo Kelly taking orders from the little lady now, is he?'

Darcy turned to face him. '*Shut your cakehole, Frank*,' she told him.

Tony sat up in his chair on hearing his boss being so directly insulted in his own home.

'As usual,' Darcy told him, 'we can leave now if you'd prefer and we can go get a warrant for you to be questioned in relation to the deaths of three boys with whom you have a direct connection.' She looked at her watch. 'It's just gone ten on Christmas Eve. I could arrest you now without a warrant under Section 4 of the Criminal Justice Act. You could be detained for an initial period not exceeding six hours, which can easily be extended. In the meantime, I will have your place ransacked – sorry, I mean *searched*, for any evidence. I reckon you'll be home sometime on Christmas Day to watch the end of *It's a Wonderful Life*. You do know that Santa doesn't visit little boys in prison, don't you?'

Frank put down his drink and came out from behind the bar. Even in his casual clothes, he was more dressed up than the majority of men in the whole of Dublin.

'We're looking for information,' Darcy told him. 'If we believe that you have nothing that will call for your detainment, then we will be on our way.'

Tony was making growling noises at her. She ignored him.

'Either way, I don't give a fuck,' she said, shrugging. 'You see, I don't have any family, Frank. Christmas Day for me is just like any other day, except the shops are shut. The TV's a bit better, I hear, but I don't have a TV.'

'What do you want?' Frank asked, any joviality gone from his tone.

Darcy took the folder from Mick and opened it. She took out the three photos of the boys. and held them up to Frank.

Mick now stepped closer to him. He took the photo of the first boy killed and held it up in front of Frank.

'Did you or anyone you know have any involvement in the death of Kevin Meehan?' he asked.

'No.'

Mick held up the second photo.

'Did you or anyone you know have any involvement in the death of Ryan Durkin?'

'No.'

Mick shoved the final photo in Frank's face.

'Did you or anyone you know have any involvement in the death of Sam Gallagher?'

'No.'

'I wonder,' Mick said, 'if it took us a day or two to find the connection between their deaths and you, how long will it take Jimmy Gallagher?'

Frank didn't move, but Mick saw his eyes narrow.

'You lot believe even less in coincidences than we do,' Mick said.

'All this for three scumbags?' Frank said.

'The law doesn't discriminate,' Darcy said. 'Everyone deserves an answer, and everyone has the right to the truth. And that includes the families of these three boys. It even applies to you.'

'Hasn't Chloe been through enough?'

'Yes, she has,' Darcy said. 'But it seems that being related to Frank Kavanagh is a fucking curse that stays with you till the day you die.'

They stared at each other. Each pair of matching blue eyes boring into the other's.

Darcy's phone buzzed in her pocket for a full ten seconds before she reached in and took it out. She saw the caller ID and walked to the glass doors. She slid the door open and stepped into the garden.

'Yes, Chief?' she said.

'We have Ciara Ward's location,' he told her.

Darcy looked back inside at Mick. 'And the boy?'

'He's with her.'

'Where?'

'Blessington.'

'We're leaving now.'

'No, wait! She was spotted in her car by a woman walking her dog by the lake shore. The woman called the local press before calling us and now Ciara is on a bridge threatening to jump off it. With the boy.'

'*Fuck!*' Darcy yelled, loud enough that everyone behind the glass looked out at her. 'Mick and I will be there in twenty minutes. If it's not too late.'

'The ERU are on their way to your location. Bike riders will clear the road for you. You'll be there in ten minutes. Hostage negotiators have been informed but maybe you can get there before ...'

O'Riordan didn't finish the sentence.

Darcy hung up and rushed back inside.

'*Mick!*' she said. '*Let's go!*'

'What is it?'

'*Now!*' she told him and ran out of the room.

# Chapter 43

Darcy and Mick were sitting in the back of one of the two ERU vehicles as they sped their way to Blessington, several Garda motorbike outriders clearing the way for them. Jamie was driving and maintained a steady 120 km/h on a road that was built for half that speed, while another officer sitting up front held on to the door for support. At each junction motorcycles left their location where they were blocking traffic and followed them, overtaking them at breakneck speeds to prepare the next junction.

Darcy tried to compose herself and prepare for the task ahead. She tried to put herself in Ciara's shoes. This was not a time to be angry. Any anger or thoughts of retribution would have to wait. Now, she needed only compassion and composure.

Jamie tore into Blessington's small village without raising his foot off the accelerator. Shops and houses whizzed by on the empty roads. Then their SUV slowed and took a left turn at the end of the village. Through the trees and over the lake, Darcy finally got a glimpse of a small crowd about halfway across the bridge. She looked at Mick, but his face was expressionless. There was nothing he could say or do at that moment. She would find no comfort from him. She knew his experience would tell her that the chances of this ending well were not good, but she also knew she would have his support whatever the outcome.

Jamie slowed as they approached the start of the bridge where a small crowd was already gathered. He squeezed the big SUV through the gap in the onlookers that the motorbike outriders had cleared for them and then came to a halt. Without saying a word, he and his colleague jumped out. The second ERU vehicle arrived behind them.

Darcy and Mick climbed out and followed Jamie. Darcy forced herself to walk the remaining distance.

As the small crowd parted, she saw Ciara Ward. Her heart sank into her stomach when she saw the little boy, Alfie, in her arms, his blond hair blowing in the wind like a white flag.

She looked at Mick, who signalled for her to lead the way. She took a deep breath in, released it slowly and then began to walk unhurriedly towards Ciara and Alfie. She could hear Mick walking behind her. Darcy was aware of the phone cameras as they panned across them, following their every move.

Ciara stood on the far side of the safety rail, standing on the concrete edge of the bridge, looking down at the hundred-foot drop into the lake's icy waters. Darcy hoped that someone had the foresight to have a water-rescue team on standby, although she was unsure whether anyone would even survive a fall from that height.

As she approached Ciara, with Mick close behind her, Darcy saw a worn, tired and exhausted face. Alfie wriggled precariously in Ciara's arms, but she held tightly on to him.

'Ciara,' Darcy said, in as relaxed a tone as she could manage. She remembered her training, kept her intonation low and calm. 'My name is Darcy, and I'm here to help you.'

'You don't want to help me,' Ciara said, her voice full of anguish. 'You're only interested in the boy. That's all anyone cares about.'

'That's not true. I want to help *you*, Ciara.'

'You want the boy. Look at him. He's fine. I told them he'd be fine,' she said and nodded towards the crowd of people.

'Yes, he's fine,' Darcy told her, edging slowly to her. 'He's such a beautiful little boy.'

Ciara focused on Darcy for the first time. She looked at the boy in her arms, then back at Darcy.

'We're all here to care for you, Ciara. You've had such a tough, tough time. Poor Ciara!'

Ciara began to cry. The wind whirled around her head, blowing the hair from her face. 'Yes,' she whispered. 'My poor Luke. I tried so hard to save him.'

'We know that, Ciara. And now you will get all the attention you need. I promise.'

Darcy inched closer to her, her hand stretched out along the safety rail. She saw Ciara's body relax and her hold on Alfie loosen.

'*Alfie!*' a woman's scream came out from across the bridge. '*Alfie!*'

Ciara's head swung in that direction and Darcy glanced towards the crowd. Alfie's parents were being held back by the police officers.

'*Mum!*' Alfie called out and struggled in Ciara's arms, trying to free himself.

Ciara tightened her grip on him and stepped closer to the edge. Behind them, the crowd let out a gasp.

'Forget the boy,' Darcy told her, not taking her focus away from Ciara as she continued to slide her feet closer and closer. She could hear Mick breathing behind her, while Jamie cautiously circled around to Ciara's other side.

Then Darcy stepped over the safety rail.

'*Stay back!*' Ciara screamed at Darcy.

Darcy stopped.

'It's OK, Ciara. I'm here for you. We're all here for you.'

Ciara looked over at the people pointing their phones at them.

'All this is for you,' Darcy told her. 'It's you who people want to hear from. You have everyone's sympathy and everyone's understanding. They know how tough you've had it.'

Again, Darcy inched forwards, her eyes fixed on Ciara's. She registered that Jamie had climbed over the railing some distance beyond Ciara but didn't break her eye contact with Ciara.

'*I'm the one who has suffered!*' Ciara shouted at her.

'I know. We all know.'

'*They took my Luke! And then they took my Rachel!' We were a family. I loved them so much!*'

'I know, Ciara.'

'*You don't know anything! We were going away. Rachel and me. We had everything planned. My beautiful girl! My beautiful Rachel!*'

Ciara shook her head. Alfie screamed for his mother again, but this time she didn't cry out.

'But we're here for you, Ciara.'

'It's too late,' Ciara said.

'I can help you!' Darcy pleaded.

Ciara didn't reply this time. Darcy knew instinctively that their connection had been lost. She watched a calmness come over Ciara's face as she looked out towards the horizon and closed her eyes.

Darcy was almost within arm's reach of her now and she saw Jamie closing the gap between him and Ciara.

As Ciara bent forward, poised to jump, with everything inside her Darcy lunged at the boy. She flung her arms out in front as if trying to save a ball from a goal and her hands grasped Alfie's jacket as he fell forwards with Ciara releasing her hold on him. Darcy pulled him tightly to her chest as the world turned upside down and they fell, and she could already feel her body hitting the icy water with a smack and then enveloping her in darkness as they plunged to the bottom.

Then her legs jerked sharply as if they'd caught on the rail and her body jolted to a sudden stop, but she didn't let go of Alfie. She cried out as they dangled upside down. Alfie didn't make a sound.

Then, after several moments staring down at the water, she felt herself being pulled up. She twisted her head and saw Mick and Jamie hauling her up by the ankles.

A Garda climbed over the rail and when they had raised her to his level, he took Alfie from her arms and Darcy felt as if the weight of the world had been lifted from her.

As Alfie's parents ran to him and engulfed him with their embraces, Detective Darcy Doyle turned and looked down into the freezing waters for Ciara but couldn't see even a ripple in the water below.

# CHRISTMAS DAY

# Epilogue 1

Irena opened the oven door and filled her little apartment with the aroma of the large, cooked turkey. Outside a soft rain fell on the grey Dublin streets, and it seemed to isolate them and make the apartment even cosier.

'I told you it was too big,' she said as she placed the turkey in the centre of the table. 'There's barely enough room for the plates.'

'There's only one thing nicer than cooked turkey on Christmas Day,' Mick told her, rubbing his stomach. 'And that's cold turkey sandwiches on St. Stephen's Day. Don't you worry about it – it'll be eaten.'

'Well, I hope you're hungry, Michael,' Irena said.

'I am starving,' he told her.

Mick tapped his son in the ribs with his elbow.

'Oh, right,' he said conspiratorially. He looked up at Irena. 'Thank you so much for cooking the turkey for me – and for my present.'

'You're very welcome,' Irena told him. 'And thank you so much for spending Christmas Day with me.'

'You're welcome too, I guess,' he said and Mick and Irena shared a smile.

In the background Celine Dion sang them a ballad. Earlier, when Mick and Michael had arrived at Irena's apartment to the sound of 'Jingle Bells', he had immediately asked her to 'turn off that shite'. Then, as a Christmas gift before dinner, Irena had given him a Celine Dion compilation CD. He had initially acted surprised and feigned disinterest, but she had just winked and walked away. Mick had blushed a little and then put the disc on as Irena cooked.

For his part, Mick had bought her a voucher for a return flight to Zadar in her home country of Croatia. She had joked that he wanted to get rid of her. He confessed that he couldn't think of a worse thing than for her to leave Ireland. She invited him to come with her to visit, and he told her that perhaps he would.

Then they stood for several moments in awkward silence until she reached up on tiptoes and kissed him on the lips.

'I'd like that very much,' she told him, and Mick felt happier than he had in a long while.

After dinner, Michael sat on the sofa watching *Home Alone* and laughing loudly. Mick sat beside him, pretending not to actually watch it but occasionally bursting into laughter. He got more pleasure in seeing his son happy than anything else in the world.

Irena busied herself cleaning up, despite the protests and offers from Mick to help her. As she pottered about, Mick enjoyed the homely sounds of dishes and plates clinking off each other in the kitchen, and the laughter of his son beside him.

He thought about Darcy and her comment yesterday to Frank about not having a family and it being just another day for her. He didn't think he'd ever feel sorry for such a beautiful woman twenty years younger than him. He wondered how Seán was getting on. He hadn't been a good enough colleague to him since he'd been shot. He vowed to make up for it in the New Year. And to Darcy too.

His phone beeped. At first, he thought it might be work, and he ignored it. If it was urgent, they'd call him. Then he thought it might be Darcy, so he pulled himself off the sofa and picked up his phone.

*Happy Christmas, Dad x*

He stared at the message from Lucy and reread it ten times before replying.

*Happy Christmas, Sweetie. Love you.*

He turned his back on Irena and took a moment to himself. He felt such a fool that a simple text could make him well up so easily. He breathed in and out slowly.

'Mick!' Irena called to him.

He turned around to her. She was looking out of the window.

'Michael!' she called. 'Come look!'

Mick walked over to her as Michael paused the television and pulled himself off the sofa to join them. The three of them stood there peering out.

'How wonderful!' Irena said. 'Isn't it the most beautiful thing in the world?'

The afternoon had brought a drop in the temperature, and the soft rain had turned to fluffy white flakes of snow. They all stared out as the music serenaded them.

'I told you it would snow,' Irena said. 'Now a miracle will happen.'

Mick looked at her on one side and at his son on the other and thought of Lucy also looking out her window at the falling snow.

'Perhaps,' he said. 'Perhaps.'

And as they stood there looking out at a grey Dublin landscape as it slowly turned to white, he put his arm around Michael and then he reached down and took Irena's hand in his.

# Epilogue 2

From her living-room window, Darcy watched the snow fall. She drank black tea and listened to Seán moving about in the bedroom. He was packing. His parents were due to collect him at any moment.

She sipped her tea but then noticed her house had gone quiet. She turned around. Seán was sitting in his wheelchair, his suitcase on his lap, looking at her.

She held his glance and forced herself to smile.

'I wish,' he said. 'I wish ...'

'I know,' she told him, and meant it. 'I'm sorry.'

'I'm sorry too.'

'You've nothing to be sorry for,' she told him.

'Thank you,' he said.

'For what?'

'For everything. For taking me in, even though I wasn't what I once was. Thank you for trying.'

'Can I call you?' she asked.

'Best not to. At least for a while anyway. You will always be a reminder to me of everything that I could have been. Of the life I could have led.'

She wanted to argue with him but didn't want them to part in anger.

'I do love you,' she said. 'And I will miss you terribly.'

'I know. But you have suffered greater things than this, Darcy Doyle. And those awful things that happened to you give you a strength that sets you apart from others. I know you don't like to talk about your past, and that you hide your pain from everyone. But know that those who love you, see it. One day you will find someone who has suffered like you and only they will really understand you.'

Darcy smiled at him. 'Are you a psychologist now?'

'No,' he said, returning her smile. 'But I've had a lot of time to think while I'm sitting around staring at the wall and at the ceiling. Thank God my parents at least have a fecking television.'

Darcy laughed. A car horn beeped, and she looked out.

'It's them. I'll tell them you're coming.'

'Please don't,' he said. 'I want to go out by myself. If this is going to be my new life, I want to start it on my own.'

He took a moment, a moment for himself, and he looked around Darcy's small house one last time. Then he looked at Darcy. Whatever his last thought was, he chose not to share it with her. And then he pushed himself forward in the chair, the suitcase balanced on his lap.

It broke Darcy's heart not to help him. She could feel her tears coming but wanted to wait until later when she would be alone.

When he got to the door, he reached out for the handle.

'No, wait,' she said.

And then she bent down and kissed him on the mouth. He returned her kiss and it seemed as if the kiss would never end. And for that small amount of time, they were both dragged back to the past when the whole world lay at their feet and when life itself was as rich and as sweet and as timeless as their kiss.

When Darcy pulled away from him, she saw that his face was wet with her tears. She used her sleeve to wipe them away.

She opened the door, and he wheeled himself out into the falling snow. His father had turned the car and parked close to Darcy's door. She watched as his parents got out and hugged him. Then they escorted him around the car and helped him into the passenger seat.

His father folded the chair and stored it in the boot while his mother made sure he was comfortable. Then his dad got back into the car.

His mother closed the door on Seán and opened the door into the back. She looked over the car at Darcy and gave her such a gentle and warm smile that Darcy knew Seán would be OK. Then his mother waved but before Darcy could return the wave she was back in the car, and they were driving out of the square.

Darcy stood in the doorway and did not go back inside until the last tracks of Seán's wheelchair had completely disappeared, covered by the falling snow.

Back in her living room, she shivered with the cold. Perhaps she had stood at the door too long and the heat had left the room, and the cold had gone into her bones. She had wanted her home back just for herself, and yet now it felt as empty and silent as the snow-filled square outside.

She looked back out at it and tried to cry in the hope of some release, but the tears didn't come. She thought of Seán in his parents' car, driving home to a house filled with well-wishers, and warmth and love. A man struck down in his prime and how she envied him his loving parents who would do anything for their son.

Her phone beeped on the coffee table. She went to it.

**Happy Christmas, Darcy.**

It was from Mick.

**Up yours too,** she replied.

**You're welcome to join us. Irena bought vegan mince pies by mistake!**

**Thanks for the offer but I'm OK.**

**Good choice. They taste like cardboard.**

Darcy smiled, typed **Happy Christmas to you all.**

She closed her phone and was about to throw it on the sofa, but she opened it again.

She found a different number and typed **Happy Christmas**.

Then she bit her lip and stood looking at the SEND button for a full minute before she pressed it.

It beeped in her hand almost immediately.

**Happy Xmas. U comin over?** her mother replied.

Darcy was surprised at how much she had hoped for that text.

It beeped again.

**I was just going to eat. I'll wait for u.**

Darcy typed: **I don't eat meat.**

**So just eat the fuckin veggies then.**

The snow had stopped falling by the time Darcy had turned out all the lights in her house. Her feet crunched in the snow. She looked out at her footsteps when she sat in her car, new tracks in a new direction. She wondered how long they would last.

When she started the car, she had a sense as if she were about to drive home, but she pushed the thought from her mind.

She reversed the car and drove out of the square just as the snow turned back into rain.

## Also available on Poolbeg.com

# IN PLAIN SIGHT

## JOSEPH BIRCHALL

Darcy has always dreamed of joining the serious crime detectives of the NBCI. She finally gets her chance to prove herself on what should have been an open-and-shut case, but which quickly turns into a race against time to stop the multiple sadistic killings of women on the streets of Dublin.

To show her the ropes, she is assigned a once-brilliant but now washed-out detective, Mick Kelly, who should have retired years ago. Darcy fears that if, or rather when, he screws up, she will crash and burn along with him.

So far in her career, she has always managed to keep her secretive past hidden but, as they close in on the killer, her past is coming back to haunt her.

**Can she save the next victim from the relentless killer but, at the same time, save herself from her own past?**

ISBN 978-178199-661-4